REBEKAH'S WAY

Kirsten Lawler

Rebekah's Way is a work of fiction. Where real people, events,
establishments, organizations, or locales appear, they are used
fictitiously. All other elements of the novel are drawn from the
author's imagination.

Book Cover by Melody Fulone Design
Illustrations by Melody Fulone Design

First edition 2023

ISBN: 979-8-218-28363-6 (Paperback)
ISBN: 979-8-218-28364-3 (E-Book)

For Jesus and Sean
(In that order)

CONTENTS

PART ONE

"And Rebekah arose, and her damsels, and they rode upon the camels, and followed the man: and the servant took Rebekah, and went his way." Genesis 24:61

CHAPTER ONE

"**W**ill you go with this man?"

The world stood still as I weighed the enormity of the question. Looking back, I'll remember hearing nothing but the vastness of complete silence. Time, movement, and the very breath in my lungs seemed to halt; even the dust particles paused their motion, suspended midair in the otherwise unremarkable beam of sunlight that filtered through my family's tent.

The gentle click of a stone dish on our breakfast table brought the present back into motion. Did they understand what they were asking of me?

CHAPTER TWO

J ust yesterday, I'd walked the familiar path to draw water for the evening from our local well. I had always taken comfort in that walk, never minding the exertion of the few kilometers, or the weight of the heavy—and then heavier—clay pitcher on my shoulder. In fact, I'd come to love the few trips I took each day. They offered me a moment to think, to dream, to visit with our neighbors, and, when time allowed, to play a quick game with their children.

But yesterday was different. As I'd walked the dusty, unevenly paved path down to the well, I'd felt the sense that I was being watched. The feeling was different than the typical appreciative—if not unthreatening—male gazes that Mother had always warned my fair complexion and almond-colored eyes would garner. Expecting to see a man nervously hopping from foot to foot while attempting to strike up a conversation, I glanced up to find a little man calmly standing on the other side of the well. Aside from the fact that I'd never seen him before, I was puzzled over his appearance. He was dusty, as if he'd just endured several days of travel, but his garments were woven in a resplendent blend of indigo, violet, and bronze. His weary eyes offered something other than mere appreciation. They carried hope, and potentially a bit of amusement.

Smiling at him in greeting, I attached my pitcher to the rope and dropped it into the well. After drawing water and turning to walk home, I heard rapid footsteps approaching me from behind.

"Please, may I have a bit of water from your pitcher?" the stranger said with a rasp just a few feet away from where I previously stood.

Upon closer inspection of the man, I could see just how worn and exhausted he was. Of course he was thirsty, and didn't have a pitcher of his own to use to draw water. Why hadn't I offered him some water and a proper greeting in the first place?

Mentally chiding myself on behalf of my mother, I held my

pitcher out to him. "Please, drink. Do you have any cattle in need of water as well?" Finally taking a moment to observe my surroundings, I saw a pack of camels kneeling under the palms one hundred yards away. Their riders stood to their side, giving the camels the better part of the shade. Surely a group this large couldn't be his, I thought.

He wiped his mouth with the back of his hand and turned to look in the same direction as I had. "I have ten camels resting down the way. I'll need to find a few pitchers to bring them water, too."

"Oh, allow me to do that. Here, drink and rest. I will see to your camels as well." Before the stranger could say anything in response, I poured what was left of the water into his jug, before dropping it back into the well to refill it.

Two hours and several trips later, my shoulders and hands were searing with pain. I silently thanked the Lord that this man arrived in the evening, saving me from the heat and glare of the afternoon sun. As I walked back toward the well, I began to wonder whether he had a place to stay, or anything to eat. Realizing that I'd drawn near to the little man, I looked up and saw that he was holding a large woven satchel, composed of the same rich colors of his garments. He met my eyes and furtively beckoned to come closer. Somewhere in the back of my mind, I could hear the light tinkle of alarm bells. What if I had just helped a mad man who planned to attack me? Most of the village had already drawn their water for the day—would anyone hear me, or be near enough to help?

My heart began to race, and I inched forward. He reached into his pack and pulled out a handful of gold jewelry. Against my better judgment, I gasped and leaned forward; I'd never seen such beautiful, opulent jewelry in my entire life. Realizing I'd been staring a bit too long, I looked up and took a step back. Who was he, and what could he possibly mean by showing me a handful of gold? My family's prosperity in recent years was widely known in our village, but surely he couldn't think that I had the means to buy the jewelry he had to sell.

Gently, as if reading my thoughts, he held his hand out to me with imploring eyes. "I want you to have these as a gift."

I stared at him in stupefied silence. He chuckled and took

two bracelets, placing them on my wrists. They were made of plaits of gold, one thick and ornate, and one delicately fine. Then, he offered me a hooped earring, which was engraved with the finest details of fig, pomegranate, and olive leaves. Growing up, I used to sit in my mother's tent and watch as she adorned her wrists and ears with bands of gold—but these were different.

"Sir, I can't accept these, nor can I pay for them. Please, take them back."

He held up his hands to silence me. "My name is Eliezer. Whose daughter are you? Might your father allow me to lodge for the night?"

My father, Bethuel, always welcomed visitors with open arms. Surely he would allow this pleasant, albeit strange man to stay for the night. I took a few moments to consider my answer, unknowingly staring down at the two bracelets that adorned my wrists. When I looked up, Eliezer was smiling kindly, patiently awaiting my response.

"My name is Rebekah, and I am the daughter of Bethuel, the son of Milcah and Nahor. We have more than enough room for you, and straw and food for your camels—is something wrong?"

In the middle of my sentence, Eliezer dropped his head to the ground in silence. Raising his hands up to the sky, he began to speak loudly, saying, "Blessed be the Lord! I've been led to the house of my master's family." He squeezed my cheeks and chuckled before turning to walk back to his camels.

Dumbfounded, I stared at him as I wracked my mind for who he might be referring to. My uncles on my father's side all resided in or around our village. I doubted that any of them would send a servant to travel such a short distance, or have access to such fine jewelry. Aside from that, I would have remembered if our family hired a man like Eliezer—he certainly left an impression. Unable to keep my curiosity at bay, I called after him. "Your master's family? Do you mean that you have been sent by one of my father's brothers?"

Eliezer stopped and turned around in surprise, as if realizing all over again that I still stood there. "Ah, Rebekah! Many apologies, I wandered off ahead of myself. I have been sent by your father's uncle, Abraham."

I gasped and nearly dropped my pitcher. Abraham was known among our people as a great and powerful man—one who God had blessed bountifully. While I had never had the opportunity to meet him, I'd heard stories of his prosperity and character from my father and grandfather. Growing up, I'd overheard the whispers that worked through our village containing tales of his fortune, sometimes laden with jealousy, but always dripping with admiration. To happen upon one of his servants at the well was nothing short of a miracle.

Hurriedly pulling my pitcher up from the bottom of the well, I turned and ran home to find my family. Hearing only the patter of my feet on the packed dirt and the regular sloshing of what water remained in my pitcher, I flew past our neighbors, past the children playing in the road, unable to contain my excitement. It wasn't until our tents came into view that I realized that the clinking sound that followed me was from the gold Eliezer had given me.

As I drew nearer to our home, my brother, Laban, stared at me in bewilderment. "Where on earth did you get those?" he said, grabbing my wrist.

"You'll never believe who I just met!" I gasped and massaged the cramp in my side before continuing. "I was drawing water and a man named Eliezer approached me to ask for a drink. I gave him and his ten camels water, and he told me that he was sent by our Uncle Abraham. He wants to know if he can lodge with us for the night."

"Are you sure?" Laban said, still staring at my wrists and ear in disbelief.

"Yes, I promise. I nearly fainted when I heard, but when I realized he was telling the truth, I raced back to tell you. We must make room for him, Laban."

"Of course we will. We would never deny a visitor of Abraham's. Hurry, tell Deborah and the servants to prepare the guest tent and to lay fresh straw in the stables. I'll go meet him at the well."

Laban ran to meet Eliezer, leaving me to wonder over the meaning of Eliezer's arrival. Hosting a member of Abraham's household was something of an honor, one that would typically come with weeks or months of planning. That this visitor came on behalf of Abraham with no prior notice was something of a mystery.

Meanwhile, it was as if our home had erupted like an angry ant hill—every one of our servants and family members jumped into action, rushing to prepare our tents for Eliezer's arrival. Carpets were slung over lines and rocks before being beaten with a fervor; dust flew through the air as every surface was swept clean. Far away, I heard the bleating and braying of our livestock as they were herded back to their fields. The scent of fresh bread wafted through the air, and I watched as the sky turned dusk pink.

I'd always loved seeing our home in a rare flurry of activity. It reminded me of the many marriage celebrations we'd been honored to host and attend. As children, Laban and I had busied ourselves with slipping past the skirts of visitors to sneak extra bites of bread and meat from the servant's proffered platters. Adults ate and danced the night away while us children frolicked and played, free from the rigidity of our normal curfews.

I smiled as I remembered what it felt like to wake up early the day of a village-wide celebration, only to find a new dress sitting on the chair beside my bed. I'd slip it over my head, turning slowly as I wondered over it, feeling absolutely regal, before running out of my tent to find Father. I'd cherished those festivals, not just for their amusement, but because they afforded me a full and leisurely morning with him. Typically, he was out of the door far before dawn, sometimes letting me tag along, sometimes leaving me to sleep. But on celebration days, we breakfasted lazily before playing games out in the cool morning air.

"Rebekah, come here and welcome our visitor with me and your father." Mother's voice jolted me from my memories, and she grabbed my arm to pull me closer to her. I craned my neck to look for Father, finding him just behind Mother, prepared to step forward to greet Eliezer.

Eliezer and Laban arrived, arm in arm, chuckling as they exchanged pleasantries and news from both sides of the family. Upon seeing my father, Eliezer bowed deeply in greeting.

"Welcome to my home. We are honored to have you here. How were your travels?" Father held out his arm to welcome Eliezer inside.

I followed closely, marveling at the changes that had taken place in such a short amount of time. Our dining tent, customarily clean and tidy, had been outfitted with fresh cushions, candles, and our finest dishes. My stomach grumbled at the smell of steaming stew and bread. I hadn't realized how hungry today's efforts had made me.

"The pleasure is mine, and tenfold! To have found an answer to prayer in your daughter is more than I could have ever hoped for, and makes the ten days of travel but a blink of an eye," Eliezer said as he bowed dramatically over Father's hand.

Mother and I looked at each other quizzically. What did he mean by my being an answer to prayer? I fought the rising trepidation that seemed to press itself into my ribs, figuring that all he referred to was my bringing him water, and helping him find a place to stay.

I watched as Mother ushered Eliezer to the honorary spot at the table that we reserved for guests. When he was finally in place, we all took our seat. I played with the intricately embroidered hand towel that sat neatly folded to the right of my bowl as the servants began to ladle stew into Eliezer's. He smacked his lips appreciatively, relishing the steam that rose to meet his face, before looking up suddenly. "As delicious as this looks, I will not eat until I have told you why I am here." He waved his arms over the table with a flourish, as if to further his point.

Curiosity tinged Father's eyes as he studied him for a moment. Finally, he nodded hesitantly. "Please, speak on."

Eliezer sat back with a loud exhalation and folded his hands in his lap before continuing. "As you know, I am Abraham's servant and overseer. I have served Abraham for my lifetime, and over the course of that lifetime, I have watched Abraham be blessed by the Lord. He is a great man, you see."

We nodded in agreement—that fact was hardly a secret.

"Well," he continued, "with that greatness, Abraham accumulated quite the collection of flocks, herds, precious metals and jewels, servants, land, and livestock. His wife, Sarah, bore him one son when she was quite old. His name is Isaac, and Abraham has given him everything he has."

We sat quietly, as if entranced by the story he told. Much of what he said was simply a confirmation of the stories our people had exchanged about Abraham over the years. It was known that Abraham had spent decades without a son, and the rumor had been that his wife, Sarah, had finally given him one when she was past childbearing age. Many of the women who heard those rumors were quick to deny them, claiming their impossibility.

Eliezer waited a few more beats to examine each of our faces as if he were searching for missing clues. "Abraham made me swear to him that I would not give Isaac a wife from Canaan, where they now dwell. He sent me here to find his son a wife from his kindred. And so, after ten days of brutal travel under the heat of the scorching sun, I arrived at your well and found Rebekah."

Pinpricks spread throughout my palms, and I swallowed the lump that formed in my throat. This story was headed in a direction that I wasn't entirely sure I was comfortable with.

"As I stood near the well after a long and exhausting journey, I prayed to the Lord for guidance, asking Him to make the wife he's chosen for Isaac clear." Eliezer glanced around the room as if to ensure that everyone was listening.

"Please go on," Father said quietly.

Eliezer placed his hand on the table, palm up, and met my eyes. Hesitantly, I rested my hand in his. He gave it a gentle, if not reassuring, squeeze before continuing. "In my prayer, I tested the Lord, so to speak. I asked Him to send the right woman to the well; if she offered a drink of water for not only me, but also my camels, that was to be the Lord's way of showing me that she was the woman he intended for Isaac. Before I had finished my prayer, Rebekah appeared. She gave me her pitcher of water to drink, and offered to water my camels without my asking. She worked tirelessly to take care of them while I rested. It became immediately clear that she was the woman God intended for my master's son, Isaac."

I heard the breath rush out of my lungs before I felt it. Mother, having done her best to remain quiet throughout the story, finally spoke. "But surely this is a coincidence. Rebekah was raised to be hospitable—"

"Hush. You heard him, he prayed to God for a sign, and Rebekah was the one to give him that sign," Father said while casting a disapproving look toward Mother before turning back to Eliezer. "If you were a man from any other place, I would question the validity and truth of your statement. However, I know Abraham to be an honorable and righteous man, and if he sent you, then surely the Lord's will is in this. If this has proceeded from God's mouth, then I cannot pass judgment over whether it is bad, or good."

I snatched my hand from Eliezer's and ran to kneel by my father. "Father, please, what can you mean? Surely you can't expect me to just leave and marry a man I've never met?"

His eyes were filled with a mixture of sadness and acceptance. He placed his big, rough palm on my cheek as if to reassure me before turning to look at Eliezer. "The Lord brought you to this land to find a suitable wife. You asked for a sign, and Rebekah provided it. It is not my right to stand in the way of the Lord's will. You have my blessing."

Shock and betrayal coursed through my body. I turned to look at Laban, who refused to meet my eyes as he nodded in agreement with what our father had said. My father, the one who once held me so lovingly on his knee, who never spoke a cross word, who had been my place and person of refuge, had just promised my hand in marriage. While I wasn't surprised that Laban had been so quick to give his blessing, I had never expected the same from my father. Witnessing the exchange that happened was surreal. It felt as if I were watching some other woman's life be traded away, so detached was I from the reality of the scenario. I stayed by his knee, staring at the ground, until the rattle of metal and stone broke through my thoughts.

I looked up to find two of Eliezer's servants carrying in a large wooden chest. Eliezer was crouched with his face to the ground as he murmured a quiet prayer. At the sound of the chest being placed by his head, he bounced up and took his seat again. "Because you have blessed me and my master so greatly, I have brought gifts for each of you to cherish." He tipped his head, and his servants opened the chest to reveal a pile of gold, silver, gemstones, and stacks of glimmering linens. He studied the chest of treasure carefully, before retrieving two bracelets similar to mine, two earrings, and a ruby ring for my mother. Her eyes widened in appreciation, momentarily too absorbed by the glittering objects in her hands to remember that her daughter had just been given away in marriage to a man she had never met. To Father and Laban, he gave an assortment of gold jewelry. Before I knew it, he was kneeling before me with the chest extended in his hands. "And for you, Rebekah, I give garments of the finest and rarest quality, and precious jewels." He nudged the chest toward me, as if hoping that by accepting them, the shock and horror written on my face might disappear.

Immobilized by the thoughts and questions that raced through my mind, I continued to stare down at him. As I studied his small, weathered face which boasted wrinkles and lines from years of work and laughter, I realized with a pang that he had been given an impossible task. It wasn't his fault that Abraham had sent him here, and that he had prayed, and I had happened to answer that prayer. If anything, the fault had been entirely mine. I mentally chided myself for the second time that day for going to the well at all. What if I had skipped my duties for just one night? Would we be enjoying a quiet family dinner, free of jewels and marriage propositions?

I thanked Eliezer for his generosity before slowly rising from my seat. My feet carried themselves out of the tent and down the long, dark corridor to my room. I heard my mother's muffled, fervent tone as she argued with my father. As I neared the entrance to my tent, I felt a hand grip my arm.

"I've been trying to speak with you, but it seems like you couldn't hear me. Are you all right?" Laban said while peering at me in concern.

"Father has just given the blessing of my marriage to a man I've never met, and you did nothing to stop it. In fact, you gave your blessing, too. So, no, I'm not."

"I know this sounds like a hard and terrible thing, but you must remember that this is Abraham we are discussing. This isn't a man you deny, nor should you want to. By marrying his son, you'll not only have the world at your fingertips, you'll bring greater honor to our family." He raked his hands through his hair and looked around us as if indecisive about whether he should continue to speak. "Aside from that, Rebekah, you heard him say that he prayed to the Lord right before you showed up. It is not our place to speak out against the Lord, no matter how much it may hurt or scare us."

I looked up at Laban's big brown eyes, feeling the sting of the loss of our childhood work its way through my veins. When had we stopped laughing and playing as we ran through our village, hiding behind every rock and tree we found? I couldn't remember the exact moment when we had grown up and faced the reality of adulthood—I couldn't pick a time when we decided that I was ready to leave our nest.

I choked back a sob. "I'm not one to speak out against the Lord, but how can we trust that what this man says is true? What if I'm just one of many who would have offered him water? What then, Laban? Am I to believe that because I was the first woman he met at the well, that I'm the intended wife for Abraham's son?"

"Rebekah, you and I both know that it's no coincidence that you appeared before he even finished his prayer. For whatever reason," he whispered, "you were the Lord's choice."

Tears stung my eyes. "But what if I never see you, Mother, and Father again? Canaan is a lifetime away. I can't just leave, what will I do? I'm not prepared to be a wife."

"You'll learn and make do, just like so many other brave men and women have before you. Isaac will give you a good life. You can do this, Rebekah."

Without another word, I turned to enter my tent, leaving Laban standing in the dark.

❋ ❋ ❋

I blinked to adjust my eyes to the darkness of the early morning. My cheeks, temples, and eyes pounded from the aftermath of crying myself to sleep. I sat up and stretched my arms before reaching up to rub my tender neck. Mornings had never bothered me; in fact, I typically enjoyed waking up before the heat of the sun. But yesterday's physical labor and emotional turmoil brought a fresh level of exhaustion and soreness.

Deborah, my personal maid and closest friend, went about the tent tidying and folding linens before setting out my garments for the day. While she had always been my maid, Deborah and I had grown up together, becoming as close as sisters. Father had given Deborah to me as a gift when I was only seven years old, and since then, we'd shared secrets, laughed until we cried, and fumbled our way through the trying years of adolescence and early womanhood.

I swung my feet out from the bed covers and placed them on the cool earth. I wiggled my toes before letting out another yawn, then wobbled my way to the obsidian mirror to plait my hair. It was only then that I noticed just how quiet Deborah was this morning. Soft spoken as she was, Deborah and I typically used our mornings and evenings to catch up on the day's activities, as well as any news the other maids might have brought her from the village.

"Is something wrong?" I tried to meet Deborah's eyes in the mirror. She continued to vigorously fluff the pillows in her hands without looking at me. "You know, don't you?"

Deborah's dark eyes finally rested on me before flitting away. "Yes, Selah told me. Is it really as—as bad as she makes it sound?"

Sighing, I finished tying my hair before turning to face her. "Yes, I believe it is. Or if it's not bad, it is, at the very least, a surprise."

Deborah, still holding the pillow she was previously fluffing, began to twist the tassels in her fingers. "What will you do?"

I took a moment to think about my answer, still bemused that in the space of just a few short hours, my future had been decided, and my fate had been traded away. Last night, after crying quietly into my pillow, I'd had a moment of clarity and mournful acceptance. No matter how much I wanted to stay with my family, I knew that deep down, I couldn't go against Father's wishes. I had never been able to. If I stayed, I stayed with the knowledge that I'd disappointed him. I couldn't—I wouldn't—live that way.

Regardless of my decision, all peace in my life as I knew

it had been lost the moment I stepped up to that well. Eliezer was kind, and from what I knew of Abraham, marriage into his lineage would be beneficial—not just for myself, but for my family, too. My palms began to sweat, and I rubbed them against the sides of my nightgown.

"Are you all right, Rebekah?" Deborah cut in tentatively while furiously twirling a pillow tassel between her fingers.

"I'm just in a bit of shock, that's all."

"Do you think they'll make you marry him, even if you say no? Do you know anything about Abraham's son?"

Once again, I was reminded that my fate affected Deborah just as much as it affected me. Where I went, Deborah would follow—and she had grown to love our family as her own. I fought to keep my sadness at bay, forcing a small smile as I turned to face her.

"I've heard very little about Isaac, only that he exists. As for my mother and father forcing me to marry him, I'm not sure." What I failed to mention was the fact that Isaac was reputed to be a handsome and hardworking man. Growing up, I had heard many of the women of the village gossiping and giggling about him, speculating over who would be lucky enough to become his wife. Secretly, I'd always been curious about Isaac. But marrying him? That put things in an entirely different perspective.

I gripped the padded stool I sat on to steady my thoughts and breath before turning back to put my bracelets and earring on. "We might as well go to breakfast. It'll do us no good sitting here and fussing over what might happen." I looped my arm around her shoulders and gave her a quick squeeze, both to comfort her, and to steady myself.

As I walked the narrow corridor to the dining tent, I pondered Deborah's question. Nearing the door, I overheard my mother speaking in her shrill voice.

"Can't you let her stay just a few more days before leaving?"

I whipped open the flap of the tent, finding Eliezer at the table with the rest of my family. All four of them hushed as I entered.

"So it's been decided for me, then? That I'm leaving?" I bent down to meet Mother's averted eyes as she looked imploringly at Father.

Father cleared his throat before finally looking at me. "After listening to Eliezer's story and hearing how the Lord blessed your encounter with him, I believe that it is His will for your life. Will you go with this man?"

Taking a slow breath, I forced myself to relax my jaw. Mother always told me that clenching my teeth would give me the jaw of a man, and little good would it do me to break them in my moment of panic and confusion. The problem was that Father, my levelheaded, kind, quiet and thoughtful Father, was always right. Growing up, I'd watched my mother question his every motive and decision, only for him to be proven correct. Where she was sharp and quick, he was slow and steady—for him to have come to such a decision so quickly spoke volumes. Was it possible that he was wrong, for the first time?

I looked at him inquisitively, and his eyes, the same color as mine, softened. "I realize that this comes as a bit of a shock. As my only daughter, you know that I want nothing more than for you to be happy, while also being in the Lord's will. So, it is my wish that you follow Eliezer to his home. But I will leave the final decision to you."

I squeezed my hands into fists as I thought about everything he and Eliezer had said, and the decision I came to last night. I thought of the joy I'd known here in my village, and realized that after today, nothing would ever be the same. I'd taken my last walk down to the well as a young, unmarried girl, and I'd returned as good as betrothed, without even realizing it. Before I could think any further, the words flew out of my mouth. "Yes, I will go."

CHAPTER THREE

My numb acceptance of my newly designed fate carried me through packing and preparing for the journey that lay ahead of me. From the moment I agreed to follow Eliezer, Deborah and the rest of our family's maids had been in a constant flurry of activity. Our journey to Canaan was urgent—Abraham was bedridden, and it was his dying wish to see his son suitably betrothed. Typically, packing for ten days of travel would require a couple of weeks of preparation. But packing for ten days of travel and my marriage with little more than a day's notice was an entirely different feat.

As a young girl, I had watched the women in my village prepare for their weddings. Weeks of feasts, celebrations, and pampering took place before the actual marriage. Mother's long-ago promises of, "That'll be you before you know it," rang in the back of my mind. I would be lucky to get the chance to bathe and wash my hair before we left.

Finding myself standing in the middle of my barren tent, I took a moment to absorb the impact and finality of everything that was to come. In just several hours, I would set off on ten long days of travel. At the end of those ten days, I would meet and marry a stranger. His family would be mine, and mine would be but a distant memory. I would be expected to raise a family, tend to my husband's needs, and look after the household.

Was I ready? Would I ever be?

As I watched the maids pack and prepare at the instruction of my mother, I took comfort in the fact that at the very least, Isaac came from a well-respected and affluent family. By marrying him, I would bring honor to my father, and by extension, my entire family. All my life, I'd heard the women around me discuss Isaac's looks and wealth. Now, knowing that I would soon marry him, my only concern was for his temperament—I could accept the idea of marrying almost any kind of man, so long as he was kind.

"Are you ready to bathe, Rebekah?" Deborah asked softly, as if the emptiness of my room made her presence too big for comfort.

"I believe so. If not now, then when? Although I know I'll be covered in dust by the time I arrive."

Deborah placed a pot of water over the fire, and prepared the soap, oils, and linens as I sat and watched the flames. Her movements and quiet chatter sounded like they came from the bottom of a well—something that happened too often lately. Once the water was warm, Deborah poured it into the wash basin and gave me a piece of soft, worn linen to wash with. "I'll keep packing up the remaining things while you bathe. Take your time, and let me know when you're ready for your hair to be washed."

I savored the sweet smell of the soap as I worked it into my skin, knowing that this would be the last time I'd experience this level of peace and cleanliness for the next several days. It was also the last time I'd ever bathe in the tent I grew up in. Emotion threatened to work its way up my throat and into my eyes, but I distracted myself by running through my mental list of items to bring for my new life.

"Did you remember to pack the two tapestries from grandmother?" I didn't have many possessions that were important to me to bring, save the gift of two picturesque tapestries given to me from my grandmother, and one other token from my father.

"Yes, of course. I made sure to wrap them myself, and they'll be attached to your pack so you can keep an eye on them. I also placed your little wooden donkey in your purse." Deborah looked at me from the corner of her eye before resuming her work.

"You know me better than I know myself. Thank you for remembering."

Father had given me that little wooden donkey when I was a small child. I'd carried it with me everywhere I went, until I became too old to do so. Since then, it sat on my bedside table, greeting me every morning, and bidding me good night every evening. I wasn't sure what Isaac would think when he discovered that his new wife had arrived covered in dust with a mere two tapestries and a tiny wooden donkey in tow, but I'd rather he knew me, as I was, right away.

After a few more minutes of blissful silence, I asked Deborah to wash my hair. I sat wrapped in a linen cloth while she dipped my hair in a bowl of clean water. Closing my eyes, I let the feeling of the hairbrush soothe my fractured nerves. As she scrubbed the soap and oil mixture into my hair, I thought about the memories I would bring with me from this home. Growing up, I'd been attached to my father's side. I was a quiet girl, with eyes bigger than my size, and I'd followed him everywhere he went. When he worked the fields, I came, donkey in hand, and watched until he had a few moments to play. When he went into the village to barter and catch up with friends, I listened intently. His serene disposition had always been a balm to me, especially when contrasted with the testy, quick-tongued nature of my mother. My relationship with my father was unusual, given the fact that I was his daughter and his youngest child. But he always managed to love and nurture both Laban and I, and secretly, I'd always wanted a husband with the same qualities as my father.

"How are you feeling, really?" Deborah asked, interrupting my musings.

"A part of me is sad, and another part of me is terrified. And lastly, there's a part of me that's come to an odd kind of acceptance. The truth is that I have been of marriageable age for some time now. I could only resist so many proposals in the hopes of finding someone I loved. At least this marriage will be one that will bring honor to the family."

"The maids have been chattering away about everything they've heard about Isaac. Everyone says that he's handsome and agreeable. It would be much worse if he were known for being otherwise." Deborah smiled timidly into the mirror as she combed out my damp hair.

"Yes, I am sure you're right. But is it too much to hope for more than that? Is it too much to hope for love, too?"

"No, of course not. With your beauty and wit, I would be shocked to find a man who wouldn't easily love you. I think it'll just come down to you loving him."

I sat in silence as Deborah added scented oils to my hair and braided it for the evening. Declining to eat in the dining tent, I had a few bites of food in bed before slipping into a fitful sleep.

I was awoken the next morning by Mother's soft murmurs. Confused, I shifted to sit up and looked around the room for Deborah. Mother hadn't woken me up since I was a small girl.

"I wanted a moment with you, in private, before you depart," she said as she reached out to play with my hair. "I know that this wasn't what you expected, planned, or hoped for. It's not what I had in mind, either. If I had it my way, you and your brother would remain in our village, sharing our family's tents forever. But I want you to know that I believe you are doing the right thing, and will be blessed for it."

Struck by her words and soft countenance, I looked at her without speaking. Even in middle age, she was a beautiful woman. Her chestnut hair, distinctive cheekbones, and thickly lashed eyes that stood out against her fair skin were what had caught my father's eye so many years ago. Stripped away from her typically shrill voice and anxious ways, I was able to see her with a fresh perspective.

"I'm scared, Mother," I admitted. "I'm not sure I'm ready to be a wife." I looked across the room at my few remaining bags that had yet to be strung to my camel, attempting to distract myself from the flood of tears that threatened my eyes.

"Rebekah, I know I haven't always told you this, but I want you to listen," she said with a deep breath. "You are ready. You are smart, and kind, and caring. Any man would be fortunate to call you his wife. I am grateful that you are marrying an esteemed member of your father's family; a man I know will take good care of you." Gently, she wrapped her hand around the back of my neck and placed a kiss on my forehead. "Go on, make your father and I proud. Be the mother of millions, and may your descendants rule over all."

"Thank you, Mother," I said as I pulled her in for a hug. "I should get ready now." I turned away from her to conceal the emotion that betrayed itself in every line and movement of my face. As I gingerly placed my feet on the cold ground, I heard her clear her throat.

"Rebekah? I have one final thing to say," she said with a sigh. "I need you to let him in. Him and his entire family. You might have inherited your father's temperament, but you have my need to control our environment. It's rooted in fear—and when we are fearful, we tend to act foolishly out of self-preservation. Doing so only hurts us, Daughter." She cupped my face with her hand. "So, promise me you'll do your best to let God do His work. He will take care of you."

While I hated to admit that she was right, I couldn't deny that I had a tendency to operate out of fear when I felt that I lacked control. Control over my environment, my safety, the food I ate, the company we kept; it was all the same. If I felt unsafe, my natural inclination was to begin creating my own plans, my own reality, and it had only served to worsen things over the course of my life. Which was why this decision, my departure, was ludicrous. I had elected to throw myself into the lion's mouth of my worst fears.

The rest of the morning was a blur of packing, goodbyes, and well wishes. As I emerged from my tent, I felt the warm and gentle morning breeze tickle my skin. The sun was just beginning to emerge over the horizon, its fiery blaze promising a sultry day. Father, Laban, and Mother stood by our camels, overseeing the servants' final preparations. Along with my two tapestries and tiny wooden donkey, I brought Deborah and ten other maids. Knowing I had these members from my home was reassuring.

Deborah came to meet me with a small bundle in her hands. "I know we want an early start to get ahead of the heat of the day, so I packed your breakfast for you. I'll put it in the basket on your camel—take your time saying goodbye, and I'll help you get comfortable."

Thanking her, I turned to face my family, hugging Mother and Laban first, avoiding the moment when I would have to say goodbye to Father. When it finally came time to look at him, I saw for the first time in my life that tears flooded his eyes.

"I love you and will miss you so much, Father," I said, choking back a sob.

"Beautiful, darling Rebekah. I miss you already." He held my head to his broad chest, as he had so many times before. Bending down to meet my ear, he whispered, "And I am so proud of you. More proud of you than you'll ever know. You are to be loved and cherished, I am sure of it. Now go, follow the Lord's will, and know that I miss you every day."

Nodding, I gave him one final squeeze and turned away to find Deborah watching me with compassion filling her eyes. Willing myself to control my tears, I made my way toward my camel. Deborah held out the step to help me up, and once reasonably comfortable, I took one last look back at my family. All three stood as bravely and staunchly as they could. Father held Mother, as if to keep her from running toward me to change my mind. Laban stood as resolutely as a palm tree, every so often swaying under the force of sadness and uncertainty, but otherwise rooted, steadfast. I gave one final nod to all three as a goodbye, and turned to face forward.

"Where is Eliezer?" I asked Deborah, who sat on her own camel next to mine.

"He's up at the front. We're to follow him closely, and he will signal when he's found a place to stop and rest."

The sun was making its steady ascent; I could already feel its warmth on the side of my face. As I searched for the words to describe all that I was feeling, the horn signaled that it was time to move, and the camels began their loping walk.

CHAPTER FOUR

B y midday, I'd drained one of two waterskins completely. The sun was brutal; it blazed through my clothing and roasted my skin. My lips were dry and beginning to crack, and inwardly, I hoped that we'd get an earlier start the following morning.

The first hour of our journey started slowly. The camels took a while to pick up speed, and given the fact that we followed a good distance behind Eliezer, his commands and messages slowly made their way to those of us in the back. I spent the first hour of our journey waving goodbye to my family, to our neighbors, and finally, to Haran, until it was nothing more than a speck of sand. I turned after taking one final look at my home, my world, and saw Deborah riding quietly beside me. She met my eyes with tears glistening in her own—a reminder that I was not the only one affected by what laid ahead.

"Well, there's nothing left to do but look forward now, is there?" I said to Deborah, while glancing around the barren desert that surrounded us. "What a view we have."

I heard the tiniest snort, and looked at Deborah to find her laughing silently as she wiped tears from her eyes. In all my life, I'd never seen her laugh like this.

"What? You don't enjoy the view of the backside of camels, and plenty of hot, scorching sand?" At this point, I'd begun laughing so hard that I couldn't breathe, nor get another word out. Hearing Deborah's repeated snorts and attempts to stop only sent me further over the edge. The maids ahead of us turned around to shoot us inquisitive looks before quirking their eyebrows and facing forward.

"Shhh! You're going to get us both in trouble, Rebekah," Deborah said as she wiped a final tear from her eye with her thumb. "I apologize, I have no idea what came over me. It must be the lack of sleep and the enormity of everything hitting me at once."

"And maybe the camels' backsides, too," I giggled. Laughing

while facing the future with Deborah by my side had released a new kind of peace in my soul. I was scared—more than scared, really—and I had no idea what to expect. But I did have my friend, my sister, my Deborah here to help get through it all. I had never been so sure that she was a blessing from God.

I snapped out of my brief daydream when my camel came to a stop. Looking ahead, I saw that our group had paused to take their midday meal and reset their packs. I clicked my tongue and my camel, whom I had recently named Chazo, bent his legs to allow for a more comfortable descent. "Thank you, Chazo," I said while patting his sweet face and looking into his heavily lashed eyes. We'd get to know each other well in our next ten days of travel, that much I was sure of.

Deborah had used a bit of canvas and a few poles to fashion a small tent for us to take shade in while eating our meal. I ducked inside and was overwhelmed by the relief from the heat; the tent felt palatial compared to the several hours we'd just experienced. How on earth would I make it through another nine days?

"Eat up, we'll both need it," Deborah said as she unwrapped the fresh bread and dried meat she'd brought from home.

I bit into the bread, and tears, no doubt attributed to homesickness, sprung to my eyes. I wiped them away before turning to Deborah. "How do I look?" I said while wiggling my eyebrows.

She laughed. "We're going to need to find a better way to shade you, or else you're going to show up for your new husband looking like this piece of meat."

"Men like meat, don't they?"

"Yes, but I believe they prefer to enjoy their meat and women separately."

My smile fell as I considered what she said. "Do you truly believe it's possible to find love in an arranged marriage?"

Since I was little, I'd dreamt about finding and falling in love with my future husband. I'd always pictured that our paths would cross at the market, or at one of our village's weddings. Our eyes would meet across the stall of fruit—or through the mass of dancers—and it would feel like taking lightning to the heart. That was how I had pictured falling in love, and I had certainly pictured falling in love before agreeing to marriage.

My, how adulthood offered its many surprises.

"I do, in fact," Deborah said. "It might not be easy, and it might feel a little strange, but I've heard and known of many happy marriages that began with an arrangement."

Quietly, I nodded and finished my meal.

"Hallo ladies, are you in here?" I jumped at the sound of Eliezer's voice outside our makeshift tent before looking at Deborah in amusement.

"Yes, we are here. Please come in," I said as I opened the tent to welcome him inside.

"I must say, you two are smarter than the rest of us. What a lovely reprieve," Eliezer said as he slowly assumed a cross-legged position and eyed the remnants of our food.

I stifled a laugh as I fought the temptation to look at Deborah. "Would you like something to eat? We only have a bit of bread and meat, but you're welcome to it."

"Oh, I really couldn't, normally—" he grabbed a piece of bread and put it in his mouth. "But since you so kindly offered, I believe I shall," he said as he chewed with a twinkle in his eyes.

I found myself wondering, not for the first time, who Eliezer really was. I knew that he was Abraham's trusted overseer, and had once been his chosen heir. How close must they be, for Abraham to have chosen him as he would a member of his own family?

"May I ask you something, Eliezer?" I said while shifting to a more comfortable position.

"Please, ask me anything. I owe you every answer you seek."

"What is Isaac like?"

"Ah, a worthy question from the bride to be. A difficult question, too," he said as he leaned back on his hands and stared at the roof of the tent. "Isaac is a rarity. He offers the patience and kindness of a man his senior, and the diligence and strength of a young boy. He is good to every one of us who serves him. The death of his mother, Sarah, affected him greatly, and he's been quieter, keeping to himself even more than usual. To be quite frank, we've all mourned the loss of Sarah for the last few years. Our home doesn't feel the same."

"Was he very close with Sarah, then?" I could only imagine

what it must have felt like to lose his mother. The mere thought of losing my father forever was enough to send me into a fit of sorrow.

"Very much so. He loves both of his parents, but he and Sarah were inseparable. It comes as no surprise that he mourns her death greatly," he said as I nodded in agreement. "However, I have a feeling that your arrival may lift his spirits a good deal."

I looked down at my hands in an effort to avoid his direct gaze as he studied my face. "I hope that you are right, Eliezer. I would hate to be a disappointment after everything we've gone through."

"My dear, if you forget all else, remember this: You were chosen by God. How could Isaac be disappointed with that?" He patted my cheek and rose with a groan. "These creaky old legs better get a move on. I'll head to the front, and we'll plan to set off again in a quarter of an hour."

Deborah and I rose and bid him goodbye before packing up what remained of our picnic, as well as our tent. As I turned to hoist myself onto Chazo's back, I heard Deborah clicking her tongue behind me.

"Don't you dare get all the way up there before I can figure out a way to shade you from the sun," Deborah said while staring at me as an artist might stare at a painting. "Let me see what I can do. We can't have the sun cooking you alive for the rest of the day, much less the rest of our trip."

I sighed while petting Chazo's cheek and neck. Undoubtedly, that bit of shade would more or less look like a blanket thrown over my head, which would stifle me while protecting my complexion. I wasn't quite sure whether I disliked the blazing sun, or the potential of Deborah's solution, more.

"That should do it." I looked up in surprise to see that Deborah had assembled a miniature tent for me to ride under.

"How did you do that, and how did you do that so quickly?" I said in awe. Never again would I doubt her abilities.

"I brought a few short poles with me from home without thinking about it. I realized while we were eating that I could use them to make a miniature tent for you. It's rickety, but it should work for a bit. I'll keep an eye out for palm branches to use as a more permanent solution."

"I don't deserve you, you know," I said as I hugged her with a squeeze.

"Yes, I do know," she giggled.

We both turned at the sound of Eliezer's horn—it was time to get going. I swung myself up onto Chazo's back and settled in comfortably under the awning. With the shade provided by Deborah's clever design, I would be able to relax and enjoy the journey.

I turned to Deborah as the camels began their slow walk. "When do you think we'll stop for the night?"

"Oh, I'm sure we'll stop for the evening once the sun has gone down."

So, another several hours to go, I thought to myself. I took a moment to steady my breath and my thoughts, before contemplating five things I was grateful for at that very moment. It was a practice I'd learned from my father, and one I knew I'd carry with me for the rest of my life. Doing so never failed to put things in perspective. My family was healthy, I was safe, and I was on my way to marry a good and reputable man. While I was apprehensive about what awaited me, wishing away the future that had been dealt to me wouldn't make that future different, it would only make it more difficult. I rolled my shoulders back and sat up straighter in my saddle. Yes, I would accept my fate bravely and honorably, if not for myself, then for Father, Mother, Laban, and Deborah.

As we continued our slow, steady walk, I couldn't help but notice that my surroundings looked markedly different. It wasn't until several hours later that I realized why.

They were shrouded in hope.

CHAPTER FIVE

We made camp long after the sun left the horizon. I stretched my aching, dust-coated legs by the fire as I looked up at the stars. Out here, seemingly in the middle of nowhere, they glittered brilliantly in the inky sky. Vast, limitless sand surrounded our caravan—all that distinguished us from our surroundings were our few fires, dotted throughout the landscape like candles in a vacant room.

I turned as I heard the sound of muffled steps shifting the sand behind me. Eliezer walked toward me slowly, and it occurred to me just how sore and exhausted he must be. He'd traveled this same route on his own for ten days, before stopping for one night of reprieve with my family. Then, he'd turned around to do it all over again. I patted the blanket I sat on and offered Eliezer a seat.

"I don't know how you are able to travel so intensely and for so many days. I am utterly exhausted," I said to Eliezer as he crouched down to join me in front of the fire. The makeshift shade concocted by Deborah had helped immensely, but that didn't change the physical impact of spending nearly fifteen hours on the back of a camel in the intense heat.

"Ah, the Lord gives me strength, and I am fueled by my excitement to bring you home to Isaac," Eliezer said with a smile as he tipped his head back to admire the stars. I smiled and pushed my feet into the warm sand while we sat in companionable silence.

After a few minutes, Eliezer seemed to remember that I sat beside him. "I can imagine that this entire experience feels overwhelming for you. Is there anything you'd like to know about your new home and family?"

Breathing a sigh of relief that I hadn't realized I'd been holding, I turned to face him. "Yes, actually. What was Sarah like?"

Eliezer studied my face for a few moments in quiet contemplation. "She was beautiful, shrewd, and unfailingly loyal to her family; a strong woman and an even stronger mother."

"I wish I could have met her," I said while studying the dying flames in front of us. If Isaac and Sarah's relationship was anything like the one I shared with my father, the more I knew about his late mother, the more I'd know him. No matter how much I tried to push past it, marrying a man who lost someone so dear to him so recently just didn't feel right.

"Your husband will have plenty of stories to tell," Eliezer said with a raise of his eyebrows.

I smiled and bowed my head, bidding him good night before walking to my tent.

Deborah was fast asleep on the blankets she'd carefully padded and folded on the ground. I struggled to keep my eyes open as I splashed water on my face, neck, hands, and feet before lying in bed, all the while thinking about home, and wondering what my family was doing at that exact moment. Had life gone on as normal without me? Were they mourning my departure, too?

My thoughts became murkier and more confused as I wiped a stray tear from my eye and faded into a deep sleep.

CHAPTER SIX

T he next nine days passed in a blur of heat and the kind of exhaustion that only a weary traveler knows. Each evening, I lingered by the fire, speaking with Eliezer and listening to his stories from home. I'd become fond of Eliezer; he felt like a long-lost uncle. We grew to have our own repartee, and I was comforted by the knowledge that Abraham, and by extension, Isaac, trusted him and held him in such high esteem.

I spent my time over those nine days thinking about my new life, and my new husband. Excitement and dread continued to build, and waking up on our tenth and final day of travel felt as much a welcome relief as it did an ominous ending.

Walking beside Deborah, I carried our final few belongings to Chazo. She and I worked quietly as we tied up our packs and checked to ensure that we left nothing behind. I slipped my hand into my purse to feel for my little wooden donkey, before clicking my tongue to ask Chazo to stoop down. He and I had become quite close, and I'd miss our daily conversations as we sauntered through the desert.

I climbed up onto Chazo's back and looked back at Deborah. "Are you ready?"

"I am. Are you?" Deborah said, peering at me cautiously.

"I believe I am. This day had to come, didn't it?" I tried to fight the fear that fluttered in my stomach and made its way to my throat. Today, I'd meet Isaac. Tonight, I'd become his wife.

Deborah and I had been moved to the front to travel with Eliezer, who claimed that he was ready for a change in travel companions. I, however, feared that he wanted me near the front so that Isaac and his family would see me first.

Eliezer sounded his final horn, and we started our slow walk. As the hours passed, I watched the desert turn to packed earth, and the packed earth turn to rocks, then intermittent grass and brush. After what felt like an eternity and also but a moment, we entered an area populated with cypress trees. The sun began its descent, its last rays tickling the back of my neck.

As I took a moment to observe and enjoy my surroundings, something caught my eye on the horizon. From afar, I could just discern the outline of a man crouched in the brush. His broad shoulders sloped forward, and after a few moments, I realized that his head was bowed in prayer.

"Who is that, Eliezer?" I said without taking my eyes off of the outline ahead of me.

"That is Isaac, my dear."

A thrill ran through my spine as we drew nearer. Even from a few hundred meters away, I could make out Isaac's muscular build. As if he felt my eyes on him, he lifted his head to look at our approaching party. He nodded to Eliezer in recognition before standing up and brushing himself off and turning to pat his mule. I took my time observing him as we slowly drew closer—he was tall, much taller than I expected, and there was something graceful and inherently patient about the way he moved.

As I watched him, I felt something in my heart break wide open; something I had kept under lock and key. Here was a man who had lost his mother, a man who continued on, faithfully, even through his pain. He could have had his pick of any woman to be his wife, but instead, he'd waited patiently for a woman chosen by his father's overseer.

Without knowing, he'd chosen me.

"Stop!" I blurted out before realizing what I'd done. Panicked, I turned to Eliezer. "Please, let me put on a fresh veil before we approach him. What will I say? How will we meet?"

Eliezer, who had originally turned around in his saddle to look at me in alarm, softened as he recognized the fear written all over my face. "Please, don't worry. I will go ahead of our group and apprise him of everything so that he is ready to meet you. Then, I'll come and fetch you. Take your time," he said as he urged his camel forward.

I looked down in surprise when I felt Deborah's reassuring hand on my calf. "Come, let us put your veil on. I think you should walk to him," she said.

I clicked my tongue and Chazo bent his long legs to let me dismount. My heart felt as if it were a tiny bird with wings, and I took a moment to pet his side in an effort to calm myself. I turned to find Deborah standing in front of me with a new veil. Tiny flowers and leaves, embroidered in gold and scarlet thread, scattered its perimeter.

"Where did you get this?" I asked her in disbelief.

"It's something I've worked on, privately, for some time. I rushed to finish it the night before we left. I wanted you to have something beautiful to wear on your wedding day," Deborah said as she placed it over my head.

Overcome with emotion, I pulled her in for a hug. "I will never, ever deserve you. But I do promise to give you the best life I can."

"You are good to me, Rebekah. All I want is for you to be happy, and something tells me that you will be. Now, let's stop our weeping. We want you looking fresh as a rose for Isaac."

I laughed as I looked down at my traveling dress. "I'm not quite sure that we'll be able to achieve that today, but I do know that your veil will make all the difference."

I scanned the horizon to find Eliezer and Isaac, only a few hundred yards ahead of us, speaking with each other. Isaac's head was bent lower to listen to Eliezer, and Eliezer's hand was on Isaac's forearm as if to anchor him in place. Both men looked up at me suddenly, and Eliezer gave me a slight nod. I took a deep breath in through my nose, and willed my heart to settle down.

After what felt like an eternity, Eliezer walked back to me while Isaac waited with his mule and Eliezer's camel. "All right, Rebekah. It is time to meet him. We must hurry if we want to get back before the sun completely sets." He offered his arm, and I placed my hand in the crook of his elbow.

Walking toward him, this man I'd never met, felt like walking along the bottom of the sea. My body was unrooted and weightless; my feet were heavy and slow. It seemed as if no matter how hard I pushed, no matter how furiously I swam, I'd get to him both too soon, and too late.

Isaac watched as we walked toward him, and in that moment, I longed more than anything to know what he was thinking, too. Was he anywhere near as nervous as I was?

We were no more than twenty meters away when my eyes met his. With my heart in my throat, I took note of his honey-colored eyes and bronze hair. It was then that I realized that I had no idea what to say to him. My steps faltered, and Eliezer gently urged me forward while patting my hand. Isaac closed the distance between us in a few steps, and I bowed my head in greeting.

"This is Rebekah, daughter of Bethuel. She has been chosen for you by the Lord to become your wife," Eliezer said as he lowered his arm and released my hand.

After a moment of silence, I looked up and found Isaac watching me quietly. He tilted his lips in a small smile and cleared his throat. "I must apologize, your arrival has caught me off guard. I knew my father sent for you, but I didn't know if, or when, you'd arrive. I am Isaac, and I am honored by your arrival."

The three of us stood there, at a loss for words, staring at one another. Eliezer cleared his throat awkwardly. "Us weary and dusty travelers are in need of respite. What are we waiting for? Come, let us take Rebekah to her new home—we'll need to tell the others to prepare the marriage feast as soon as possible." He bowed before backing away. "I'll let you two get acquainted." He practically skipped back to his camel, the joy of his job well done emanating in every step.

Isaac chuckled quietly and rubbed his neck as he watched Eliezer. He turned to look at me in bewilderment. "Shall we?"

I tried to speak, but found that my throat was completely dry. I coughed indiscreetly. "Yes, I'll follow you," I said while glancing at the darkened horizon. I had no idea where I was going, nor how far away my new home was.

"Please, allow me to offer you my mule. You must be exhausted from the trip, and we're a good few kilometers from home."

I thanked him and walked to the creature, admiring his long, dark lashes and sable coat. He seemed familiar to me in a way I couldn't place, and as I stood petting his side, I realized that he bore a remarkable resemblance to my tiny wooden toy. I smiled and looked up to find Isaac observing me from across his back. "What is his name?"

"Elech," he said while patting him fondly.

"He is very sweet, and his name suits him," I said. I wasn't quite sure where I had gotten the courage to speak to Isaac directly and alone, but I figured that Elech had something to do with it.

Isaac came to my side and held out his hand. "May I?"

I placed my hand in his, and my breath hitched when his other hand rested on my waist. Before I could say anything, I landed gently on Elech's back. "Thank you," I said before clearing my throat and adjusting my veil.

Isaac nodded and began to guide Elech in the same direction as the others. He walked slowly next to us, seemingly lost in thought. I remembered what Eliezer had said about his quiet demeanor since the loss of his mother.

"Eliezer told me about your mother, Sarah. I am so sorry for your loss. She sounded like a great woman, one I would have been honored to meet."

Even on Elech's back, I only came up to Isaac's shoulder. He looked down at me in surprise. "Thank you. She is missed," he said with a flicker of warmth in his eyes.

I didn't know what else to say; I had already spoken more than I was comfortable with, and I feared sounding too forward. We walked in silence for several minutes, and I admired the vibrant pinks, reds, and oranges of dusk on the horizon.

"I—I want you to know that I realize how uncomfortable this must be for you," Isaac said, breaking through my thoughts. "I fear I am not a skilled conversationalist, but I want to assure you that I have every intention of being a good husband to you. I grew up with the honor of watching my father and mother enjoy a happy and loving marriage, and I hope to emulate that with my own." I caught a glimpse of the color that flushed his neck before he turned to look away.

"Thank you. I can't say that marrying a man I've just met while covered in dust and filth from travel was something I hoped for as a young girl," I said with a slight smirk. "But, I'm happy to hear that we want the same thing. And I don't mind your being quiet, the quiet can be enjoyable when in the right company." I shifted in the saddle in an effort to look busy.

Isaac stopped walking and turned to look at me. The last rays of the sunset sparkled across his eyes, transforming them into liquid gold. "I see no filth, nor any dust. You are beautiful, because you were chosen by God to be my wife. For that, I am honored."

Speechless, I stared at him through my veil. Isaac urged Elech forward, and we began our final walk home.

CHAPTER SEVEN

A s twilight enveloped us, I began to see twinkling lights on the horizon.

"Is that your village?"

He looked at me in surprise. "No, that is our home."

I stifled a shocked gasp as I continued to stare forward. Even from this distance, I could see that Isaac's house alone was nearly as large as my village. I'd known that he and his family were prosperous, but until now, I hadn't been able to picture what their life might be like. There were tents and stables enough for hundreds of servants and animals.

The distant sound of flutes reached my ears first. As we entered the gates, I was utterly swept into the flurry of activity surrounding me. Men, women, and children ran around us with baskets of grain, linens, and livestock in hand. The joyful tinkling of music came from a large tent, larger than I'd ever seen, several hundred meters ahead. Everything sparkled. I glanced upward to see hundreds of lanterns strung across the tops of the tents around me.

I had never seen anything so beautiful. Was it possible that this was all for me?

I looked to my right to find Isaac watching me again. "My mother's tent was prepared for you before Eliezer departed. May I show it to you?"

"I'd like that," I said quietly.

Isaac reached up and placed both hands around my waist, and I felt that same thrill race through his palms and into my bloodstream. I caught my breath as he gently lifted me from Elech's back and placed me on the ground. Taking a moment to steady myself and ensure my knees weren't as wobbly as they felt, I gave him a nod of readiness. Isaac hesitated a moment before slowly holding his hand out to me, palm up. I stared down at it in confusion before I heard him chuckle. "I was hoping you'd hold that," he said with a glimmer of amusement in his eyes.

"Oh, I see," I said in embarrassment. Praying my palm wasn't clammy with nerves, I placed it in his. Surprised by the warmth and comfort of his hand, I took a moment to admire just how small mine looked in comparison.

"We should go. The marriage feast will be starting soon, and I want you to see my mother's room first," Isaac said quietly. I swallowed nervously and allowed him to lead the way.

We walked hand in hand through the throng of bustling servants until we reached a clearing. Across from us stood a solitary tent, surrounded with lush grass and greenery. Behind it, the moonlight glinted across a small, trickling brook. After experiencing the chaos of the preparation for this very day, the isolation of our surroundings felt like an oasis.

"It's so quiet here," I whispered to Isaac, as if we were on hallowed grounds. It didn't seem appropriate to speak too loudly.

"Yes, she always enjoyed a bit of peace at the end of a long day. My father made sure to place her tent in a secluded area to give her respite." Isaac stood at the entrance with the tent flap held above his head. "Please, make yourself at home. She wanted you to enjoy the room she created. You'll find everything you need inside for you to prepare yourself for—for the celebration. I'll fetch you for the marriage feast soon."

I stopped in the doorway and looked up to thank Isaac. He nodded with a bit of embarrassment, then gently closed the tent flap and walked away. I listened to the receding sound of his soft footsteps, before taking a deep breath and turning to take my first look at Sarah's tent.

I stood in a kaleidoscope of vibrant color. Lavender, lilac, rose, and berry-colored tapestries and linens were layered around the tent, from floor to ceiling. Candles flickered throughout the space, causing the silver and gold threads woven in the walls and rugs to sparkle. I had unknowingly walked into a jewel. My mouth dropped as I continued to take in the beauty surrounding me. The tent floor was covered with plush cushions of turquoise and cerulean. To my right hung multiple dresses of various colors and textures. Ahead of me sat my wash area, complete with a large stone bath and a dressing table decorated with glittering bottles of scented oils and soaps.

On my left was a luxurious bed, covered with what seemed to be hundreds of pillows and blankets of various colors, next to a small but cozy hearth and tea table.

I sat on the edge of the bed, weak with gratitude and shock. After the last ten days of bitter, dusty travel, sleeping on the ground, and boiling under the heat of the sun, could this possibly be mine to enjoy?

I turned at the sound of rustling behind me to find Deborah peeking in the door. "May I come in, oh great one?" She said with a smile.

"This is so beautiful," I said as I waved her in. "I feel as if I'm sitting inside a cave of treasure. I'm almost too scared to touch anything."

"The keyword being *almost*, I'm sure," Deborah said as she began to prepare the bath.

"Something happened to you on our trip. You're quite mischievous now, aren't you?"

"It must be the exhaustion. I promise that'll be the last of it. Now, let's get you bathed and ready for the evening ahead," she said while eyeing me knowingly.

I swallowed nervously before walking to the large mirror that sat behind the dressing table. "I'm terrified, you know. This is a beautiful place and I am overwhelmed by my good fortune; Isaac seems to be a kind man, but I am still terrified."

Deborah picked up the silver hairbrush. "I think it's normal to feel that way as a bride. Even if you had known your groom before the day of your wedding, I think you would probably still be this nervous."

"I hope you're right. As of now, I feel like my entire body might explode in a fit of nerves," I said with a shiver. "Well, we're here, and it's time for me to face God's plan. Please just make sure Isaac doesn't regret his decision."

After a bath scented with lavender, I sat while Deborah combed and braided my hair. I applied argan and grapeseed oils to my skin and nails while Deborah picked out a dress and veil for me to wear.

"What do you think of this one?" she said while holding up a simple dress made of white, gold, and silver threads.

"It seems appropriate, given the circumstance," I said.

She nodded in agreement. "It'll look beautiful with your hair and veil, and will place all of his attention on your natural beauty."

I turned to look at myself in the mirror. Growing up, I had been accustomed to the compliments I received from men and women alike, but those compliments weren't from Isaac. He had yet to see me without my veil—what if he was disappointed? A man like him was surrounded by beauty every day.

"I hope he thinks the way you expect him to think," I said to Deborah with a hint of apprehension in my voice. "I, at least, have had the benefit of seeing him before our marriage. He hasn't."

Deborah sighed and looked at me. "I've told you once, and I'll tell you one thousand times more. You are beautiful. I've yet to meet anyone who thought otherwise. Now, let's hurry. He'll be here soon."

She held the dress over my head, and it shimmered as it fell down my body. It was weightless, and it fit as if it had been made specifically for me. After slipping my sandals on, I turned to Deborah. "Well, how do I look?"

"You forgot something," she said as she untied my braids and stepped back with a triumphant smile. "Now you're ready."

My waist-length hair tumbled down my back in dark waves. I breathed in sharply when I caught a glimpse of myself in the mirror—I hardly recognized the woman staring back at me.

"I must say, Deborah, you've done well," I said as I bent down to let her place my veil over my head. At that moment, I heard a cough outside the tent. I made my way to the door with my heart in my throat.

"Are you ready?" Isaac murmured through the closed tent door.

I smiled; any other man would've charged inside his bride's tent unannounced. "Yes, just one moment." I turned to look one final time at Deborah. She gave me a reassuring nod before slipping out the back door.

I tiptoed outside to find Isaac standing with his back to me. "Don't worry, I'm decent," I said while stifling a laugh.

He turned to look at me, his Adam's apple bobbing as he

slowly took me in. After what felt like an eternity, he stepped toward me and gently removed my veil. Isaac's eyes shifted from shyness to awe as he looked at my hair, my eyes, my mouth. "You are even more lovely than I could have ever imagined or hoped," he said with emotion in his voice. "Thank you for choosing me."

I replaced my veil and took his outstretched hand.

"Come," he said, "there are many I want you to meet."

CHAPTER EIGHT

I peered through my eyelashes at my surroundings, catching a glimpse of the glowing embers in the hearth from the night before. The tea table, presumably set by Deborah last night, sat beside it invitingly. The faint burble of the brook behind our tent met my ears, interrupted only by the occasional chirp of a bird on its morning rounds.

My heart flipped at the sound of deep, steady breathing behind me, and I remembered for the first time that I hadn't slept alone. Ever so gently, I peeked over my shoulder. Isaac slept with his back turned to mine, and I watched the rise and fall of his shoulders until something just past him caught my eye.

In the chaos and excitement of the night before, I hadn't had the chance to take in more of my surroundings, more of the brilliant colors and textures decorating Sarah's tent. I squinted my eyes to force them to focus more clearly on the object on the table next to Isaac, and was surprised to find that it was a small wooden animal quite similar to my donkey. Not wanting to wake him, I craned my neck further in an attempt to peer over my shoulder and his to get a better look at it. Was it some kind of beast—a huge cat? My curiosity got the better of me, and I rolled onto my right shoulder to get a better view, only to realize that Isaac's deep, rhythmic breathing had stopped.

"Are you spying on me?" Isaac said, still facing the other direction.

"No, I—" I stuttered, failing to come up with a reasonable explanation for why I had rolled onto my side and stared in his direction.

Isaac looked over his shoulder, and I caught that same mirth in his eyes. "It's all right, I had my fair share of watching you sleep last night. It's only right that you did, too."

I sat up straight as heat crept up my neck and into my face. "You watched me? I fell asleep before you?" It took me a few moments to see that Isaac's shoulders were shaking, and I peered over him to find him laughing quietly.

"No, I didn't. But now I know that you were watching me, because you didn't say otherwise. How did I look?" He grinned.

I stifled a laugh as I nudged his shoulder with my hand. "If you really want to know, I was trying to get a better look at whatever that little animal is on the bedside table."

He turned to look in my same direction, inhaling sharply. "Ah, that's the lion my mother gave me when I was young. She kept it in here when I grew too old to carry it around anymore. I believe she left it on the bedside table as a bit of a joke," he said as he studied it thoughtfully.

Even in the dimness of the early morning, the light seemed to refract off of his eyes, amplifying their honey tones and accentuating their softness. After far too long, I remembered that he was waiting for me to speak.

"He reminds me of the small wooden donkey my father gave me when I was little," I said after clearing my throat. "I carried him with me everywhere growing up. In fact, I brought him along with me." I threw off the blankets and padded softly over to where Deborah hung my purse. I grabbed my little donkey and studied him in the palm of my hand, looking up to find Isaac's eyes on mine.

"May I see him?" he asked as he sat up against the pillows.

I nodded and walked to his side of the bed. Standing in front of him in my nightgown, with my tiny wooden donkey in hand, I felt like a little girl again. I lifted my palm to show him, and he held my hand between his, turning it every which way, ever so gently, to get a better look.

"He looks a lot like mine, you're right. Don't you think they should live together now? They'll probably get a bit lonely otherwise," he said without letting go of my hand.

"You're probably right. Wooden animals can cohabitate, right? Even if one is technically a predator, and the other is prey?"

Isaac chuckled as he pulled my hand toward him. "Yes, I believe you're right. If nothing else, I won't tell if you don't." He patted the space on the bed next to him, inviting me to sit.

My mouth went dry as I studied his face, reminded once again that not only was I in the presence of a respected man, but I was now his wife. On the long journey to meet him, I hadn't known what to expect, not in his appearance, nor in his demeanor. That he was handsome was a given, but there was something about his gentle and welcoming manner that drew me to him.

The evening before had passed in a haze. Isaac had taken me to meet his father, Abraham, who blessed our union from the comfort of his bed. We were married in the peace and solitude of Sarah's beautiful tent, and later joined hundreds of Isaac's family, friends, and servants at the marriage feast.

I had never witnessed such opulence in my life. Isaac had walked me to our table at the head of the feast, his hand in mine, propelling me through the joyful crowd as I stared in stupor at the food and decoration. The tables had been covered with rich silks, and laid with gold and silver plates. Candlelight had sparkled and bounced off of every surface, and vines of tiny, fragrant blossoms hung in the air overhead. It was only at the gentle squeeze of Isaac's hand that I remembered that all of it had been done for me, for us.

Gratitude and awe filled me as I squeezed his hand and looked up to meet his eyes. "I can't believe that they did all of this for us," I said. "It's spectacular."

Isaac bent down to get closer to my ear, his breath tickling my neck in the process. "You deserve it all, my wife. I hope you enjoy it."

A wheezing laugh interrupted us, and we looked down to find Eliezer, tears glittering in his eyes, his arms outstretched as if awaiting a hug. When we didn't move, he bounced forward, encircling us with his thick arms. "Aside from my own marriage, I have never been happier. What a blessing to us all!" he cooed.

We laughed, remaining trapped in Eliezer's arms until the procession of well-wishers came to greet us. After the marriage supper, we mingled and danced as the night spun by in a whirl of glowing color. It had been the wedding of my dreams, even without my family present.

My breath came out in a rush as I sat next to Isaac and stared down at my feet, remembering with sadness that my father hadn't been present to give me away, and that he wouldn't be here to greet me at breakfast. This was the longest I'd ever gone without seeing my family, and adjusting to the time apart so suddenly was proving to be more difficult than I'd anticipated. I took comfort in remembering that Isaac missed someone dear to him, too—someone he wouldn't get a chance to see again in this life.

"Is something wrong?" he said as he cupped my chin with his palm.

"I was just thinking of my family, and your mother. I'm missing those I love, and someone I never had the chance to meet."

Isaac took a deep breath and sat back in thought. "I imagine that you miss them very much. I have the burden of missing my mother, but you have the burden of missing your family. For that, I am sorry."

"I am grateful to have the blessing of knowing that I may see them again soon. I am only sorry that you have to mourn the loss of your mother. I can only imagine how difficult that must be," I said gently.

Isaac searched my eyes before taking the little donkey out of my hand and placing it next to his lion on the table. He held both of my hands in his as he caressed my palms with his thumbs. "It is true that I have mourned the loss of my mother for quite some time. We were close, and I loved her. But having you here—for the first time, I feel as if I have found happiness again."

I blushed as a small smile made its way across my lips. "If nothing else, you've gained a friend for your lion," I said with a playful nod at the figurine.

"You have a point." I watched as his eyes betrayed his typically guarded smile.

"Come," I said, "Let's find breakfast."

❋ ❋ ❋

We'd risen to find two trays of food just outside our door, arrayed with bread, fruit, cheese, three small jars of tea, and freshly boiled water in an elaborately engraved clay pot. I'd have normally preferred to dine with the rest of the family, but I appreciated Deborah's thoughtfulness. Everything felt so new and foreign, the prospect of enjoying a private breakfast with Isaac before venturing out to learn more about my new life and home seemed fitting.

While I was quickly learning that Isaac truly was a man of few words, I was relieved to find his silence companionable, and even comforting. It was almost as if he reserved speech for the most important moments, and I found that my ear was becoming increasingly attuned to those times.

After breakfast, I washed my face and hands before brushing and plaiting my hair. Doing so had always been therapeutic to me, a ritual that I enjoyed every morning and evening, one that allowed me to sit with my thoughts in peace. Normally, I'd hear Deborah bustling around the room behind me, her movements a welcome and familiar sound. The quietness of the room struck me, and I turned around to find Isaac observing me from our table by the hearth. "Now you are truly watching me, and you can't deny it," I said with a lift of my eyebrow.

He leaned his elbow against the table, his hand covering most of his mouth. "You've caught me. To be fair, it's nearly impossible for a man not to stare at a beautiful woman as she brushes her hair. It goes against the laws of nature," he said as his eyes shone with amusement.

"You're free to admire as you'd like, it's your right. Anyway, it's nice to know that someone gets to see all of this hair before it's covered for the day." I wound the end of my braid with a piece of leather before slipping my veil on. "May I ask you a question?"

"Of course, what is it?"

"What were you doing out in the fields when we arrived, if you didn't know we were coming?" I rose and walked back to where he sat, toying with one of the bracelets Eliezer had given me.

"Each day, I make my rounds and oversee our head farmers as they tend to our flocks, herds, and crops. I end the day visiting our southernmost well. In all, it's a several kilometer distance I travel each day. You arrived when I was on my way home."

A several kilometer journey with multiple stops to speak with his family's farmers and servants was likely a far more strenuous day than he was letting on. That he did so each day was astounding. I hesitated a moment before asking him the one question that had lingered in my mind since the evening before. "It looked like you were kneeling on the ground, or bent over something when we arrived. Were you meditating?"

I looked up to find Isaac studying me, and realized too late that I likely allowed my characteristic curiosity to get the best of me. Relief flooded through me when he nodded and smiled.

"Yes, I was. One of my favorite parts of each day is meditating before I return home. I enjoy the vastness and silence of my surroundings, and it affords me the opportunity to speak with the Lord." He reached out for my hand, tracing the lines of my palm. "Would you like to come?"

"Come meditate with you?" I asked, struggling to stay focused on our conversation with my hand in his.

His laugh came out in a breath, and he paused to look up at me. "Sure, that would be fine. But I meant to ask if you would like to join me on my daily rounds, to meet our farmers and get a better understanding of the land."

It'd been years since I last joined my father on his daily visits and work in the fields; something I missed dearly. Joining him granted me the luxury of being out in the open air, visiting the animals, and greeting our neighbors. I hadn't expected to be able to do the same as a new wife, especially so soon after my arrival.

"I'd like that," I said with a smile.

❊ ❊ ❊

After we readied ourselves for the day, we left our tent in search of food and water to pack. Isaac opened the tent's flap, letting in the dazzling morning light. As my eyes adjusted, I was able to fully appreciate the beauty of my surroundings. Having arrived late the evening before, I hadn't had time to admire the lushness of the fig trees that lined the happy little brook just behind us. I smiled and allowed myself to enjoy the first instance of true and utter peace that I had felt since the night before I left home.

I turned to look for Isaac, who leaned patiently against a tree. "Shall we?" he said, and I nodded in response.

As we walked by the tents, I couldn't help but wonder over the difference the morning had made. What was now tranquil had been boisterous the evening before. The tables, though they were now clear of dishes and food, displayed the remnants of the decor that had graced our party. I couldn't help but wonder just what else the following six evenings of the marriage supper and celebration would bring.

I followed Isaac closely as I surreptitiously looked in the entrance of each tent we passed. All were decorated with fine furniture and lined with woven tapestries and linens of all textures and patterns. Each tent boasted its own unique appeal, far more elaborate than anything I'd ever seen, though none came close to Sarah's tent.

As I looked in on what appeared to be another servants' tent, I found Deborah kneeling over a basket of laundry.

"Oh! Here you are," I said. "I was wondering where you were."

Deborah looked up in surprise before casting a glance above my head and bowing slightly. "Good morning. Are you both off for the day?"

"Yes, I am joining Isaac as he makes his daily rounds. We will be back in time to prepare for this evening's festivities, of course."

"Very well. May I go to your tent to straighten up and unpack the rest of your belongings?" Deborah said with another nervous look at Isaac.

"Of course, please do. And Deborah?" I looked back at Isaac before stepping into the tent so as to speak with her privately. He seemed to understand my cue, and tilted his head to Deborah before walking down to the next collection of tents. "Please don't act so strange, you have nothing to be afraid of. You are being unusually shy, even for you."

"I'm sorry, Rebekah. I've just never been around a man like him. Doesn't he make you nervous?"

I paused in thought, surprised to find that I no longer felt the nerves I had just yesterday. Meeting Isaac had put all of my fears and anxieties to rest. His calm and steady demeanor, his solid presence, they'd been a balm to my soul. "Actually, no he doesn't. At least, he doesn't anymore. He's a good man, and I enjoy his company, though I will miss sharing a tent with you," I said with a giggle.

A hint of a smile crossed her lips. "All right then, I'll do my best to be less shy in his presence."

"Is your new room adequate? If you need anything at all, please tell me. I want to make sure you're as comfortable, if not more comfortable, than you were at my father's." I faltered as I spoke, feeling a jolt of homesickness wash over me. It had been Deborah's home, too—one that she undoubtedly missed every moment, just like I did.

"Actually, my new room is even better than I expected. It's not far from yours, and I share it with Lydia, another handmaid. It's twice the size that you and I shared before. I'll be very comfortable," Deborah said with a smile. "Now, go. Your husband must be wondering what we're up to, and I'm determined to stay in his good graces."

I gave Deborah's hand a gentle squeeze, promising to find her before dinner. I walked out into the sunshine to find Isaac waiting for me.

"Thank you for your patience while I spoke with Deborah," I said as I stepped closer to him.

"Is she settling in well?" he said, a touch of concern tingeing his brow.

"Quite well. It seems that your welcome extended past myself and included everyone I brought with me. I am grateful." I smiled up at him, enjoying our proximity and the comfort we already had in each other's presence.

Isaac smiled and nodded before offering me his hand. "Come," he said, "we must get to the stables now if we are to make it back in time for supper." With one hand in mine, and the other carrying a basket of our provisions, he drew me forward.

❊ ❊ ❊

The remainder of the weeklong marriage celebration was over as soon as it had begun. We enjoyed the sunshine by day, and the luxuries of decadent food and dancing by night. Wearing new, intricately embroidered dresses while laughing and twirling in the candlelight had been unforgettable, but I'd loved my time alone with Isaac, when I'd watched him work and learned about his life, even more.

The week of merrymaking left me craving the comfort of a familiar meal. So, after Isaac left in the morning, I set about gathering the supplies I needed for a dish as familiar to me as the back of my own hand, one that Mother had taught me to make as soon as I could be trusted at the hearth.

Deborah crouched next to me, stoking the fire as I chopped the herbs for the venison. We'd spent the morning catching up and exchanging stories about the past week. It was a comfort to spend time as just the two of us again; it felt like home. As I added the herbs and venison to the mixture in the stone pot over the fire, my stomach grumbled with anticipation.

"Does he like venison?" Deborah asked, interrupting my thoughts.

"He said he does. Here's hoping he likes mine." I stared into the pot, lost in thought. "Well, I haven't met anyone who didn't love Mother's venison recipe. We'll just have to wait several hours to find out."

While the food simmered over the fire, we set about preparing the tent for dinner. Aside from our breakfast the morning after our wedding, this would be my first time enjoying a private meal with Isaac. I wanted him to enjoy it.

Deborah had salvaged a smaller tablecloth from the previous night's festivities, and we draped it over the small table in my room. While she began placing candles around our table and hearth, I polished the stoneware, pausing every so often to check on the food. We worked in companionable silence, and it wasn't until she spoke that I realized how deeply I had been lost in thought.

"What will you wear tonight?"

We turned to eye my growing wardrobe. Prior to my arrival, I would have never dreamed that it was possible to live in such luxury. Every day, new apparel and jewelry even finer than the last were brought to me as a gift from Isaac. Growing up, I'd been accustomed to making do with three main dresses, which took care of everything I needed. While we were well off, it was important to my father that we didn't stand out too loudly among our neighbors. He'd always made sure that Laban and I had clothes made out of quality, if not slightly plain, materials. Standing there surrounded by jewels, gold, and shimmering garments, I couldn't help but think that Father would be pleased to finally see me adorned in the beautiful things he'd always wanted to give me.

"Oh, I'm not sure. Every night has been one elaborate dress or another. I think I'd like to wear something simple tonight."

Deborah nodded in agreement while appraising the options in front of us with her hands on her hips. "I think that's a good idea. However, you have to wear the jewelry he's given you."

I rolled my eyes playfully, wondering whether other handmaids had the same amount of input over their ladies' attire as she did. Even so, I wouldn't have it any other way.

We spent the next several hours talking, sewing, and intermittently checking on dinner as it simmered over the fire. As dusk began, I took my hair out of its braids while Deborah chose my clothing and jewelry for the evening. She selected a simple dress made of cerulean linen, pairing it with a mixture of gold and silver bracelets, earrings, rings, and necklaces. After one final look at me to ensure her work was done and a quick squeeze of my hands, she left for the evening.

I sat by the hearth, enjoying the glow of the fire, when I heard Isaac enter the tent. Standing up to greet him, I watched as he took in his surroundings. When his eyes found the hearth and table, I saw the room as he saw it—its coziness paired with the inviting scent of stew wafting throughout the space serving as the perfect combination. I couldn't help but laugh to myself as I watched him place his staff and shoes by the door. Even after a long day of traveling in the heat, he looked as handsome as he had in the morning. His olive skin, tanned from countless hours spent in the sun, set off his golden eyes.

I realized a moment too late that I was staring. In my attempt to find something else to focus my attention on, I grabbed the nearest plate, which only made me feel even more foolish. Determined to avoid Isaac's attention, I picked at a nonexistent piece of dust. Noticing the silence, I glanced up to see Isaac facing me, his hand covering his mouth, his shoulders shaking.

"Are you laughing at me?" I said, clutching the utterly clean plate in both hands.

"Never," he said, visibly working to remove any trace of a smile from his face. "Did you get the plate clean?"

I huffed out a sigh of irritation and swallowed my laugh. "I'd caution you to watch what you say to your cook this evening. Unless you weren't hungry after all?"

At my words, Isaac peered over my shoulder and into the simmering pot, sniffing appreciatively. "No, I'm quite hungry. Is it ready to eat?"

I shooed him away, failing to hide my pleasure at his excitement over my cooking. I refused to admit to myself just how nervous I had been to prepare my first meal for him. Over the short time I'd had to get to know Isaac, it had become apparent just how much he loved food. Sitting across from him as we ate each night allowed me to learn more about him, his childhood, and his vision for his father's land. Normally taciturn, he opened up quite naturally when we shared a meal. It was as if he took off his invisible armor, if even for just a short while. I'd come to crave that side of him, and had committed myself to helping him open up, little by little, dish by dish.

We sat across from each other while the fire flickered to our right. After allowing him a few minutes to enjoy his venison in peace, I finally decided to ask him the question that had been sitting in the back of my mind since the moment I'd arrived. "What was she like—your mother? What was Sarah like?" I'd asked Eliezer the same question on the first night of our journey, but I wanted to hear Isaac's perspective.

He sat back in his chair, playing with his spoon while studying me. Heat crept up my cheeks, and I instantly regretted asking him. What was I thinking, reminding him of the mother he missed every day, and in whose tent we now sat?

Before I could apologize and change the subject, he leaned forward. "She was a lot like you, actually. Strong, resilient, a natural leader. While our servants would swear that it was my father they feared, each would secretly admit to the fact that it was she who managed to make our land a home. She was also beautiful. I never grew accustomed to the stares that followed her everywhere we went."

"Is it difficult for you to be here, to stay in her tent?" I asked, forcing myself to speak above a whisper.

"In some ways, yes. But in other ways, it's healing to be here. This place was her pride and joy—she spent many years acquiring the finest linens and tapestries so as to make it what it is now. Before she died, she made me promise to bring my future wife here. Who am I to go against her will?" His mouth twisted into a rueful smile as he turned to grab the ladle. "Now, I am absolutely famished and this is the best meal I've had in a long time. Am I free to eat more?"

Giggling, I nodded before coming around the table to serve him what remained of the venison. "You may always have as much as you'd like," I said as I handed him his bowl, hesitating ever so slightly before bending down to give him a light kiss on the cheek.

While I was nowhere near the example of a perfect woman, I did know that I would do anything it took to make Isaac smile each day. Seeing him mourn the loss of his mother, watching him soldier on through his pain, moved my heart in inexpressible ways. We both missed those we loved deeply—a feeling that seemed impossible to overcome, but one that could be easily vanquished through true, whole, and unconditional love.

Silently, I vowed to fill the void that Sarah had left in his heart and home in any way I could.

PART TWO

"And the LORD said unto her, Two nations are in thy womb, and two manner of people. . ." Genesis 25:23

CHAPTER NINE

Twenty years later

Deborah and I stood under the cool shade of the fig trees, each of us holding baskets brimming with fruit at our sides. I brushed the back of my hand across my forehead, breathing out a sigh as I leaned against a tree trunk. "We really aren't as young and agile as we once were," I said as I used as little energy as possible to turn my head to look at her.

Deborah leaned against an adjacent tree, fanning herself with a large leaf. "We're hardly approaching middle age, Rebekah. I think it's probably time for us to admit that we've always been this way, especially after a strenuous harvesting season."

I laughed with her, though the dull ache of the reminder of how quickly time had passed threatened to resurface. Twenty years had floated by in a gentle breeze of laughter and love, and a fair amount of heartache. Isaac and I had grown close, building our love for each other over the bittersweet memories of people we missed. Before long, we fell into a routine—Isaac started his day before sunrise and ended it with meditation at sundown; I learned my way around the land and household, becoming fond of my new family and comfortable with my responsibilities.

Together, Deborah and I oversaw nineteen harvests just like this one. We labored tirelessly in the heat, picking and preserving fruit and vegetables, and planting for the season ahead. While we had plenty of servants to do the work for us, I preferred to work alongside them, rather than waiting at home for Isaac to return each day. Working gave me a sense of purpose, and I enjoyed the feeling of stretching out my sore, tired limbs at the end of the night with the satisfaction of knowing that another day of productive labor was behind me. Deborah had often commented on my inability to enjoy the luxuries of the new life given to me, but we both knew that I worked to keep my mind off of the fears that haunted me.

After our wedding, Abraham regained his strength, remarried, and fathered more sons. Each passing year and new child bore a reminder of the life I had yet to create. While I was happy to be Isaac's wife, while I enjoyed managing our household and land, I heard the echoes of the laughter of the children I didn't have. They followed me when I woke up, and as I walked in the brook. They shimmered through the leaves, sometimes tricking me into believing that they were real, that my loneliness was a product of my own tragic imagination. Isaac never complained about the fact that we hadn't yet conceived, nor did he blame me, as so many other men would. Instead, we started and ended each night in prayer, asking the Lord to bless us with a child. Isaac's patience and calm, steady confidence in the fact that we would one day bear children was just one of many reasons why he would forever have my heart.

Even so, the pain and fear of failing him and his family nagged at me each day. Without an heir, where would Isaac's inheritance, Abraham's blessing, go? While Abraham was in good health, he wouldn't live forever, and I had begun to wonder if I'd already reached the last of my childbearing years. I was quite young for that to be a concern, but it wasn't impossible. It was the only way I could make sense of my twenty years of barrenness. Isaac had never expressed a wish to take a concubine like his father had, but I couldn't help but wonder if one day the wait for a child would have been enough. I couldn't bear the thought of the shame; I couldn't bear the thought of sharing him with someone else.

Approaching voices broke through my reverie. I jumped up, brushing off my skirt and readjusting my veil. "What do you think, Deborah? Would you say we're safe to end our day here and head home?"

Deborah appraised the rows of fig trees, her mental calculations showing on her face. "I believe that would be fine, yes. It is probably a good idea to let everyone go home and rest, so that we can finish out the season within the week."

I nodded in agreement before turning to greet the approaching group of women and children. Our company of laborers had grown noticeably in the last several years—we now had over one hundred women and children to assist with harvesting, drying, and planting each year. While there were many of us, I enjoyed spending each day with them, and made it a point to get to know each individual over the course of the three-month season.

After making sure that everyone was present, I sent them home with instructions on what time to return in the morning. I left out the fact that a feast awaited them at home, preferring to surprise them instead.

The breeze loosened what hair remained in my braid, causing it to tickle my neck as we began our slow return home. I watched as children wove in and out of the throng of women, tapping on each other's shoulders and squealing with delight. Earlier in the day, an elderly woman had whispered her offer of yet another mandrake fertility recipe. Her offer was kind if unbidden, and she hadn't been the first or even the tenth to offer some form of cure for my failure to conceive. I often wondered if Isaac experienced the same. I doubted it.

After returning home to enjoy the feast, Isaac and I shared a warm blanket by the little fire we'd built in the clearing outside our tent. The evenings had begun to cool, and we'd come to cherish these moments of quiet together at the end of each day. Stars glittered overhead, and I listened to the distant laughter of the few remaining children who had managed to avoid going to bed.

"Do you blame me?" I said while staring into the flames.

"For what?"

"For our lack of children. It's been nearly twenty years, Isaac. I started to give up hope long ago."

He shook his head, putting his heavy arm around me and pulling me to his side. "How could I blame you? While I would love to have as many children with you as there are stars in the sky, it's not our will we follow. It's His."

Several minutes passed in silence as I studied the way the flames fluttered in brilliant tones of blue, orange, and yellow. Without realizing that I spoke aloud, I said, "You aren't thinking of taking a concubine, are you?"

Isaac froze in the middle of caressing my arm, turning slowly to look at me. I felt his eyes bore into the side of my face, studying me in the way that he always did. When I didn't meet his gaze, he put his hand under my chin, turning my face gently to look at his. "You are the only woman I have ever loved, and will ever be with. Has this been bothering you for long?"

I brushed an errant tear from my cheek, nodding while looking down at my lap. "I—I just know how important it is to you, and how important it is to your father to carry on his blessing in our family. I don't know what I'll do if I can't bear you a child after all." My voice broke and I forced myself to breathe in deeply.

"Rebekah, I have no fears or concerns as to our lineage, or whether or not we have children. It is my hope that we will conceive, and I have no doubt that the Lord can and will bless us with a child in His time. If He doesn't, I accept that outcome, too."

I picked up a stray twig, balancing it in my palm as I considered what he said. "Most women my age have a job, a purpose. I keep busy, but I don't feel that I have fully grasped either of those things. No one needs me in the way that a child needs their mother. I watch the women work each day, tending to our crops while nurturing their children, and I want so badly for that to be me. What have I done wrong to deserve this?" Tears spilled down my cheeks and neck and onto my dress.

Isaac pulled me into his chest, cupping my jaw with one hand, and stroking my hair with the other. "If you do nothing else in this life other than be my wife, you will have done enough. You oversee our land, our servants, our household; you keep our books. You make me and our hundreds of servants happy. Don't forget that."

I was tempted to bite back and complain about the well-meaning comments and insinuations about my inability to conceive. Instead, we sat quietly, listening to the crackle of the fire as frogs trilled and crickets chirped behind us.

❊ ❊ ❊

The bed shifted, and I felt the empty space behind me. I sat up, blinking my eyes in the darkness. It certainly wasn't dawn, or anywhere near it.

"Isaac?" I croaked.

"Please, go back to sleep," he whispered. "I won't be long. There is something I need to tend to outside." He stroked my cheek with his thumb before turning to leave. A brief flash of the night sky showed through the opening of the tent flap before it quickly disappeared.

I sat in the dark, trying to work through the murky waters of my drowsiness. For as long as I had known him, Isaac had strictly adhered to structure and routine. He had never left in the middle of the night to tend to something on our land, or in our household. Everything waited until dawn.

What was he up to?

I tiptoed through the darkness, blindly pulling on my sandals and day dress. Peeking through the door, I found Isaac on his knees at the end of the clearing, his face turned up to the sky. His indistinct murmurings were enough for me to realize that he was in the middle of a prayer. Struggling between wanting to join him to find out what he was praying for, and knowing he deserved his privacy, I paused a moment before letting the tent door drop in front of me. After slipping off my sandals and dress, I crawled back into our bed, lying in the shadows of my questions and fears.

CHAPTER TEN

We expect to experience change at a certain, specific, and special moment in time, as if life decides to earmark a moment and deem it suitable. But oftentimes, that's not the case. Oftentimes, we experience those course-changing shifts while performing our most mundane, everyday tasks. Like drawing water.

I'd drawn water for my family every evening for years, never knowing that one day I wouldn't again. That evening at the well had slipped past my awareness, parading under the guise of a morning and day like so many mornings and days before. The only difference being that that night, I had walked down to the well and drawn water for my family for the last time.

In the middle of an unseasonably cold winter, I stood over a pot of boiling water while stirring in the dried figs we'd harvested. I planned to use them to make a cake for Isaac for dessert. The room smelled sweet, fragrant with spice and fruit. As I bent over the pot, sniffing it appreciatively, I felt them for the first time.

Tiny flutters, microscopic bubbles. Then realization, then joy.

* * *

Overwhelmed with happiness, Isaac had commanded that a weeklong feast be held in celebration. The last time we had dined and danced at that scale had been for Abraham's marriage, and our marriage before that. This reception was different, but in many ways, it was better.

Rather than join the merriment, I sat at our table and hummed along to the music with one hand placed over my stomach. Initially, Isaac hadn't wanted to leave my side. But things were different now—even alone, I no longer felt lonely. I'd never seen him display his feelings, this level of joy, outwardly. So, I encouraged him to join in the dancing and mirth, with his promise to fetch regular refreshments as each night wore on.

As dancers twirled by in a flash of color and tinkling bells, I felt my stomach flip. Once, then twice. I looked down to see it moving rapidly, though I sat still. With a gasp, I bent over to steady myself as I felt what could only be described as a struggle inside of me. It stopped and started intermittently, before halting as quickly as it began.

"Are you all right?" Deborah whispered in my right ear, making me jump.

"I'm not sure. I feel strange. I was enjoying the festival, but then it suddenly felt as if something were kicking me from inside. It felt as if—as if the baby were fighting me. Or fighting something else."

Deborah stared at me in concern before leaning forward to pat my hand. "Let's get you to bed. This has been a wild evening for everyone, much less you in your condition. I can send for a midwife in the morning, if you wish."

I stood up to follow her, feeling like a small child, but grateful to be taken care of. We walked back to my tent arm in arm, the music and laughter fading with each step.

❊ ❊ ❊

Concerned by my disappearance, Isaac had come to find me shortly after I'd gotten into bed. After I'd assured him that all was well, he'd fallen fast asleep.

I listened to his rhythmic breathing as I laid on my back and stared up at the ceiling. In the dim light, I could just make out the gentle swaying of the roof of our tent in the breeze. Something about those movements, those kicks, hadn't felt right. Knowing that I wouldn't be able to sleep, I crept outside. The coolness of the fresh air soothed my rattled nerves, and I knelt down in the damp grass, sitting back on my heels to look up at the sky. I realized with amusement that I was sitting just as Isaac had only months before. Hadn't he been praying when I found him?

Without knowing what I intended to say, or what I was hoping to understand, I closed my eyes and began in a whisper. "Lord, I do not understand what it is that I am feeling. It doesn't feel normal, and I am worried about the baby. I waited so long to have a child, I don't know what I'll do—" my voice broke with a sob as I allowed the fear to wrap its grip around my neck. A sudden burst of wind slammed into my back, pushing me forward before it stilled. The hair on my arms stood up as I looked around in bewilderment. The night, while quiet before, was now utterly silent. I could no longer hear the trickling of the brook, or the chirp of crickets.

I waited for a few moments, refusing to move. A light breeze ruffled my hair, and I heard the delicate tinkling of what sounded like thousands of bells. Abruptly, a voice broke through the sound.

Rebekah.

I fell backward, catching myself on my hands while wildly searching for the speaker. Seeing no one, I called out, "Who is it? Who are you?"

My heart raced; all at once, every sense was magnified. The grass became needle sharp, its dew seeming to stand still, as if awaiting what happened next. At the sound of a distant rumble, I closed my eyes and held my breath, only to realize that I heard my own blood flowing through my veins.

In wonder, I waited.

The struggle that you feel inside you is from two children, not one. Two nations are in your womb, bringing with them two manners of people. One nation will prove to be stronger than the other; the elder shall serve the younger.

I stared at the clearing in front of me, stupefied. "Do you mean to tell me that I am carrying two sons?"

The bells began again, tinkling past me in a gust of wind before disappearing completely. I struggled to understand what had just taken place, and how I would explain this experience to anyone else. Isaac had told me a story of how the Lord had appeared to Abraham when he was ninety years old to form a covenant. But Abraham was different—I was different. Aside from that, bearing twins was rare. I had yet to meet any woman who had done so in my time.

Was I a fool to believe that God had actually spoken to me?

As I watched dawn begin to break on the horizon, I knew in my soul, however much I wanted to doubt what I had just experienced, that I carried two hearts, two souls, inside of me. I felt it in their daily movements, their little kicks and games of tug of war.

Elation coursed through me as I thought about everything I had just learned. After twenty years of waiting and praying, I was blessed with not one son, but two. In the midst of wondering what they'd be like, one single sentence kept echoing in my mind.

The elder shall serve the younger.

CHAPTER ELEVEN

A distant scream pierced the air. I looked up at the ceiling, watching light flecked with dust particles float through the small gap at the top of my tent. Clutching Deborah's hand, the sounds of the nurses and midwife met my ears again in a rush of noise. It was only then that I realized the scream had come from me.

* * *

I'd been sitting with my back against an oak tree, enjoying the cool shade and gentle breeze, when it was finally time. The day I'd been hoping and praying for these last twenty years had come. I'd looked at Deborah with a gasp and mute nod, unable to breathe.

She and Isaac had ordered me to rest for the last sixty days, allowing me short, daily walks with one or both of them by my side. While I had originally been frustrated by my incapacitation and guardianship, I was relieved when the time came to find Deborah close by. Without a word, Deborah had run to fetch Isaac, before ordering the midwife and nursemaids to ready the tent.

Just a few months prior, Isaac had given Eliezer and his son responsibility over the daily management of our land, agriculture, and livestock, so that he could remain nearby for the impending birth of our sons. After twenty years of spending each day apart, I had cherished the time we'd had together as my pregnancy drew on. Aside from his daily meetings with servants and overseers, he'd had time to tend to things at home. He'd built and prepared the nursery, while I wove and sewed. In between our work, we spent any free time we had splashing in the brook, watching the sun glint off of the tiny waves we made with our feet.

Isaac had come running, fire in his eyes, with Deborah

trailing far behind. After giving me a kiss on the forehead, he'd lifted me gently, and carried me to the birthing tent.

Now, hours later, I squatted close to the ground, bathed in a pool of my own sweat and riddled with unbearable pain. In between my feverish daydreams, I remembered that night I had spent in the clearing, the prayer I had prayed, and the answer I had received.

"Deborah," I gasped, before breathing through another round of contractions. "There are two."

Deborah's warm, brown eyes rounded as she realized what I had said. She bent down, shifting to face me while blocking the others out. "Are you sure?" she mouthed.

I nodded frantically before closing my eyes.

Once again, sound dissipated as the contractions overwhelmed my body. I heard the distant echoes of Deborah urgently ordering the midwife and nursemaids to prepare for two babies. Then, the ensuing sounds of muffled panic.

❊ ❊ ❊

What could have been several minutes or hours later, I awoke to a cool palm pressing on my forehead. I opened my eyes to see Isaac, a broad smile on his face.

"Are they healthy?" I said while holding his hand to my cheek.

"Yes, my love. They're perfect."

I struggled to sit up, looking around the room frantically. I remembered telling Deborah that there were two children. I remembered the contractions, and the torment of desperately wanting to lie down and sleep—but that was it. The rest had become a gauzy memory.

I looked to my left to find Deborah and another maid from my childhood, Selah, walking slowly toward us with small bundles in their arms. My breath hitched. In all my life, I'd never felt the joy and yearning that I did now. Twenty years of prayer, of tears, of hope, of heartbreak, had led to this.

Deborah placed the first bundle in my arms, and I looked down at the shock of hair that peeked out from the swaddle.

Bewildered, I glanced at Deborah, and then Isaac, finding amusement in both of their faces. "He's so. . ." I searched for the words, unable to describe the child I held in my arms. I'd never seen anything, or anyone, quite like him. Finally, I tore my eyes away from his furious little face to look up at Isaac. "Red. He's so red, Isaac. How?"

Isaac laughed quietly. "I said the same thing. He reminds me of a fox," he said as he gently stroked his hair.

Throughout the pregnancy, we'd discussed potential names with the assumption that just one baby would arrive. Whether it was due to shock, or fear, or both, I hadn't told Isaac what the Lord had told me that night in the clearing. Rather, I'd let him assume we'd have one child, preferring to give him the surprise of finding two, instead of the heartbreak of meeting just one or none. We hadn't been able to come to an agreement on a name in those nine months, but here, looking down at the small, glowing face that stared up at me, I had a moment of clarity. "Esau," I said. "His name should be Esau."

Isaac continued stroking his head, finally stopping to nod and look at me. "It suits him."

A throat cleared, and I looked up at Selah, remembering the second child she held. Gently, I passed Esau back to Deborah, before holding my arms out to the small, squirming bundle.

As she placed him in my arms, I stared down in wonder. He was smaller than his brother, with coloring like Isaac's. His tiny mouth opened and closed in defiance. "Jacob."

"A fitting name," said Isaac in bemusement. "He came out on the heels of his brother, quite literally. When Esau arrived, the midwife was surprised to see that Jacob held onto Esau's heel until he, too, made his entrance into the world. He's stubborn like his mother." Pride flooded Isaac's face as he looked down at me, and then his son.

Shame washed over me as I remembered the same six words that had echoed in my mind these past months. *The elder shall serve the younger.* Not fully believing or understanding what I'd heard, I'd neglected to tell Isaac, or give it any further credence. But here, now, while holding Jacob and hearing about his birth, certainty grew in every fiber of my being.

For reasons unknown to me, I held the future heir of

Abraham's blessing, of Isaac's inheritance, in my arms. And I would do everything in my power to protect him.

CHAPTER TWELVE

As was customary with an eldest child, much less the eldest son, Isaac and Esau were inseparable from the moment of his birth. As soon as the boys were weaned, Isaac resumed active management of our land, agriculture, and livestock, bringing Esau along with him each day.

While in diapers, Esau had already begun to show his strength and size. He was inarguably taller and stronger than any toddler I'd met, with boundless energy and the same zest for the land, and for hunting, that his father had.

Jacob was different from him in every aspect. While he was smaller than his brother, he caught on quickly, learning to speak weeks before Esau, and taking interest in the things I did early on. Initially, Isaac tried to bring both boys with him on his rounds. But after a few days, he decided it would be best to leave Jacob at home, as Esau showed interest and boundless energy that Jacob lacked. Inwardly, I was pleased to have the gift of Jacob by my side as I wove, harvested, cooked, and managed the house. As he grew, he took to those tasks, learning them with skill. And as I watched his brother grow stronger and more adept in the ways of his father, my trepidation grew, too. How would he usurp Esau's position and inheritance with plain household skills?

As both boys grew from infants to toddlers, and toddlers to children, I questioned whether I'd misunderstood the Lord's message. It had been years since that prayerful night, long enough for me to question whether that encounter had really even happened. Deep down, however, I knew it had. I just didn't know how the plan would be realized.

✳ ✳ ✳

Deborah and I sat under the shade of that same oak, enjoying the relief from the sweltering summer morning. Esau and

Jacob, now seven, ran through the grass toward us.

"Mama," Esau said proudly, "look what I've found you." He reached me several paces before Jacob did, breathing evenly as he lifted his upturned palm to show a smooth, white stone.

"It's beautiful. Where did you find it?"

Esau began to answer as Jacob joined us, breathless and waving his closed fist overhead.

"I got one even better, Mama," said Jacob with glee. "Mine sparkles." He opened his hand to reveal a rough, black stone with iridescent purple, green and blue veining throughout.

"That is beautiful, Jacob. Here, show that to Deborah," I said as I urged him toward her. Even though Deborah had raised him alongside me, he was still shy in her presence.

As Deborah bent her head over Jacob's small palm, Esau began to whine. "That's not fair, you said mine was beautiful, but you didn't have me show Deborah. He told me we were in a race to find the prettiest rock we could find, and that the first one to make it to you wins. So I won. Now I want his rock instead!" He kicked the dirt for emphasis, sending twigs and leaves scattering around us.

"Now, Esau—"

"Do you really want mine instead of yours?" Jacob wheedled.

Esau's copper head of hair nodded furiously.

"Fine. Give me your rock, and I'll put it behind my back with my rock. If you guess which hand mine is in, you can have it."

Esau cast a questioning glance at me, and I shrugged. I was just as interested to see where Jacob was going with this game as he was.

Jacob put his hand out, palm up, waiting for Esau to give him the stone. Once he did, he covered both with his tiny hands, shaking them as if he were casting lots, before separating them into two fists behind his back. "Now, guess which one my rock is in, and you can have it."

Esau stared at him with a furrowed brow. "It's in that one," he said as he pointed to Jacob's left hand.

Jacob's back was to me, and I watched as he swapped the rocks in his hands, before offering the correct one up to Esau. "You guessed right. Here you go."

Giddy over his spoils, Esau skipped away, hooting and

tumbling through the grass and into the sunshine. Jacob watched him quietly, his shoulders slumped.

"That was very nice of you to play that game and let him win, Jacob," I said gently.

It was then that he turned to me, triumph written across his face. "I wanted the white rock all along," he said with pride.

Deborah and I exchanged a questioning glance, and I told Jacob to go and play with his brother. We watched as he walked away slowly, proudly, studying the prize he carried in his palm.

Once he was out of earshot, Deborah turned to me. "He's quick-witted, that one. We'll have to keep an eye on him." She arched her brow.

I nodded in agreement. "He needs to be that way, if he'll ever outshine his brother."

Shortly after their birth, I told Deborah what the Lord had told me. I had been unable to continue to carry the burden of the knowledge alone, and Deborah had known my every thought, fear, and dream since we were young. I'd trusted that she would believe me, and she hadn't let me down.

"Yes, I suppose you're right," she said, deep in thought. "But how will that be? Shouldn't you tell Isaac?"

"No. I love my husband, but he keeps to his traditions. The eldest always inherits. Telling him so many years later would not only confuse him, it would worry him," I said while neglecting to answer her question of how Jacob would take Esau's rightful place.

The truth was that I didn't have a clue. But I knew that with his upbringing and future left to me, it would come to pass. One way or another.

❋ ❋ ❋

"The boys are becoming quite the contrasting pair," I said as I looked at Isaac in the mirror while brushing my hair. One of his favorite things to do after a particularly strenuous day was to sit on our bed and watch as I unplaited and brushed my hair in the evening. It had become our ritual.

I saw the shadow of a smile cross his face as he closed his

eyes and leaned his head against the pillows. "They each have their own set of strengths, those two. With time, I am certain they will become great men."

"Yes, I am sure they will," I hesitated while staring at the bottle of oil in my hand. "Though, I am a bit concerned about Esau's impudence. Aren't you?"

Isaac opened his eyes and studied me intently. Slowly, he got out of bed and made his way to me. I watched him in the reflection until I felt his hands on my shoulders. "He's young, my love, but he's brave. He has everything he needs to be a great leader of our future nations. Just look at his skills as a hunter, and how he feeds us. Don't you worry." He bent down to kiss the top of my head. "I'll make sure he gets better with time."

I leaned back into Isaac, taking comfort in his presence and surety.

"And let's not forget Jacob's cunningness, either. I know that he is dear to you, Rebekah, but he presents his own set of weaknesses, too." He squeezed my shoulders, his eyes twinkling playfully in the mirror.

"You're right, he can be artful in getting his way. But he is intelligent, and slower to anger—" I cut myself off, realizing how ridiculous I sounded comparing my own two sons to each other. "I apologize. You know I love them both. It's a mother's job to worry."

"And that," Isaac said with a kiss, "is one thing you will never do poorly."

CHAPTER THIRTEEN

After the birth of the boys, Abraham lived for fifteen more joyful years. He spent each of his remaining days making them smile with his stories, and enjoying time with his wife, Keturah, as well as his sons.

Just when we were beginning to think he'd outlive us all, he died peacefully, quietly, one afternoon when he laid down to rest. Many mourned the thought of him dying alone, but Isaac was quick to remind them that the Lord had been next to him, guiding him each day, until it was time to take him home.

Watching Isaac absorb the loss of his father while assuming the mantle of his inheritance left me in awe. In comparison to others in our household, I had only known Abraham for a handful of years, yet I missed him deeply. I could only imagine the pain that my husband felt. Isaac and his half-brother, Ishmael, laid Abraham to rest with Sarah in the Cave of Machpelah, with Eliezer trailing closely behind them. Thousands came to pay their respects and to say their tearful goodbyes—their presence covered the hills and spread over the valleys as far as the eye could see.

I stood at the head of our receiving line, among hundreds from our household who were there to do the same. Together, we bowed over the hands of each visitor, thanking them for coming. Near the end of our sixth day, I bent over a pair of hands that looked alarmingly familiar. Looking up, I gasped as the shock and elation of seeing Laban's face again, thirty-five years later, hit me.

He had matured in ways I couldn't quite put my finger on. He looked the same, just as youthful and vibrant as he had the day I left, but he carried himself as if he had finally come into his own. His warm, playful expression was still there, and he had grown a full beard. The only signs of his age were in the smile lines around his eyes, almost certainly from years of laughter.

"I do hope you recognize me, Sister?" he said cautiously.

It was only then that I believed he was really there, standing in front of me. "Of course," I sobbed. "Of course it is you. I just couldn't believe that you really came, after all of these years."

Deborah approached from behind, smiling as she greeted Laban. "Why don't you two go and catch up? I'll oversee greeting our final visitors for the day," she said.

Overwhelmed with happiness, I walked beside Laban as we made our way across the warm sand. Watching the sun start its slow descent was a relief; it had scorched us these last several days, and every evening came as a welcome reprieve.

"How are Mother and Father?" I asked without preamble.

Laban hesitated before answering. "They're aging, but well. They wanted to come and pay their respects, and also to see you, but I wouldn't allow it. I didn't think the trip would be wise."

I nodded, remembering the bitterly long journey I had undergone as a young woman thirty-five years prior. "Please tell them I miss them so, and that my sons are growing stronger, taller, and hungrier by the day. Speaking of which, here they come." I was pleased to see both Jacob and Esau walking toward us.

At fifteen years of age, Esau was well over six feet tall, and broader even than his father. He had the beginnings of a copper-red beard sprinkling his face, and he walked with the confidence of a seasoned hunter. Jacob had surprised his father and I by growing tall, if still short in comparison to Esau. He had his father's height and a strong, athletic build. Where Esau was loud and brash, Jacob was quietly confident. The two could not be more different.

Laban studied them as they approached. "You were right in describing them as contrasting, Rebekah. I have never seen two brothers look so unlike. Are you sure they are twins?" he joked under his breath.

I stood to hug them both, before gently pushing them toward Laban. "Esau, Jacob, this is your Uncle Laban."

Laban stood and shook each of their hands, before inviting them to sit with us. Over the years, I had apprised Laban and my parents of the boys' growth and interests through servants whom I'd sent with gifts and provisions after each harvest. It touched me to see that Laban had paid attention to those messages, asking Jacob about his studies, and Esau about his hunts. The four of us talked until sundown, and I was pleased to see that Esau and Jacob had taken quickly to their uncle. As the evening's campfires began to dot the horizon, I realized that we had yet to eat supper.

"Come," I said to Laban. "You must join us for a bite to eat."

"You know I'm never one to deny myself a good meal," he said as we stood up, both groaning before looking at each other and laughing.

"Time hasn't exactly been kind to us, has it?" I said as I rubbed my aching neck.

"I wouldn't say that, exactly. You're still as beautiful as the day you left, and you have two strong and capable sons. If anything, I'd say that time has blessed you greatly."

I pondered his words as we began our slow walk back to camp. Esau and Jacob had gone ahead, and were already out of sight. Thirty-five years had come slowly and gone quickly; with them, they had brought an abundance of growth, change, love, and heartbreak. For twenty of those years, I had mourned my inability to bear children. Now, my two sons were nearing adulthood, and I'd have the chance to watch them build families of their own. I wasn't sure when the young, naive Rebekah had disappeared—likely sometime between the walk home from the well, and the journey to meet my husband—but in her place was a strong, capable woman. A survivor.

"Do you remember when we were young, how we'd share secrets?" I turned my head to look up at Laban as he walked beside me. The starry sky framed his outline, and I could just barely make out the glint of his teeth as he smiled at the memory.

"Of course I do. I never did tell anyone those secrets of yours, you know."

"Well you couldn't, under threat of death," I said with a smile. "I ask because I have one more to share with you, if you are willing to hear it."

Laban stopped and turned toward me. "What is it?"

I swallowed to push down the familiar panic that began to

build in my chest. Was it right to tell him? More than anything, I needed Laban's advice and wisdom. He had always been an excellent listener, and he also offered a man's perspective and insight. While Deborah's confidence had been a welcome relief, the secret I carried these fifteen years had only grown heavier with time. I looked up at the constellations overhead, admiring their brilliance, and remembering that evening as vividly as if it had happened just yesterday. "A few months after I knew that I was pregnant, the Lord. . . spoke to me while I was praying." I stopped, waiting to find out if Laban would interject. When he didn't, I continued. "At the time, I had been experiencing the strangest feelings. It felt as if the children were wrestling inside of me. That very same night, the Lord told me that I would not only have twins, but that both would represent two different nations."

Laban nodded. Even in the darkness, I knew he was deep in thought, studying the ground before him.

"But that wasn't all He said, Laban. The surprise of carrying twins would have been enough, but then He said something else. He told me that the elder would serve the younger."

Laban's sharp intake of breath startled me, and I jumped back. "I apologize," he said. "It is a heavy amount of information to take in at once. What happened next?"

"After that, He disappeared. Our conversation was done. I didn't know what to do, and I had a hard time believing that what I had experienced wasn't just a result of my imagination, so I kept it to myself. It wasn't until they were born that I realized my error in not telling Isaac. I should have told him that very evening, but instead, I waited. Then, months became years, and, well, here we are."

"Having met both of my nephews, it is interesting to hear what you have told me. Esau displays all of the attributes of a natural leader, hunter, and warrior. As the firstborn by even minutes, it is only right and natural by our culture that he step into Isaac's place one day. Even so, there's something different about Jacob, Rebekah." I watched as he tilted his head to look up at the sky. "While he may not be Esau's match in size and strength, he is wise beyond his years."

I nodded in agreement. "He has been this way since before

he could talk. Knowing what I do, I've tried to encourage him to spend time in the fields and to hunt with his father and brother, but he isn't interested. He'd rather stay home and learn, cook, help the household. That's why I bring the subject to you, because I don't know what to make of it all. How can I possibly ensure that Isaac gives his blessing to Jacob, instead of Esau? This many years later, I fear telling him what the Lord told me. It would hurt him to know I hid it from him for so long, and I also worry that he will believe I misunderstood. Giving the blessing to the youngest just isn't done, Laban. What do I do?"

After years of asking myself that very same question, it was an overwhelming relief to be able to ask my brother instead. I'd watched the boys grow and play while trying to solve the puzzle that had been given to me. I believed that the Lord had told me for a reason, but whether that reason was to charge me with the task of making sure it became a reality was something that I was still uncertain about.

Laban sighed deeply before reaching out to pat my hand. "Rebekah, you must do what you think is best in order to follow God's will. It seems He has told you how He wants things to be, and He has chosen Jacob. You must make sure that Jacob gets Isaac's blessing, not Esau. However"—he squeezed my hand in reassurance before letting it go—"I do not think it is wise to keep this from Isaac. He is a wise and understanding man. You should tell him."

I let my hand drop to my side, staring at the ground in horror. What had I been thinking by hiding this from Isaac for so many years? My husband, the one person I trusted most in the world? The truth was that my disbelief that night had turned into astonishment, then denial, then fear, and finally, shame. Shame in the fact that I had kept the knowledge from Isaac as we raised our two sons, shame in the fact that I hadn't trusted him enough to listen to me without judgment. Isaac had never betrayed my trust, nor had he ever given me reason to believe that he would deny me anything I wanted or needed. But now, so many years later, it felt as if reopening that door, that secret, would uncover more pain than it was worth.

I would have to make sure that Jacob got what was due to him—and Isaac could never find out.

CHAPTER FOURTEEN

T he years after Abraham's death passed slowly, like one long, extended summer. The boys continued to mature, with Esau spending more of his time outdoors than in, and Jacob becoming increasingly skilled in his studies, as well as the management of our house and property. Esau was a renowned hunter and marksman. Servants and friends would bring with them tales of his bravery, his vigor, his skill. Many of those stories were true, if not inflated, but all of them pleased Isaac and Esau immensely.

By the age of eighteen, Jacob had learned how to butcher and clean all manner of animals, as well as cook. Standing over the fire while stirring a simmering pot of some new, fragrant recipe had become our favorite thing to do together. Aside from that, he was skilled with numbers, and had learned to manage the books and servants for our household and land.

Where Esau was gruff and forceful, Jacob was gentle and cajoling. He had a way with people that was unlike anything I had seen before. He had Laban's wit; Isaac's quiet, steady presence; and as Deborah was quick to add, my craftiness. Combined with his good looks, he had quickly become a man who could easily capture the hearts of many. But the difference was that while Esau took advantage of that gift, Jacob didn't.

As the boys grew older, I couldn't help but notice that more women came to call on us than ever before. Where I might've attributed their visits in earlier years to genuine curiosity about Isaac's new wife and home, it amused me to realize that one day, the intentions of those visits had shifted to focus on my sons instead. It seemed as if every day some young woman would arrive alone, or with her mother, to bring about a recipe or basket of freshly baked bread. They'd linger, having first completed their customary and expected visit with me, watching the entrance of our tent as if waiting for Esau to come crashing through, or for Jacob to happen upon us unannounced. While most women came with the intention of drawing Esau's attention, they left with Jacob on their mind.

Many times, Esau would burst through the door at the perfect time, delighting the women and humoring me. He would impart any number of compliments on the ladies, before exchanging pleasantries that inevitably led to stories of his bravery and skill. They'd laugh, admire him, blush demurely, and beg for the promise of his visit. He always promised, though he rarely visited. It was usually at this time during their call that I would take the opportunity to remember to find Jacob, partly for the fun of it, and partly because there was a side of me that hated the thought of him being overlooked. In my eyes, my dear Jacob was more handsome and skilled than Esau in the things of our world that truly mattered. With his wits, diligence, and wealth, he could hire any number of hunters to feed his family. "You must forgive me," I would say. "Now that you've met my eldest son, you must do me the honor of meeting my youngest."

The ladies would tear their eyes away from Esau to glance at me and nod politely. I'd hasten to find Jacob, who was likely poring over books or speaking with our servants, pulling his arm as he protested until we found our way back to our company. With a small shove, Jacob would find himself in the room, looking at another set of appreciative, doe-like eyes. Perhaps it was my cruel humor as I grew older, or my deep-seated pride in him that made watching the moment they truly looked at him my favorite. Without fail, their faces would transform from that of surprise at his sudden entrance, to admiration. Their eyes would dart over him, before transfiguring back into their guise of shyness. Jacob, unfailingly polite and well spoken, would strike up conversation with them about their interests, home, and family, and within just a few minutes, all thoughts of Esau—who at this point would excuse himself out of boredom—would be forgotten.

While I knew that it was wrong to favor one son over the other, I couldn't help but feel a burden for Jacob that I didn't have for Esau. As the eldest son, Esau was born into privilege and partiality, not only from his father, but from everyone he met. He was viewed as the next great patriarch, and thus, he was respected as such. Because of that, Jacob was left to pave his own path of success, to find his own way to build a legacy and feed his future family. I didn't want that for him, and every time I remembered those same six words from so many years ago, I knew that the life our world had planned for him couldn't, and wouldn't, happen.

* * *

I stood in the shade outside the servants' quarters, bent over a basket of fresh linens. Normally, Deborah would bring them each day, but I had wanted to pay her a visit instead. It gave me the perfect excuse to look in on the others, and spend some time catching up.

As I began to walk back to my tent, I heard a rustle behind me. I turned around to find Esau, covered in sweat and blood, panting for breath. "How was your hunt?" I asked with a quirk of my brow.

"It was excellent, as always," he said with a jovial slap of his chest. "I am famished, though. Have you cooked anything for me to eat?"

"No, not yet. However, Jacob has prepared your favorite pottage," I said with a nod toward the nearby servants' tent. "Why don't you go and ask him for some?"

Esau nodded before sauntering away. I watched him whip the tent flap open, startling a couple of servants, before letting it drop behind him.

Normally, I'd leave him and Jacob to work things out among themselves. Today, however, I felt a strange urge to listen to their conversation. I'd done so in the past, and had always been amused by what transpired. Even as adults, the two were night and day, and their discussions typically followed in the same suit. Creeping forward, I shifted my basket to my right hip and pressed my ear to the side of the tent.

"I am starving," Esau shouted. "You've made plenty for everyone, just give me a bowl of pottage. I'm so tired after my hunt, I could faint."

Even from the outside, I could hear Jacob's silent frustration over his brother's brazen behavior and demands. Jacob had worked on this recipe for a couple of days, carefully selecting the right cut of meat, gathering his herbs and vegetables, and then waking early today to start it in time for supper. Esau's demands were not the first of his kind. I listened to the gentle clinking of Jacob's ladle in the pot, imagining him working slowly, methodically, as Esau stared in defiance.

"Give me your birthright for it," Jacob said coldly.

My mouth dropped. While Esau was known for his foolishness in the face of a good meal, I doubted that he would ever consider what Jacob asked for. Given Esau's temper, I feared that he would kill Jacob then and there.

Where had Jacob gotten the idea to ask for his birthright?

I fought to steady my breathing as I recalled a time when Jacob was young, not more than nine years of age. We had sat by the fire and watched as Isaac and Esau carried in their kills for the day. Jacob had turned to me, asking in his small voice, "What's a birthright, Mama? And why does my brother get it, but not me?"

In my surprise, I had shifted to look at him closely, examining the concern etched on his tiny face, the worry lines already forming between his golden brows. "A birthright is something that you are entitled to receive because of your birth. In your brother's case, he is the eldest, so he is entitled to your father's land, home, and possessions. But that won't happen for a long time, Jacob. Your father is young and healthy," I'd said, working to conceal the worry in my voice.

Jacob had pursed his lips and kicked at the grass, deep in thought. "I want a birthright too, Mama. How can I have one?"

"Well, my dear," I'd said as I kissed his forehead. "To get one, you'd have to have been born first. I suppose"—I laughed—"you could also ask Esau to share a bit of his." The moment the words had left my lips, I regretted them. While I had my own reasons for wanting Jacob to receive what I believed he was due, it had been a mistake to plant that seed in Jacob's mind. "I'm sorry, Jacob. That was a poor joke. You are smart and diligent—keep up with your studies, and I promise you that your father and I will not let you go without."

"All right," he'd said. Then, we'd stared at the fire in silence, both lost in our own thoughts.

I snapped out of my reverie at the sound of Esau's gravelly voice.

"What does it matter? I'm about to die from hunger—some good that my birthright will do to me in my death."

"Swear that I can have it, and you can have all of the pottage you'd like," Jacob said quietly.

After a few beats, Esau answered. "I swear it."

The wind rushed out of me, and I dropped my basket, staring at it in shock. Could it have possibly been that simple? Was this what the Lord had meant?

I knew that the moment Esau satiated his appetite, he'd be furious with Jacob, with me, with anyone but himself. I had to find Isaac.

* * *

Remembering that Isaac had chosen to come home for his midday meal, I found him crouched at the brook behind our tent, splashing water on his face and neck. Even now, after decades of marriage, he still managed to make my heart swell with admiration. While his face boasted a few more lines that hadn't been there when we met, his hair still shone like burnished copper in the sun. He still possessed the stature and rugged good looks that he'd had all those years ago.

I approached him quietly, not wanting to disturb his moment of reprieve. He looked up at me, blinking the water from his lashes, and smiled gently. "My beautiful bride. I didn't expect to see you until supper." He studied me for a few moments, growing concerned as he took in my appearance and silent panic. "What is wrong, Rebekah?"

"Something has happened, and I came to find you before Esau's fury did." I paused to catch my breath before telling him what I had overheard.

Isaac listened intently, the furrow in his brow growing deeper with each passing second. "Esau has been unwise. I am disappointed in him, though I can't say that I am surprised," Isaac said.

"There's—there's something else I've been needing to tell you, something that casts a different light on this altogether. But you must promise to forgive me for my impudence. I only wanted to do what I thought was best for our sons, for you," I struggled to hold back a sob as Isaac crossed the little stream to hold me.

"What is it, little one? Nothing you could do or say would ever make me think less of you." He kissed the tears that fell down my cheeks.

Ten years ago, we'd experienced a season of rain unlike ever before. It had looked and felt as if the heavens had wrung themselves out in an endless, terrible downpour that stretched well into our summer harvest. Standing in front of Isaac now, I couldn't help but think back to that rain, that downpour. I began to speak slowly, picking up speed as every word, every passing beat felt as if I were digging into an old, buried wound. I recounted everything that I had experienced that night in the clearing, all of the hopes and fears I had hidden from him for so many years, and I watched through tear-flooded eyes as the downpour struck and then devoured him.

Isaac's face transformed from concern, to hurt, to anger. By the end of it all, he had stepped away from me, staring in cold disbelief. I felt the last, thin pieces of my heart shatter; he had never looked at me with anything less than love and admiration before. What had I done?

"How could you hide this from me, Rebekah? I am your husband, their father. I had a right to know." He raked his hands through his hair in frustration. "The worst of it is that I would have acquiesced. I would have gone into prayer, seeking guidance from the Lord and asking for His will to be shown to me," he turned to me with fire in his eyes. "You forced me to go eighteen years without doing so, Rebekah. I've spent that time treating and training Esau as my heir, the inheritor of my father's blessing and my birthright. You have made a fool of me, and you've also planted ideas in Jacob's mind."

I had no words—there was nothing left to say. "I am so sorry, Isaac. I know it is too much to ask for your forgiveness right now, but I vow to you that I made the decisions that I did, however foolish they were, out of my wish to protect you and the boys. I know now that I was wrong." I sobbed quietly, feeling as if each ragged breath loosened yet another piece of myself, my facade of strength, and tossed it into the water beneath my feet. Here I stood, watching as the man I loved, the man who had accepted and adored me, who had waited patiently for a child for twenty years, saw me for who I was—crafty, manipulative, controlling.

"Rebekah," his gentle voice broke through my thoughts, and I looked up to find him standing in front of me. "I shouldn't have reacted so harshly. I forgive you." He spoke with quiet restraint.

I reached out for his hand, lifting it to my lips. "What do we do about Esau? I fear he will kill his brother once he realizes what he has done."

Isaac sighed, looking over my shoulder before meeting my eyes. "I will speak with him. I expect that he will be angry, and will likely need to be sent away from Jacob for a while to ensure no further contention comes between them."

I nodded my head in relief.

"However, I will ask you to trust me with the outcome of our sons' lives from here on out. If it is truly the Lord's will for Jacob to have my blessing in place of Esau, He will make that happen. I will pray and seek God's will and direction. Otherwise, I intend to follow the standard customs passed down to us by our fathers, and bless Esau as my firstborn."

Relief followed by hurt shot through me as I digested his words. While I had wanted him to trust me implicitly, I knew that I had broken his trust by keeping my knowledge a secret. I had masqueraded as one thing, while binding my thoughts, yearnings, and beliefs close to my heart. The fact that he was willing to consider, and even pray over, the matter would have to be enough.

For now.

CHAPTER FIFTEEN

T rue to his word, Isaac sent Esau on a three-month-long hunting and foraging expedition after speaking with both him and Jacob, and remedying things as best he could. While he couldn't break Esau's sworn promise to Jacob, he did pacify Esau with the reminder that he had yet to give him the Abrahamic blessing. After weeks of ill humor and brooding, Esau left on his excursion. Everything around us seemed to breathe a sigh of relief. I had forgotten what it was like to not wake up in fear of some furious outburst or threat, and I relished the opportunity to spend time at home with Isaac and Jacob.

Jacob, for his part, did not gloat, nor did he acknowledge the fact that he now held Esau's birthright. Esau's promise, and subsequent confirmatory anger, had been enough for him. In the weeks of his brother's quiet, then loud, rage, he had worked studiously, intently, continuing to learn while managing our servants and estate.

The stress of our environment and our shattered trust sat heavily between Isaac and I. For the first time in our thirty-eight years of marriage, our silence at the dinner table, or while I prepared for bed each night, was not companionable. Instead, it was fraught with tension and heartache. I hadn't known how much I would miss Isaac's gentle teasing and admiring glances until they were gone.

One morning, Isaac stood over the wash basin, splashing water on his face before dressing. I had been watching him quietly from the confines of our bed, afraid to speak and make things worse than they already were. Suddenly, I was overcome with a sense of boldness, both out of sincere desire to reclaim the relationship we once had, and exhaustion from the weeks of strain.

"I miss you, Isaac. I miss the woman you used to think I was. I want to be that woman to you, and I'll do anything to earn your trust again."

He paused in the middle of drying his face with a linen cloth, lowering it slowly to meet my eyes in the reflection of our mirror. "It is I who should be ashamed, Rebekah. When you told me, I admitted that I behaved wrongly, before slipping back into my anger. That anger has subsided, but I haven't known how to move away from the hurt, and into trust with you again. I shouldn't have made you feel this way."

Swinging out from under the covers, my feet found the cool, soft rug. I padded to him quickly, quietly, before throwing my arms around his neck. "Let us both stop being upset with each other, and with ourselves. It is doing us no good. Can we move forward in peace?"

He grabbed my face with both hands. "I give you my word, my love. There is peace between us."

As I looked into his honey-colored eyes, the same ones that had captivated me so many years ago, I couldn't help but wonder at all the Lord had brought us through, and all that would come. What had once started as childish, giddy admiration had blossomed into a deep love. A love that withstood sorrow and betrayals, a love that remained unbreakable, even when we were broken.

We were older now, more full of life, of pain, of shared experiences. The future I had envisioned when I walked across that twilit field nearly four decades ago hadn't looked remotely close to this one. This was even better.

PART THREE

"And I will make thy seed to multiply as the stars of heaven, and will give unto thy seed all these countries; and in thy seed shall all the nations of the earth be blessed." Genesis 26:4

CHAPTER SIXTEEN

After years of abundance, famine arrived—the first of its kind since Abraham's time. Desolation swept over our surrounding hills, through our plains, taking with it our last harvests, our only method of survival. What was left of our livestock was nearly too diseased and malnourished to eat. We had lived this way for two years, doing our best to support the needs of our neighboring families, without starving our own. Every servant and family member had a part in our survival, with teams of women and children leaving before dawn to dig roots and find grass while the earth was still soft, and men hunting for game that didn't seem to exist.

One evening, after a particularly meager soup of wild asparagus and celery in boiled water, Isaac set off on his own again, this time not stopping in our little clearing, but walking slowly, deep in thought, out to our dusty fields. I watched him, remembering times where I could hardly make him out between the lush crops of wheat and corn. This time, he told me where he was going and what he was doing, explaining briefly that he needed uninterrupted time with the Lord.

I waited for him, watching as the sun made yet another trip down our horizon, witnessing its descent, and wishing for its delayed arrival, if only for a day or two of rain. We needed rain above all else—rain to water our crops, rain to fill our wells, rain to nourish our livestock. Instead, each bitter day had been drier and sunnier than the last. Once the stars began to perform their introductory twinkles, I blew out the candles and extinguished our fire, climbing into bed to stare at the deepness of my surroundings, ignoring the grumbling of my stomach and the dryness of my throat.

Some time later, I drifted into a fitful sleep, waking in the wee hours of the morning to Isaac climbing back into bed beside me. He gently put an arm around me, holding me close to him. "I have good news, Rebekah," he whispered into my ear. "The Lord has given me an answer. We are to go to Gerar as soon as day breaks. He will take care of us there."

I listened to the way his steady breathing clashed with the rapid thumping of my heart. For forty years, I had called Canaan my home. How were we to start over as strangers in a new land? I had heard stories of Gerar, of their living in excess, and their roughness toward outsiders. The men were rumored to be greedy, hungry for wealth and women that weren't their own. The women were hardly better, known for their viperlike tongues and beauty. How could that possibly be the future the Lord had designed for us?

I focused on my breathing in an attempt to quiet my thoughts. What Isaac needed now was my support, my belief in him, and in what the Lord had told him to do. After everything we had gone through over the last several years, I owed him that much. So, I turned over, shoving the terror and concern aside, and pressed a kiss to his nose. "It'll be an adventure."

❊ ❊ ❊

True to his word, Isaac ordered our departure at daybreak. It took little time for us to pack up what remained of our home and livelihood. Once, we were a small metropolis; now, we were barely more than a collection of tents.

Sweat rolled down my back as I tied up what remained of Sarah's room. Decades of her love and work had come down in just a few short hours. With every tapestry and linen I had removed and folded, I felt the sadness and permanence of Isaac's decision. Should we ever return to our home, it wouldn't be the same sparkling, brilliant place that it had been the evening I had arrived as a young bride. I felt as if what remained of that part of me was being ripped away, taking with it the memories we'd made as a young and growing family. Here, we were married. Here, we raised our children. Here, we said goodbye to Abraham, and then Eliezer. If I looked hard enough, I could find my heart buried deep within the disheveled dirt of what used to be our home.

"Are you ready?"

I looked up at Deborah, studying the tracks her tears had

made through the dust on her slender face. My own likely looked the same. "I remember you asking a semblance of that question many, many years ago," I said, smiling as yet another tear trickled into my mouth.

"And just like I was all those years ago, I'm here with you, ready to go where you go. I'll miss this place, Rebekah," her voice was thick with a level of emotion that I was unaccustomed to seeing in her.

"As will I, more than anyone will ever know. It's strange, I remember feeling heartbroken about leaving my home. Looking back, I was nothing but a child—this feeling, leaving here, feels infinitely worse."

We looked at the remains of our home, its tents lying in the dirt, collecting dust. After a while, I drew a deep breath and turned to Deborah. "Well, we have to be ready, don't we?"

She nodded, reaching out to squeeze my hand. "Let's start our new life."

CHAPTER
SEVENTEEN

O ur journey was brief. After three long days of walking and two short nights of restless sleep, we stood outside the glittering gates of Gerar.

Esau and Jacob had volunteered to bring up the back of our company, while Isaac and I had led the front. We had traveled quietly, solemnly, as if we were mourning the loss of a loved one, and were on our way to their burial. In a way, we were.

I studied the busy, foreign city ahead of us, looking up to draw strength from Isaac's resolute face. "What do we do when we arrive?" I asked. My voice was barely above a whisper.

"We will need to come before the king and request his permission over our stay. Then, we will need to find a place to pitch our tents." He spoke with the same quiet, enduring confidence that had drawn me to him over four decades ago.

I reached out to take his hand, squeezing it in a show of solidarity. He took a sharp breath, turning to look at me with that same playful twinkle in his eye, before facing the rest of our group. "My friends, my family. We have come to Gerar by the Lord's direction, and it is here that we will sojourn and await His blessing. I have every confidence that what He has promised will come to pass, and I thank you for your faith and perseverance." I was near enough to hear his voice break slightly before he resumed his speech. "We walk through those gates strangers in a new land, at the mercy of their king and country. I ask that you behave in a way that my father would approve of, and that you make our ancestors proud." And with that, he turned, drew himself up to his full height, and began to walk.

As we passed through the gates, I gasped at the scenery around us. It had been years since I had witnessed this level of grandeur and wealth. Food stalls surrounded us, boasting ripe fruits, vibrant vegetables, and more grain than I could fathom.

Choice linens were laid out on accompanying booths, seducing the women to come in for a closer look.

I looked around me and felt a rising sense that I was being watched. I glanced upward, finding a group of men leaning out from a second-story window, leering down at me suggestively as they waved bottles over their heads. One hiccupped as the other nudged him in his side, dropping his bottle with a loud shatter in the process.

"Hello, pretty thing," said the man who nudged his companion. He was covered in dust and grime, and even from where we stood, his stench assaulted my nostrils. "Why don't you come up here for a visit?"

My cheeks burned as I turned to look at Isaac. His mouth was set in a thin line, his pallor white with strain.

"They aren't—they aren't speaking to me, are they? Can't they tell I am your wife?"

Isaac grabbed my upper arm, pulling me into a small alleyway while hushing me. "I feared this would happen, as it happened to my mother when she arrived. These men—they will kill me if they find out you are my wife, and then they'll take you for their own. You must tell them you are my sister, Rebekah."

I stared at him in silence, horrified by the thought of masquerading as his sister, and the potential threat to his safety. It had been many years since I had experienced strangers' appreciative, if sometimes threatening gazes. It hadn't occurred to me with our move to Gerar that this would be a possibility.

"Isaac, I can't do that. I've been your wife for over forty years. I wouldn't know how to pretend," I stuttered while looking around us with wild eyes. "Please, don't make me do this."

"Would you have me die instead?"

"No!" I stifled a scream. We had left our home, and walked into what could only be described as a nightmare. Even if I claimed to be Isaac's wife, could I be guaranteed safety as a seemingly single woman? "I will do what you ask, Isaac, if only for your safety. But something tells me that it is not the right decision."

A look of relief crossed his face, and he squeezed my shoulders in appreciation before we stepped back into the street.

We made our way to the king's quarters, our eyes fixed on the road ahead of us. It wasn't until we reached a set of smooth stone steps, each of which as tall as my shin, that I looked up to see a group of soldiers staring down at us coldly.

"I am Isaac, the son of Abraham. I have come to seek the king's blessing and protection." Isaac stood straight as a rod, bending only to give a slight nod to the commanding officer he spoke with.

The officer—a tall, weathered man—took his time examining Isaac, and then me. My skin burned as his eyes traced my face and body, and I felt Isaac stiffen beside me. "I will pass your message along, but I cannot promise you more than that. Wait here." He turned on his heel to speak quietly with another officer before marching through the front gate.

After what felt like an eternity, he returned, giving us a slight nod to follow him. "Just you two," he said. "The king is not interested in the rest of your party."

Isaac nodded, and we followed him inside. Each echoing footstep on the cold stone only furthered the tightening of my chest. I felt that familiar panic shoot from my toes and into my throat, only to settle near my heart with a nervous flutter. I had never met a king before, nor had I any idea what this one had in store for us.

I offered up a silent prayer as we turned the corner to find ourselves in a vast, cavernous space. My eyes adjusted slowly, finding a portly little man sitting on a large granite throne at the end of the lengthy walkway. Though it was midday, the palace had no natural light or visible windows. Lanterns and torches lined the path to where he sat.

"His Highness, King Abimelech, grants you permission to approach his throne," the officer said before bowing and stepping into the shadows.

I looked up at Isaac, hearing only the thunder of my pulse in my ears, to find him staring back at me. We had learned to communicate wordlessly; the look he gave me was charged with urgency, and a reminder of the promise I had just made. I tipped my chin up slightly, as if to affirm his thoughts, before turning to the king.

The walk down the corridor to his throne felt nearly as long as our journey to Gerar. While he had appeared menacing from the end of the corridor, the king took on a kindlier appearance the closer we drew. He had lines around his eyes from years of smiling, and folds on his neck, wrist, and ankles from even more years of indulgence. Even so, his was not a threatening presence.

We came to the end of the corridor, standing at the base step of his throne. Isaac bowed his head slightly, and I followed suit, offering a small smile. The king studied us both, his eyes lingering on me. "Welcome to Gerar, Isaac, son of Abraham. What is it that you request of me?"

I fought the urge to duck as his voice echoed around me.

"Your permission and blessing for our inhabitance in your fine country, Your Highness," Isaac said, his eyes resting on the floor in front of King Abimelech's feet.

"Your father and mother came to our land with that same request many years ago. Abraham served our people well. It is my honor to welcome you as one of my own," he said with a grand sweep of his hands.

Isaac raised his right hand and placed it over his heart, lifting his head to look at the king for the first time. "Thank you, Your Highness. We will do everything in our power to be a blessing to you and yours."

Relief washed over me as I began to turn, expecting us to take our leave. Instead, the king broke through the silence, freezing me in place.

"And who are you, my dear?" He said with a quirk of his brow.

"I am Rebekah, the daughter of Abraham. I am Isaac's—sister, Your Highness." The lie tasted like poison as it left my lips.

"You are very fair, Rebekah. We always welcome beautiful women such as yourself," he said with a chuckle that rustled the folds of his tunic. "Don't be shy, my dear. Make yourself at home."

I swallowed the bile that rose in my throat, doing my best to smile appreciatively.

Isaac cut through the tense silence. "Where may we take up residence, Your Highness?"

The king slowly shifted his eyes back to Isaac as if remembering for the first time that he was still present. "There is a large plot of land to the southeast, roughly ten kilometers from the outside gates. You'll find wells and fertile land that should give you what you need to prepare for harvest."

Knowing that we would be away from the prying eyes of the city was enough to make me weak with joy. We would be able to pitch our tents, build our home, and survive off of the land while making only necessary trips into the city for supplies.

"Once again, Your Highness, I am grateful." Isaac bowed his head slightly, and we walked back down the stony corridor and into the fading light of the outside world.

It was only when we were clear of the city gates that I turned to Isaac with a look of triumph. "You did it," I said with a smile.

"We did it, Rebekah," he murmured quietly. "We did it."

❊ ❊ ❊

The land the king had given us was fertile. It would never compare to our home in Canaan, but it had everything we needed to begin planting and preparing for future seasons. After two years of famine, the knowledge that we would soon have grain for bread and vegetables to feed our livestock felt akin to finding a cave of treasure. We were giddy with relief, and ready for the new life God had chosen for us. Even so, the knowledge that Isaac and I would have to pretend to be siblings in the presence of anyone outside of our home weighed on me heavily. Not only would we have to ensure that we never showed any familiarity above that which a brother and sister would exhibit, we would need to create stories to explain Esau and Jacob's existence, and ensure our servants did the same. Aside from that, any acquaintances or friends I made would know me as Rebekah the unmarried woman, rather than Rebekah, wife of Isaac, and mother to Esau and Jacob. I had built so much of my worth and identity around being a wife and mother. What was I without those two things?

In a matter of a few short days, we managed to rebuild our tents. I took special care to replace each linen and tapestry as Sarah had, smiling as I set Isaac's lion and my donkey on the bedside table. Standing inside, it almost felt as if I were home again—almost.

Isaac returned to his daily management of our land, agriculture, and livestock with renewed vigor. After two years of scant hunting, Esau relished our new landscape, spending dawn until dusk trapping, hunting, and cleaning. Jacob was as steadfast in his responsibilities as ever, and I cherished the fact that I could trust him with the task of overseeing our household, books, and servants.

With the weight of much of our former responsibilities off of our shoulders, Deborah and I spent our days before harvesting season weaving linens and tapestries to be sold in the marketplace, and entertaining the small number of visitors who came to call. While many of the women in town remained cordial at best, a few had ventured out, at first out of sheer curiosity, and then genuine friendliness. I always welcomed them with open arms, and sent them away with baskets of baked goods for their families. Of those visitors, I grew close with a woman named Diana, a mother of three whose husband had died some years before, and Lilah, a newlywed whose husband served as one of the king's sentries. Diana was open, if not a bit too forthcoming, but welcoming and understanding of our differences. Lilah was timid, with eyes bigger than her size, and a heart of gold. I counted myself blessed to have found two such women in a new land.

One afternoon, Diana, Lilah, and I enjoyed our tea as we sat under the shade of a pomegranate tree. We watched as a speck on the horizon grew larger, and I realized with a start that Esau must have ended his hunt early for the day. I hesitated mid-sentence, not knowing how to introduce him. Thus far, I had managed to entertain visitors without interference from either son. Now, I would have to explain the huge, red man who waved with warm familiarity as he walked toward us. And I would have to make sure he didn't accidentally give away my identity.

"Ah, my nephew!" I said with animated joy as I stood up

to welcome him home with open arms. "It is good to see you, and so early. Come, meet my friends," I pinched his arm as I guided him to where the ladies sat, pretending not to notice his look of confusion as I propelled him forward. While Isaac and I had explained that he and his brother would need to grow accustomed to referring to me as their aunt, that conversation had happened months ago. I could not trust Esau to remember to assume the act without a bit of a reminder. "Diana, Lilah, please meet my nephew, Esau." I watched as both women exchanged glances of confused admiration before smiling pleasantly at him.

"Ladies, it is a pleasure to meet you," he said before turning to me. "You are right, my hunt today ended early. The snares brought in a healthy number for today, and I thought I'd give the other animals a rest before starting back up tomorrow." He smirked, always happy for an opportunity to boast about his success.

After he and the ladies exchanged pleasantries, he excused himself to wash up for his meal. I sat back down beside them, looking out at the horizon in an attempt to avoid their gazes.

"When were you going to tell us you had a big, strapping nephew?" said Diana, her brow shooting up into her hair.

"Oh, hadn't I? How strange, I thought I had. Anyway, if I didn't tell you about him, I likely forgot to tell you about his brother, Jacob. He's usually nearby, so you may meet him soon," I chanced a look around me, attempting to appear casual.

"Are they. . . Isaac's sons?" Lilah asked quietly.

"Yes, they are. Their mother died some time ago." That same bitterness entered my mouth, and I washed it away with a gulp of tea. My lies were not by choice, they were told at the request of my husband. While I hated living this way, there was nothing more I could do.

"Well, they are lucky to have you in her stead," said Diana. She didn't appear to believe my lie as quickly as Lilah had, but she had the grace to go along with it anyway. I murmured my thanks, before changing the subject.

Later that evening, I took my time washing my hair, relishing the smell of the clean, soapy water, and the feeling of removing the week's dust and grime. "Will we need to hide our marriage forever?"

Isaac, who lounged with his feet outstretched by the fire, turned to look at me in surprise. "For as long as we are here in Gerar, yes. Admitting our deception would only serve to infuriate the king. Why do you ask?"

"Diana and Lilah met Esau today," I said. "It was difficult to introduce him, and I fear that they might have sensed I wasn't being completely honest with them." I worked the soapy water into my hair, using a boar-bristle brush to scrub my scalp. Normally Deborah would help me, but lately I'd enjoyed doing so myself.

Isaac appeared to consider what I said before sighing heavily. "I don't know another way around this. I may have acted rashly when we first arrived, but I do believe that I would have been killed, and that you would have been taken by some other man. Now, the only option is to live with the decision I made. That or run the risk of punishment."

I studied the handle of my brush, unwilling to admit that I agreed, but able to see that what Isaac said was right. However much we disliked doing so, we would have to continue pretending to be siblings, for the safety of each other. I could only hope that one day we would leave Gerar and go home to Canaan, free to be known as husband and wife.

CHAPTER EIGHTEEN

Our first harvest in Gerar was more abundant than we had expected or even hoped for, and every year after that continued to be more plentiful than the one before. The marvel of our ten prosperous gleanings after years of famine was not lost on us, and Isaac decided to host a feast at our first opportunity to celebrate and give thanks.

As newcomers in our land, we had grown and harvested ten times more than our neighbors, and our livestock had expanded rapidly as well. We were acutely aware of how our arrival and success appeared to the people of Gerar, and while we couldn't change that fact, we did want to remain in their good graces. Isaac, fortified by the blessing we'd been given and cognizant of our testimony, had decided to invite all of our neighboring farmers—and their families—to join in our festivities.

I stood in the clearing, blinking as the first rays of morning sun shimmered through my vision. Contentment, then longing, flooded through me. While I was overjoyed by our success and grateful above all else, there were moments when I missed our old home. I'd catch myself tuning my ear to listen for the babble of our little brook, only to realize that it was no longer there—that we were no longer there. No matter how much God blessed us in this new land, a part of me would always wish we were home.

I breathed in deeply, stretching my neck and shoulders for the day of preparation ahead. Along with all of our available servants, Deborah and I had spent the better portion of the last week preparing for tonight's feast. Every rug had been beaten, every surface dusted, every pillow and table located and arranged. Esau and Jacob had overseen the slaughtering and dressing of our choicest livestock according to the menu I had prepared.

"Finally, a day for us to celebrate our accomplishments and blessings," said Isaac as he walked up behind me. "When I think about where we were even a year ago, I am struck with awe. The Lord is good to us, and I hope that tonight, we may be good to those around us."

I nodded, leaning back into his chest and savoring the momentary feeling of weightlessness. I watched as the sun rose higher, slowly peeking its way through the leaves overhead. A memory of a time when I'd sat on my father's shoulders and watched the very same thing rose to my mind. How long ago that was. How much I missed him.

"Well, it'll be evening before we know it. I must get to work," I said, forcing myself out of my own memories. "And you, sir, have plenty of preparation of your own to get to." I poked Isaac's chest playfully.

"What would I do without you to remind me of my duties?" His eyes shone as he looked down at me. We stood there, smiling at each other for a few brief moments, before hearing a throat clear behind us.

"I apologize for breaking things up, but I came to find Rebekah," said Deborah as she fought to hide the smile on her face. Even decades after our wedding night, she never failed to tease me anytime we showed any sign of affection. She also never failed to remind me of how unhappy I'd once been about the prospect of leaving my home to marry Isaac.

I sighed, forcing down a giggle. "Thank you, Deborah. I was just on my way." I turned to place a kiss on Isaac's cheek before walking toward her. "Now, shall we?" I pinched her side to quiet her laughter, biting my own cheeks to keep from smiling.

She squeaked, jumping like a small girl before attempting to resume a normal walk a good distance away from me. "I hardly think I deserved that," she said.

"Not yet, you didn't. But I knew what was coming."

"Well, fine, so you did. Let's move on from that, yes? We have much to do today, but you'll be happy to know that much of the work has been divided among the rest of the servants and household, leaving you with the opportunity to prepare yourself for the evening."

"Prepare myself? What for?"

She arched her brow knowingly while staring straight ahead. "Let's just say that your usual attire and grooming might be sufficient for a busy harvest, but not for an evening of celebration. It's my job to make sure you don't keep covering up your beauty with plain clothes, so you and I are off to bathe, prepare, and adorn you with jewelry."

"Honestly, Deborah, isn't this all a bit too much? I've been married long enough now, who is going to pay attention to what I'm wearing and how I look tonight?" I couldn't help but find Deborah's outspoken nature amusing. She used to be so timid. Secretly, I was pleased to realize that after decades of friendship, she felt comfortable enough to speak to me as she would a sister.

"The fact that you ask that question is enough to tell me how clueless you are. You are a beautiful woman, Rebekah. You are still desirable, especially now that you are married and a mother, and I refuse to let you dull yourself because you think it's 'too much' to do otherwise. Now"—she nudged me into my tent—"hop into the bath I drew for you, and I'll be back in an hour to wash your hair."

My momentary irritation at Deborah's accusations subsided when I saw the large, luxuriant bath. She had filled it with oils and spices, and topped it with beautiful flowers. It had been years since I'd indulged in such a treat, and while I felt guilty for relaxing while the rest of our home was abuzz with activity, I also understood that Deborah often knew what I needed more than I did.

A few hours later, after having my hair washed, brushed, and plaited, I looked in the mirror, nearly jumping in surprise at the woman who stood before me. While I could see the fine lines from mirth and worry beginning around my eyes, I looked almost as I had the evening I had married Isaac. Looking at myself in this way felt like meeting an old friend. I hadn't realized how much I missed feeling beautiful—special, even. For years, I had convinced myself that doing so was just a sign of selfishness. But tonight, I remembered what it was to feel like myself again, unafraid of being seen, happy to be admired by those I loved. If nothing else, I wanted to always remind Isaac of the woman he had married. We had changed and endured much over the years, but at my core, I was still the same. His Rebekah.

"Well, you certainly made your point." I turned to look at Deborah, who stood proudly behind me. "Thank you for forcing me to do this. I didn't realize how much I needed it."

With Isaac's permission, Deborah had gone into town to purchase fabric to make me a new dress. It was finer than anything I had owned before, woven in threads of gold and cream. It floated over my body, and every time I turned to look at it, the candlelight made it shimmer. Deborah had chosen to pair the dress with the bracelets that Eliezer had given me when we first met, along with a variety of other pieces of gold jewelry I had acquired throughout my marriage.

I looked down at the bangles that adorned my wrist and felt a pang at Eliezer's memory. He had been so good to me, so good to our family. I missed his laugh, and his wheedling ways.

The sun had already set. Deborah and I had whiled away the day, enjoying every minute of our luxurious preparations. It was now time to greet the guests. Normally, the thought of doing so wouldn't send a shiver of fear up my spine, but the fact remained that those who would be joining our feast tonight would be doing so with the belief that Isaac and I were no more than siblings. I had never had to endure a party while separated from my husband.

"If you think about it," I said to Deborah, "it's almost a bit cruel for me to be dressed like this. We're supposed to be preserving the facade, you know." I peered at Deborah suspiciously, who appeared to be studying the floor with intensity. When I continued to look at her, she sighed and finally met my gaze.

"Once again, it is my job to let the world see your beauty. Just because Isaac can't behave in the way a husband would while guests are around does not mean he shouldn't admire you from afar. If anything, it'll keep things fun," she said with a smirk.

I swatted at her before turning for one last glimpse in the mirror. She had a point, after all.

We walked outside, admiring the scene that seemed to have magically unfolded while we were away. Tables stretched as far as the eye could see, boasting a multitude of linens in a vibrant array of jewel-toned colors. Lighted candles snaked throughout the tables, their flames momentarily blinking and wiggling in the breeze. For the first time, it felt like we finally made ourselves at home.

I turned to see Isaac approaching us. He appeared to be deep in thought, studying the ground as he walked. When he looked up, I watched as his eyes transformed from recognition to admiration. My heart fluttered and I shifted my weight to offset the nervousness I felt. It was as if we were meeting for the first time, all over again. After what felt like an eternity, he finally stood next to me as Esau, Jacob, Deborah, and the rest of our servants lined up beside us. "You look as beautiful as you did the day we were married. I'm not sure how I'm supposed to pretend to be your brother now," he whispered in my ear, sending a tickle down my spine.

"Hush, you'll get us in trouble with that talk." I hid a smile as I tried to focus on our approaching guests.

We greeted every family as they arrived, all of whom refused to come without bringing their own refreshment or delicacy to share. While many families brought fruit, bread, or eggs, one farmer brought a goat. I accepted each dish or gift with thanks, before bringing it to one of our tables. The goat received a family-wide welcome, before being sent to live with his new friends.

When I returned from placing another dish on one of the many tables, I was overjoyed to see that Diana, Lilah, and their families had come as well. While they were not farmers, it had been important to me to include them in our festivities. Both women had turned out to be good friends to me, and for that, I was eternally grateful.

"Diana, Lilah, it is such a pleasure to have you both. I've told Isaac so much about you," I said with a smile after making a conscious effort to avoid referring to him as my husband.

Diana and Lilah both greeted Isaac in turn, before saying hello to Esau, and meeting Jacob for the first time. I watched as Lilah and Diana looked Jacob up and down before exchanging knowing glances with each other. Were they merely appreciating his good looks, or did they see the obvious signs of him being my son?

"Rebekah," Lilah said quietly as she touched my arm. "I want you to meet my husband, Paul."

I turned to find her standing with a man who was nearly as broad as he was tall. Next to petite Lilah, he was positively enormous, and equally intimidating. His eyes had a hard glint to them, and though he couldn't be more than forty years old, his skin was weathered from years of battle in service to the king. "It is a pleasure to meet you, Paul. I have heard so much about you. Welcome to our home," I said with a small tilt of my head.

Paul held my gaze for a moment too long before nodding silently. Knowing that he worked as a sentry for the king and did not seem to appreciate my connection to Lilah did not sit well with me. While I hoped that I was merely mistaking his behavior, my instincts rarely misled me.

I shook off my thoughts before escorting Lilah, Paul, Diana, and her children to their tables. As I thanked the servants who stood guard at the front door in case of any late visitors, I felt a gentle tug on my elbow.

"We need to talk, Rebekah," whispered Diana. I turned to find her and Lilah looking at me. Lilah's eyes were as wide as an owl's.

"Of course," I said with a nod. I led them to an area that afforded us more privacy from the rest of the party. It was only once we stopped walking that I noticed my heart was thundering in my chest. "What is it?"

Lilah looked at Diana with pleading eyes, before Diana began. "I think it is time that you be honest with us, Rebekah. We've done our best to mind our own business and believe you when you say that Isaac is your brother. We even gave you the benefit of the doubt when we met Esau, who looks unlike anyone we've ever met. But after meeting Jacob, who might as well be the mirror image of you and Isaac, it's become too clear to us that you are not who you say you are. Why have you lied to us?" Even through Diana's tough exterior, I could hear the hurt in her voice.

What could I do? Telling them would go against Isaac's wishes. But I couldn't lie to them any longer. If I did, they'd know what I had done, and could very well tell others out of anger. Lilah's husband was the king's sentry—his knowledge of our marriage could be catastrophic. I closed my eyes and offered up a silent prayer and apology before speaking. "You are right. I have not been truthful with either of you, but I have my reasons. Isaac and I have been married for many years. Esau and Jacob are our sons, our twins."

Lilah's eyes rounded even more at my admission, and I absentmindedly wondered whether they could widen any more.

"The truth is that when we arrived in Gerar, we were met with hostility. It became clear early on that the men of our city didn't take kindly to Isaac's arrival, nor the idea of him being married to me. So, we devised a plan to present ourselves as siblings, just to protect him, and in turn, to protect me." I forced myself to stop, listening to the suffocating silence and Lilah's small, irregular breaths. Diana stood as still as a statue.

"I understand," Lilah said. Relief swept over me, and I looked at her in appreciation.

"I can't say that I do," Diana said. "Living in that lie, after so many years of marriage, cannot be much easier than the alternative. However, I can understand why you thought you needed to do so. The men of Gerar are merciless. They take any beautiful woman they want, and they kill whoever they need."

"Please forgive me for lying to you. It felt terrible to do so, and I hated every moment of it." I looked at the ground before finally asking the question that had sat in my mind for months. "Will you please keep our secret?"

Lilah nodded furiously, before turning to peer at Diana. I watched as Diana's face softened, and she dropped her arms with sigh. "You have our word."

Tears flooded my eyes as I pulled them both into a hug. Lilah squeaked with delighted surprise, while Diana stood stiff as a board. "I know that you don't like hugs," I whispered in her ear. "But that doesn't mean that you are any less deserving of them."

We walked back to the feast, Lilah and I arm in arm, while Diana remained at a comfortable distance behind us.

"Rebekah?" Lilah whispered.

"Yes?"

"If you're supposed to be brother and sister, you're going to need to tell Isaac to stop looking at you like that."

It was rare for Lilah to be anything more than timid, so I was thrilled to hear notes of playfulness in her voice. I looked at the head of our family's table, and saw that Isaac was watching me as we approached. His eyes glittered with mischief and appreciation. "If I were a better woman, I would agree with you. But it is quite fun to hold him at arm's length for the evening," I said with a smile.

Diana hushed us both, before taking Lilah's arm and steering her in the direction of where their families sat.

The evening passed joyfully, and our music, food, and laughter lasted well into the early morning hours. We bid the final family goodbye as the sun rose, waving until they were nothing more than specks of sand in the distance.

"I am far too old to still be awake," Isaac said with a yawn.

"As am I. But wasn't it lovely?"

"You were lovely, my dear. Come, let us get ourselves to bed."

I slipped my arm around his waist, leaning my head against his shoulder as we slowly walked to our tent. A voice broke through my trance, and I realized it was Lilah's.

"Rebekah!"

I stepped away from Isaac and turned to look at her. She stood next to Paul, glancing between Isaac and I in panic. "We—we forgot my shawl and came back to retrieve it."

After a moment too long, I realized that my devastation over being seen by her husband was likely written all over my face. I forced myself to smile before speaking. "Of course! I remember you getting too warm when we danced, and you setting it aside. Here, let me help you." I walked with Lilah to help her search the tables where she and her husband had sat.

Once we found her shawl, we returned to find Isaac and Paul standing in tense silence. It was clear that something had been said when we were out of earshot, something that would be too uncomfortable for her or I to ask about until after they left. We bid each other good morning, and Isaac and I watched as they walked away.

Once they were out of sight, Isaac turned to me, his voice quiet, but stern. "Is there something I need to know?"

While I had known I would need to tell him that Diana and Lilah knew we were married, I hadn't expected to have to tell him this way. "Yes, actually. This evening, Diana and Lilah drew me aside and told me that they knew about us. They had been suspicious for a while, but it wasn't until they saw Jacob that they knew that he had to be our own. They promised to protect our secret. Unfortunately, her husband saw us when we didn't know he was still here. While I can trust Lilah to keep this to herself, I don't know whether her husband will, or can."

He exhaled through his nose, and I watched as his jaw worked furiously. "While I didn't want anyone to know, I can understand that you couldn't continue to lie after being caught. My concern is that we were unwise in being affectionate. We should have waited until we were sure everyone had left."

"We were sure," I said. "We couldn't have known that they would forget something and come back. Plus, while we were certainly more affectionate than most siblings, they didn't see anything more than us walking arm in arm. Maybe he won't think anything of it."

"No, Rebekah. He was immediately suspicious. When you two walked away, he began to ask about my life, Esau and Jacob's mother, and why you weren't married yet. He knows."

My throat went dry as I considered the magnitude of what he said. Paul worked for the king. He spoke with him, walked with him, stood guard over him every single day. It was not only likely that he would pass his knowledge along to the king, it was his duty.

CHAPTER NINETEEN

W e watched the horizon for twenty days, expecting to see a group of sentries or horde of townspeople galloping our way. Instead, each evening closed as gently and serenely as each morning began.

It had been months since our last visit to the city, and it was time for us to stock up on provisions, sell the textiles that the women and I had woven, and prepare for the autumn and winter seasons. While Isaac would normally go into town with Deborah and a few other servants, I decided to come along to see Diana and Lilah, whom I hadn't visited since long before our feast. I missed them, and I was also eager to find out what Lilah's husband had made of our unfortunate encounter.

We crossed the city gates and my heart leapt as we were swept into the excitement of our surroundings. Entering the city felt like walking into another world; the commotion reminded me of an anthill. Everywhere I looked, I found a woman peddling her wares, or men slinging lines of dried meat and fish. There were no available stalls left for us to utilize, so Isaac disbanded our group, ordering those that had joined us on our excursion to partner up and begin going from stall to stall to barter and sell. To my surprise, he chose to have me stay by his side. I had assumed he would want me to leave with Deborah so as to avoid suspicion.

As the others walked away to see to the goods they carried, I looked up at him with a wry smile. "Are you sure of your choice of partner?" I teased.

"Always. Plus, while I'd rather not raise suspicion, I can't fathom the notion of leaving you on your own in the midst of these wolves." He looked around us, and for the first time I noticed the suspicious leers of the men and women nearby. For some reason, I had forgotten just how unwanted we were within the city gates. Lilah and Diana had made me feel so welcome, and spending time on our own land, away from the fold, had given me enough space to forget just how foreign Gerar still felt.

It was unsettling.

I squeezed his arm gently in response and followed him as he made his way through the rows of stalls, greeting familiar faces, and introducing himself to new ones. Within hours, we sold everything we brought, and profited tenfold. It was only after we thanked our last merchant that I looked up at the sky and noticed just how late it already was. We hadn't eaten since before dawn, and it was nearing time for supper.

"If you're anywhere near as hungry as I am, you must be starving," I said to Isaac as we headed back to the city's center.

"I've worked up an appetite. I didn't expect for us to be here quite so late. We should round up the others, and find some food before we head home."

I found Deborah and Selah bent over a table of incense and oils. After asking them to find the others, Isaac and I made our way to the market near the city's gates. My mouth watered as I inhaled the aromas of fried fish, freshly toasted bread, roasted vegetables, and succulent fruit that surrounded me.

"I think, after all of our hard work and the success of today's sales, we should feast. Would you agree?" Isaac looked down at me teasingly. He knew how much I had wanted to try the food in Gerar since our arrival.

"I'll order the vegetables and fruits. You take care of the rest." I poked him in his side as I walked hastily past him, stifling my laughter at his quiet grunt.

We met, baskets of food in hand, at the center of the market. Deborah had led the rest of the servants to a small copse that lay between the market and the city's gates. True to form, she had remembered to bring linens for us to lounge on. After a collective groan of relief, Isaac and I began passing out food and drink.

"Now, it's time for you to eat," I said as I held out a plate of food. Knowing they were his favorite, I had separated the grapes I'd found at the market and saved them for him. As he reached to accept his plate of food, I snuck my other hand out from behind my back, and held out the small basket of grapes. I loved seeing his eyes light up, just as Jacob and Esau's had throughout their childhood when given a new toy, or their own favorite sweet treat. "A gift for you," I said as I bent to give him a swift kiss on the cheek, "and a gift for me."

"Thank you, my love," he said as he pried the basket from my hands. He placed it on the ground, and cupped my cheek affectionately. I watched as Isaac's expression transformed from appreciation to alarm; it was only then that I realized what we had done.

I felt the wind rush out of me, and I looked up and met Deborah's panicked eyes. Somehow, between the busyness of the market and the relief of having had such a profitable day's work, I had forgotten to mind my behavior. Instead, I'd behaved immaturely at best, recklessly at worst. I couldn't even remember the last time I had been so playful with Isaac. I couldn't believe how ridiculous I had been.

And now, my ridiculous behavior could very well be the cause of my husband's imprisonment or death.

"Forgive me," I whispered. "I allowed myself to become comfortable with our surroundings, and I forgot. Do you think anyone saw?"

Isaac put his finger to his lips, before looking upward at the walls that surrounded us. I followed his gaze, my heart dropping when I noticed two sentries watching us closely while speaking with each other. While I wanted to comfort myself with the reassurance that few people likely saw or took note of our behavior, the truth was that we had been outsiders since the moment we had arrived in Gerar. Our every movement, our every conversation, was watched, discussed, and analyzed. The question now was whether we would be able to get home before word spread.

"It is my fault as well, I returned the affection. It is time that I deal with the consequences of the decision I made." Isaac said quietly.

The rest of our meal was a somber affair, with each member of our group staring down at their food, only to glance up nervously at each passerby. As I stood up and brushed myself off, I heard the chilling sound of a familiar voice behind me.

"His Highness requests your presence immediately." I turned to look into Paul's cold eyes.

"Please allow me to send my family home, as it is growing late," Isaac said.

Paul looked between the both of us, his irritation growing with each passing moment. "He wants to see you both."

My pulse fluttered, and I felt my palms grow clammy. Not knowing what else to do, I turned to look at Deborah. "We do not know what the outcome of this meeting will be. Please, go home."

Deborah stared at me before slowly and stubbornly shaking her head. "No. We will wait for you here, and then we will all go home. Together."

I tried to smile, but only managed to achieve a pained grimace. Paul and Isaac were waiting for me on the path that led to the king's quarters, and I knew that if I were to say anything more, I would disintegrate. So, I turned on my heel, drawing myself up to my full height, and walked resolutely ahead.

The distance to the king's quarters was short, though we walked it with leaden feet. My vision blurred as I listened to the dull tapping of our steps on the cobblestones. Memories from the early years of our marriage flooded my mind—our tiny wooden animals sitting together on our bedside table, the moment he first introduced me to Esau, and then Jacob. We had been blessed, we had done well. Even in my fear, I knew without a shadow of a doubt that I would die before being forced to live my life without him.

Finally, we arrived at those same huge stone steps. Paul held out his palm to tell us to wait, before walking ahead to speak with the head sentry, who nodded before coming to us.

"Come with me." He turned and marched past the row of armed guards, not stopping to ensure we followed him. I looked up at Isaac, grieved by the forlorn look in his eyes. He nodded gently, and we began to walk forward.

I thought I had experienced terror when we first met the king. In retrospect, that had been nothing more than discomfort. Walking down the long, echoey chamber to his throne with Paul's unforgiving glare floating in my vision brought on a terror unlike anything I had ever experienced. We stopped just short of the steps that led to the throne, and I finally looked up into his rotund face. His small, black eyes shone down at me, and then Isaac, before he slammed his staff on the floor.

"In front of me, I see a man and his dear and loving wife. Why did you tell me she was your sister?" He held up a firm hand, stopping Isaac from speaking. "Before you attempt to offer your excuses, I saw your behavior with my own eyes today. At first, when my sentry reported his observations from your feast, I assumed he was merely jealous or paranoid. But then, today, I happened to be paying a visit at the front of the city, when I looked down to see none other than the two of you displaying more than an acceptable level of sibling affection." He clicked his tongue. "How unfortunate it was to realize that I had been fooled. You were quite thoughtless. And you, my dear," he shifted slightly to eye me, "you are quite the little fox. A kiss in the market? My, what a surprise." His laugh bounced off of the red granite walls, sending a chill down my spine.

At this, Isaac slowly drew himself up to his fullest height before looking challengingly into the king's eyes. "Your Highness, passing as brother and sister was the only thing I knew to do. My wife is a beautiful woman, and it became clear that she was wanted by many of the men in our city. I feared that our marriage would be the cause of my death."

The king reared back his head in fury. "What have you done? What if one of my people had taken your wife under the assumption that she was your sister?" He took a deep breath, his voice softening. "My friend, you would have brought guilt upon all of us."

My mouth dropped, and I looked up at the king in disbelief. His initial anger had transformed into something akin to disappointment and confusion. Where I had expected him to order Isaac's execution, he had simply admonished him.

"You are right, Your Highness. Ever since that day, I have regretted my foolishness. I beg your forgiveness," Isaac said as he bowed his head.

The king studied us while gently tapping his staff against the side of his throne. "While I do not condone your behavior, I understand it. My people do not take kindly to strangers, nor their pretty counterparts." He looked at me with amusement. "You have been a prosperous addition to my kingdom, and for that, I am willing to overlook your imprudence."

Unable to believe what I heard, I chanced a glance up at the king. He was still watching me, barely containing his laughter. Heat rose to my cheeks as I looked back down at the ground.

"Thank you, Your Highness." Isaac's voice was thick with emotion. "I will never forget how kindly you have treated myself, and my family." Isaac bowed his head again, and I followed suit.

"You," the king said with a point of his staff to the head sentry who still stood at the end of the corridor. "Charge anyone who touches this man, or his wife, to death."

The sentry looked at us in disbelief, before remembering his role and bowing to the king. "Yes, Your Majesty."

"And as for you two, do ensure that you don't hide something like this from me again. Understood?" His voice was stern, but he continued to smile.

"Yes, Your Majesty," we said together, before turning to follow the bewildered sentry out of the room. Of all of the outcomes I had expected, this had certainly not been one of them. It was unheard of to gain the king's protection as foreigners in his land, much less after begging for his forgiveness.

Deborah, Selah, and the rest of the servants who had traveled with us for the day stood at the base of the entrance, watching for us expectantly. Joy broke across their faces when they saw us emerge from the dark corridor.

"Oh, thank God, you're all right! Is everything all right?" Deborah said as she clutched my arm and propelled me away from the sentries.

"Yes, by a miracle only God himself could have done, we have been granted pardon and protection. The king has ordered that anyone who hurts Isaac or myself be put to death." Just then, the realization hit me that my days of pretending to be Isaac's unmarried sister were finally over. For the first time in nearly a decade, I would be able to fully be the woman I had been for the majority of my life: A wife and a mother.

"Oh, Deborah," I said as I choked back a sob. "I'm so relieved."

She patted my back before turning to signal to the others that it was time to go home. I watched the town fade away and night climb across the sky through blurry eyes. A massive weight had been removed from my shoulders, one that I had grown so accustomed to, I no longer noticed. Living so discreetly, so secretively, while constantly looking over my shoulder in fear for Isaac's life had taken its toll on me. Knowing that we were to be accepted, to be truly known, was more than a relief.

It was bliss.

CHAPTER TWENTY

Autumn became winter and winter became spring, and through it all, we worked in preparation for the harvest ahead. With the fear of the king learning about our marriage behind us, it felt as if nothing was keeping us from fully and completely find our footing in Gerar. While our previous harvest had been plentiful, Isaac believed that we had only just achieved what the land promised to provide.

Before we had the chance to look up from our work, summer arrived and brought with it our most bountiful harvest yet. Our crops and livestock not only flourished, they grew a hundredfold. We could scarcely believe our good fortune, and our storehouses were filled within the first month. In just one month of harvest, we had gleaned and grown enough to carry us through the next five winters—and we had another few months to go.

Looking at the abundance surrounding us after hearing word from Diana about many farmers' inability to have a healthy harvest unsettled me. While the king had ordered our protection, it didn't change the citizens' sentiments toward us. If anything, it made many dislike us even more. While we didn't need to fear for our lives, we still faced the leers and uninvited comments of those who disapproved of our presence. I feared that our sudden yield and subsequent wealthiness would only serve to bolster their anger. As it was, I was no longer able to visit Lilah, as Paul had forbidden her to keep company with someone he deemed grossly corrupt. Diana had seen no issue in continuing to visit me, all thanks to her rebellious and oftentimes foolhardy nature. She brought with her secret messages from Lilah, and seemed to enjoy her job as intermediary.

One afternoon, I found Isaac, Esau, and Jacob standing

outside the storehouses while deep in thought. As I approached, I overheard a bit of what Esau was saying.

"I say we take what's left of our gleanings and sell it in the city for a profit. With that money, we'll be able to do anything we want, including expand our land, and add on more servants and workers."

Jacob rubbed his neck before shaking his head. "While I can see your point, you're forgetting that our frequent presence in the city will not be appreciated. The people of Gerar are already unfriendly. Imagine their anger when they watch us bring more and more supplies, crops, and livestock to be sold every single day. It'll appear as if we are flaunting our riches."

Esau huffed in frustration before turning to face him. "At a certain point, you're going to have to stop fearing every—"

"He's right," Isaac said, cutting Esau off. "We'll need to find a more suitable way to sell what we've gleaned, without further upsetting our fellow citizens."

"What if, instead of selling everything at the market, we split up our gleanings and traveled to sell them to farmers and landowners individually?" I said as I grew nearer to them. All three turned to look at me in surprise, causing me to smile.

As if remembering himself, Isaac's shoulders relaxed when he saw me. "Ah, my beautiful wife with her brilliant mind," he said affectionately as he put his arm around my waist. "Leave it to you to come up with an idea that us men wouldn't have ever considered."

"It sounds like far more work than it is worth," Esau said, his brows knitted together in a scowl.

"We have the resources and the help to do as she says," said Jacob. "We've bred more working animals than we need for the fields, which we can give to our servants to use for travel. We'll just need more wagons to carry everything, and to train everyone on bartering and negotiation."

I gave him a smile of appreciation, before sneaking a glance at Esau to see him roll his eyes. I had lost hope of curing his jealousy of his brother long ago. Instead, I had learned to accept that though Esau had many strengths, his jealousy and resentment were his greatest weaknesses.

"I will pray about this for the next fortnight. If it is the Lord's will, we will proceed with Rebekah and Jacob's plan. We will still sell in the market as well, but just at a smaller amount. My hope is that in spreading out the physical evidence of how the Lord has blessed us this harvest, the people of Gerar will have no reason to further resent us," Isaac said.

And so it was. Before long, our servants were trained in bartering and negotiation, and given detailed instructions and travel plans. Each week, they returned to us with reports of their success, their pockets jingling cheerfully. Our women, including myself, traveled into the city one day out of each week to sell our textiles and grain. I was pleased to see that aside from the occasional angry, belligerent man or hissing woman, we were otherwise unnoticed.

That harvest closed, bringing on eight more years of abundance. Our scheme of selling to individual landowners had paid off, but this current year, our twentieth harvest in Gerar, felt different. Servants reported that farmers met them on the road, asking them to return at nightfall, and then asking them again to keep their connection private. Those who purchased from us behaved as if they feared what might happen if others found out what they had done. It wasn't until I ventured into the market myself, for the first time in months, that I felt the animosity that was now outwardly shown toward us in every face and in every interaction.

I stood with Deborah at our stall, watching as shoppers passed by. Women who stopped to visit with neighboring stalls were quick to speed past ours while avoiding eye contact. Some of them had been acquaintances, even friends, to us in years past. Bolder men eyed us angrily, some spitting at our feet. After a few hours, it became clear that not only were we no longer welcome, we were wasting our time.

"Can you and Selah manage packing up our goods? I have a quick visit to make," I said to Deborah. It was not even noon yet, and I wanted to catch Diana before she settled into her afternoon work.

"Of course. But please be careful, and meet us under the palm trees just outside the gate?"

I nodded in agreement before tightening my veil and walking briskly to Diana's home. I kept my eyes on the dirt road beneath my feet, stopping when other pedestrians drew near, and letting them pass before resuming. I rounded the corner to find Diana's small, squat home. Smoke plumed out of the top, carrying the inviting aromas of her famous lentil soup.

"Is anyone home?" I called quietly through the open door, looking around as my eyes adjusted to the dim light.

"Is that you, Rebekah? Come in! Why are you behaving like a little mouse?"

"I came to ask you that, actually," I said as I sat down on a stool, groaning in relief. While it was warm outside, the fire in Diana's dark, cool home was comforting. She handed me a cup of tea, and I accepted it gratefully.

"Ah, that," she said as she rubbed the back of her hand over her forehead. "I've been meaning to talk with you about that. You see"—she peered over the lid of the bubbling soup on the fire, avoiding my eyes—"over the years, more and more people have grown frustrated with your family's wealth and success. Though you've been here nearly twenty years, there are many who have lived here for generations. They are frustrated, and feel that the king gave you preferential land."

"That is ridiculous, he gave us what he had available at the time. We were blessed with abundant harvests in Canaan, too."

"You know that and I know that, but to them, you are outsiders who paid the king off, or worse, in order to get the land that you now have. They see you as outsiders, and as a threat to their livelihood. The truth is, if you were native to Gerar, they still would be angered by your success. But being that you are foreigners, it makes it that much worse."

I stared into my cup of tea, contemplating everything she said. Were we no longer safe here, in the home we had grown to love? Fear wrapped its claws around my throat as I remembered the pain I had felt in leaving my home, and then in leaving the home I had made in Canaan. The thought of having to endure that again was more than I could handle.

"Do you think we are no longer safe, even though the king ordered the people of Gerar to leave us alone?"

At this, Diana slowly met my eyes. "Of course, it could be nothing more than drunken talk, but there—there have been rumors that some men have discussed staging an attack on

Isaac and your sons, and making it appear as if an outsider did it." Tears filled her weary eyes as she watched me absorb the impact of her words, and it took me a moment to remember to breathe.

Where I had initially felt fear, I now felt fury. To have my husband and my sons threatened after everything we had done, everything we had provided? My cheeks grew hot with rage as I stood up abruptly. "I must go." I turned with a shaking hand to place my tea back on the table. "Thank you, Diana, for telling me. I don't know if this will be the last time I see you for a while, but I need you to know that I will always be thankful for our friendship." I pulled her into a hug, taking a split second to catch the pain that pooled in her eyes before I fastened my veil. "Please tell Lilah the same."

It took everything in me to calmly walk back to where Deborah and Selah waited for me, both of whom looked relieved to see me again. When they tried to ask me where I had been, I shook my head at them, placing a finger over my mouth before beginning to walk.

It wasn't until we arrived home that I told them, and Isaac, everything Diana had told me. I watched as horror worked its way across Deborah's face, and Selah began to cry. Isaac stood to the side, his hand resting heavily on his staff, his face turned away from me.

With a glance back at Deborah and Selah, I pulled Isaac outside, under our favorite oak tree. "What will we do, Isaac? Did you not hear what I said?"

He finally looked at me, and I shivered when I saw the fire in his eyes. Normally so calm, so restrained, so thoughtful, Isaac's face was that of a warrior. Never before had I seen him so angry. "I heard. I have been praying and asking the Lord for grace ever since, as I feared what my fury might bring upon our family."

Gingerly, I stepped toward him and placed my hand over his heart.

"Before anything else is done, before our sons are made aware, I must request the counsel of the king."

I nodded, frightened at the thought of Esau learning what I had today. "I'll instruct Deborah and Selah to keep what they heard to themselves." We stood there in charged silence, listening to the sound of the wind whispering through the leaves.

Suddenly, I heard distant yelling, and we both turned in confusion to see where it came from. Even from where we stood, I could make out Esau's fiery red hair as he ran toward us at a frantic pace. As if my legs were moving out of their own accord, I broke into a run to meet him. Isaac followed closely after me, shouting things I couldn't make out through the wind that wailed past my ears. Finally, we made it to Esau, all three of us breathing heavily.

"The wells," Esau panted. "They've been filled with dirt. All of them."

"What do you mean, all of them? Every last one?"

"Yes, Father. Every last one. Filled to the brim with dirt." His chest rose and fell quickly, and his eyes burned similarly to Isaac's.

Isaac considered his words before speaking slowly. "Do you mean to tell me that they have even taken our hidden well?"

"Yes."

I gasped, tripping backward in my shock. Our wells had been dug by Abraham, and we had survived off of them for these last twenty years. Without our wells, we wouldn't be able to water our crops, nor our livestock. We only stored enough water to carry our own household through one week at a time. Our wells were our sole source of survival, and they had just been buried in the sand.

Spots of darkness clouded my vision, and I felt my knees grow weak. I heard the thunder of Esau's yell as my head met soft, spongy grass.

❊ ❊ ❊

I stared blearily at the darkness overhead, grimacing as confusion and pain swept over me. I sat up and looked to my left to find Deborah sleeping on the floor next to my bed, her head on a cushion, the fire providing a dull glow behind her. Her eyes flew open as I shifted again to reach for a cup of water.

"Stop, I'll do that," she said as she gingerly rose to fetch the pitcher. "You were asleep for some time. How do you feel?"

"Like I've swallowed cotton, and let the goats run across my head. What happened?"

"You fainted, and Isaac carried you home. I have to say, it was amusing seeing him sling you over his arms like a younger man." She grinned before looking at me in concern. "Esau tried to carry you, but he refused to let you go."

"Where are they now?" All at once, I remembered what had happened. A weight pressed down on my chest as I looked around wildly, fearing that they had gone to find and punish those who had filled our wells.

"They've gone to see if there's anything that can be done to salvage the wells. In the morning, Isaac will request the king's counsel."

"What will we do, Deborah?" My voice trembled with fear and exhaustion. "We barely have enough water left to take care of our household and livestock for another week."

She shushed me, instructing me to lie back down as she placed a cool damp rag across my forehead. I slipped back into a deep and dreamless sleep.

❈ ❈ ❈

I heard the sadness in his voice before I even opened my eyes. He sat at the end of our bed, his elbows on his knees, his head cradled in his hands. "We must go, my love," he said with a tremulous voice.

"Go where?"

"Away from here. We are no longer welcome in Gerar, and have been ordered by the king to leave immediately. With what little water reserves we have left, we will need to pack up everything we can within the next few hours."

I closed my eyes, trying to shake the grogginess and fear that threatened to creep back in. "We've been ordered to leave? We have nowhere to go, no water to survive. We will die, Isaac!" With every breath, I felt the walls of my lungs closing in, as if an elephant sat on my chest.

Isaac whipped around, and the fire that had been in his eyes was dull, but still present. "We don't have a choice, Rebekah. Staying here, death is a certainty. We've been shunned by King Abimelech, and we no longer have his protection. We must go."

I stared at him mutely, trying to digest everything he said as years of hardship, growth, and memories flitted through my mind. The roots we had lovingly, tenderly put into this soil were now being torn out, tossed to whomever wished to take them. The bitterness I felt came to a crashing halt when I looked at Isaac and saw the same worry, heartbreak, and anger written in every line of his handsome face. I shifted forward, reaching out to place my palm on his cheek. "The Lord brought us here. He will find a better place for us," I said.

Isaac patted my hand before slowly rising to his feet. "It is time for me to alert the others. Are you up to packing up the tent with Deborah?"

"I have no other choice." I gave him a small, sad smile, and watched him as he walked with heavy steps out of our tent.

In a matter of hours, Deborah and I had hastily packed up Sarah's tent. I looked at the flat expanse surrounding us, the land that had only hours previously held our entire household. While I was nowhere near as attached to this land, this home, as I had been to Canaan, the fact remained that we were being forced to leave against our will. It was this that hurt the most.

I glanced down at my palm, finding our tiny wooden animals safely nestled there. I reached down to place them in my leather satchel, before walking ahead to join Isaac and the others as they loaded our belongings onto camels and donkeys.

CHAPTER TWENTY-ONE

After a night and day's journey, we came to rest in the valley outside of Gerar. Initially, I had feared that we were still too close to the city for comfort, but Isaac had been confident that our new camp was distant enough to please the king.

I stood next to our campfire and stared into the blaze. Our household included over two hundred servants, all of whom had built their own fires that dotted across the sandy landscape, reminding me of the stars suspended overhead. Upon our arrival, each person had stopped and awaited Isaac's instruction on what to do next. Whispered questions of whether it would be safe to stake our tents again, or whether we had enough water to drink and cook with snaked their way from the furthermost person to the front. I myself felt frozen with fear and doubt—would it be foolish to pitch our tents here, in case we needed to run again?

Isaac groaned quietly as he slowly crouched down to sit next to me in the sand. "I've ordered everyone to set up their tents."

I looked at him questioningly.

"I know you are still worried, but the Lord has put it on my heart to stay here for the time being. In the morning, we will dig for water. If we find any, we will stay."

"And what of the king? Will he not mind that we are still within his territory, taking his water from his land?"

"My love, the water we consume is not his, it's the Lord's. I am just as wary as you are, but I don't think it would be wise to go against God's plan. Do you?" He studied me closely, his eyes a warm amber.

I sighed. "Of course not. I trust that you know what you are doing." I pushed my feet in small, concentric circles as I watched the sand shift below me. "And if we die, we die together."

That same, disguised smile flashed across his face. "And if we die, we die together," he returned.

Exhausted from the day's journey, we chose to sleep under the stars, blanketed by the warm summer air. I awoke as day began to break, silently watching as pink peeked over the horizon. I turned over to wake Isaac, only to find that he was no longer there.

"Good morning," Deborah whispered as she trudged through the sand to me. "I've been waiting for you to wake up. All of the men left before daybreak to dig for water."

At the mention of water, I realized just how thirsty I was. "I think I might have eaten some sand in my sleep," I said. I took a small drink of what remained in my pitcher.

Deborah busied herself around the fire, stoking it as she prepared the dried meat and fruit she brought on our journey.

"How much water do we have left?" I eyed her warily.

"Enough."

"Enough for what?"

"Enough to get us through one more week, at best," she said as she finally lifted her face to look at me. "But after that, that's it. There will be nothing left."

I looked at the women who slowly, quietly rose for the day around us as they stole past the forms of their sleeping children. The distant bleating of sheep and braying of donkeys drifted toward us in a light breeze. A stray chicken pecked at the sand just a few feet away from me. The weight of the lives that surrounded me dug into my shoulders, and I struggled to control my breathing as I considered the magnitude of what lay ahead of us. Finding water, here, was our only option. We didn't have the resources to venture any farther.

Each morning, our men left in search of water. Each evening, they returned dusty and defeated, silently shaking their heads at our questions. On the morning of the seventh day of their search, Deborah and I set about building Sarah's tent again. What my heart yearned to do was to sit and watch the horizon, awaiting good news from Isaac, or any one of the hundreds of other men in our care. But as Isaac's wife, I knew that the women in our camp looked to me for guidance—seeing me paralyzed in fear would only serve to make theirs worse.

Setting up my tent was not only a welcome distraction, it was a show of faith.

As Deborah drove the final stake into the sand, I looked up to see the beginnings of the other tents taking shape. Children who were too young to understand why their home no longer existed ran and tumbled throughout the campsite. I smiled as I watched a tiny lamb frolic behind Benny, a four-year-old boy. Watching their playful innocence felt like a necessary shot of adrenaline to my otherwise dormant faith. If they could play, and laugh, and jump, and dance while we waited and prayed for water, surely that was a sign that the Lord hadn't led us away from Gerar in vain. Surely, I thought, He hadn't walked us farther into the desert to die of dehydration.

At that moment, I heard the distinct sound of a horn and whipped around to find a small group of men running in our direction. I squinted to try to get a better view of them, unable to make out their faces with the sun streaming behind their backs. As they drew closer, I heard the garbled yell of the one word we'd prayed for these seven days.

Water.

"Deborah, is it true?" I said as I turned to clutch her wrists. "Did they find it?"

Her eyes shone with excitement, and she shook my hands off of her wrists as she began to run. "Oh, I can't just stand here. Water, Rebekah! Water!"

We met the men at the edge of our camp, their chests heaving, their faces shining with perspiration and beaming with excitement. Our head shepherd, Josiah, and two of his apprentices had set out at dawn to dig for water. After a backbreaking day spent in the blistering sun, they had dug in one final spot, where they found a spring of water.

"It is enough to take care of our entire company, as well as our livestock. With this, we can find more water sources, and begin to sow," Josiah bellowed with joy, his arms raised in victory.

The women around us began to cry, clutching on to one another for support. Many of the children, unsettled by the sudden change in their elders, began to follow suit. A few simply shrugged and returned to their games.

"Someone must find Isaac and tell him. Reu, do you know where he went today?" I looked into the small, determined face of Josiah's eldest apprentice.

"I do. I will go find him now." I watched as he took off in a sprint.

I, along with thirty other women, followed Josiah out to the well to begin filling our camp's pitchers. The strain of the several kilometer walk and the weight of our pitchers would normally have been tiresome, but we were too happy to notice. To be burdened with the weight of water again—to experience the familiar feeling of having a stone pitcher press into your shoulder—was a gift that I vowed to never again take for granted.

After our third trip back to our site, I looked up to find Isaac standing among a group of men, listening as Josiah gesticulated wildly, the excitement of his story overcoming him.

Isaac smiled and clapped Josiah on the back, before turning to raise his hand to silence the others. "Thanks to the work of these good men, we have water," he said as the crowd roared. "Now, it is our duty to use what the Lord has given us wisely. Tomorrow, we will begin to create a more efficient system to bring the water closer to our site, so as to not put such a strain on our women. We will also need it to water our future crops."

Heads bobbed in agreement, and I listened as instruments began to be tuned in celebration.

"Before we celebrate, let us thank the Lord for all He has given us, and for delivering us to this place." He bent his head and began to pray, the rest of us following suit.

As I listened to his melodic voice, my heart fluttered as I recalled having experienced a similar feeling after being granted pardon and protection by the king. It had been many years since we had experienced such an upheaval, but with today's discovery, I finally felt comfortable hoping for a better and brighter future.

After another supper of dried meat and vegetables, the men, women, and children danced around the fires, singing and laughing with glee. Isaac twirled me in his arms, and I looked up at him as I laughed and shook my head. "I'm getting a bit old for all of this excitement, don't you think?" I said playfully.

"You are but a young woman, my love," he said as he finished our dance with a slight bow before extending his arm to me. "If you're going to consider yourself old, you must then call me ancient."

"Oh, come here." I lifted my hand to pat his cheek. "You are as youthful and commanding as you were the day we met." Even being twenty years my senior, he didn't look a day older than me. "In fact, I'm not entirely sure that you do age," I said as I brushed my lips against his cheek.

"Stop it, you two. You'll make the young ones sick," Esau called from across the fire before rounding it to stand next to Isaac and I. "Dance with me, Mother."

I sighed, waving to Isaac as Esau steered me back into the crowd. After one more song, I shook my head before telling him that he had gotten all I had left in me.

He finally softened, before offering his arm and finding us a place to sit away from the others. "I feel good about this, you know," he said as he looked at our surroundings confidently. "I think this will be even better than Gerar, and it'll be on our terms. No more pandering to those who don't deserve it. We have the opportunity to build our own legacy, our own civilization, if we so choose."

I studied his broad face, watching as the fire danced through his eyes. "Be careful, Esau. You have a fighter's spirit; I worry that it'll be your undoing," I said carefully.

His brows drew together in his signature scowl, and I watched as his mental walls rose again. "You've never seen the same potential that I see, Mother. I know I'm not your precious Jacob, but I am your firstborn. It'll be me who takes care of you, it'll be me who bears our name for future generations." He stood up and began to walk away, before turning around to mutter, "Speak of the devil, your favorite has arrived."

I stared at Esau's retreating back in stunned silence. Never had he expressed such open disdain for his brother to me directly, and never had he alluded to caring about what I thought of him. Guilt crept through my mind as I thought about my relationship with Jacob, and what I knew about his future as according to God. Even so, I loved Esau, and had never wanted him to feel otherwise.

"Esau—" I called, realizing even then that if he heard me, he wouldn't come back.

I looked up to find Jacob standing next to me, watching his brother walk away with a thoughtful expression on his face. "Let him go. He must be left to come around when he is ready. It is the only way to get through to him," he said as he sat down beside me. "Are you all right?"

I nodded, swiping at a stray tear that slid down my cheek. "It is hard for me, you know. I want to be the best mother I can to the both of you. But with him, I feel that I have failed."

Jacob watched the dancers, smiling absentmindedly as a group of children ran by. "For as long as I can remember, Esau has been contrary. Headstrong. He came to this earth with strong opinions, and an even stronger heart. Sometimes, those opinions and that heart will cloud his judgment. I think, with time, he will mature and come to see how good you and Father have been to us."

I leaned my head against his shoulder, comforted by his words. "When did you become so wise?" I said playfully.

He laughed. "Well, that's the thing about me. Where he is headstrong and all heart, I am all mind. I think I was born this way as well."

I choked back a laugh, remembering his wise, concerned little face as he sat on my lap and asked questions that I hardly ever had answers for. *Why is the sky blue, Mother? Why do the stars twinkle? Where does the wind come from?* We would try our best to answer, sometimes telling him that we weren't quite sure what the answer was at all. It was then that he would crinkle his tiny forehead in concentration, as if by thinking deeply enough, he would be able to uncover the answers he sought. His thoughtfulness and meticulousness had carried into his adult life, and he had proven himself to be a caring and clever leader of our household.

"You never did quite settle into the role of being a child," I said. "You always brought the world's biggest, most complex questions to me, as if I would have the answer. When I inevitably didn't, you'd bring that same question to your father. When he didn't have an answer, you'd announce that you had a conversation with God to get to before stomping away. I so miss when you two were little," I said wistfully.

Jacob pressed a kiss into my hair before saying goodnight. I rose slowly, gently, from my place and walked to my tent, turning one last time to watch the others as they danced to their final song. While I would always miss Canaan and those beautiful, sunny days when I watched the boys run through grass as high as their necks, screaming and shouting about each new rock or twig they discovered, there was something lovely about being here, in the midst of the trial and triumph, too.

CHAPTER
TWENTY-TWO

"They've taken the well."

I blinked a few times to adjust my eyes to the dim morning light.

Deborah stood next to me, her hand clutching my arm as she shook it repeatedly. "Did you hear me? The herdsmen of Gerar, they've taken the well. Rebekah, we have no water again."

It took a moment for me to fully comprehend everything she said. I remembered the evening before, and our lighthearted dancing and celebration. It had felt like we were finally through the fire of the trial; as if we'd overcome our greatest challenge. We had water, we had livestock, we were safe.

"What happened to the men guarding the well?" I asked in a panic. I flung the thin sheets off of my feet and scrambled to dress. Always cautious, Isaac had decided to leave two men to guard our new well in case travelers came upon it. We had assumed that guarding the well was a precaution, not a necessity. If the well had been taken, what had happened to our guards?

Deborah breathed in deeply, closing her eyes as if to ward off the pain. "They killed them. We only learned about them this morning when the women in charge of drawing our morning's water found strangers patrolling the well. Our men were lying face down in the sand."

A piece of my heart shattered as I thought about the two men who had cheerfully volunteered themselves, honored to have the privilege of guarding their family's water. Both had wives and families waiting at camp for them. Losing them was like losing a member of our family.

I threw my veil over my head, pausing only to shove my feet into my sandals before running out of the door with Deborah following closely behind. Our makeshift village, while still standing, was in shambles. Everywhere I looked, women cried silently over their fires, their children tucked into the folds of their skirts. Our men had followed Isaac to meet with the herdsmen, leaving only a few behind to guard the women and children. Unsure of what else to do, I began to sit with each family, listening to them as they expressed their fears, crying with the two women who lost the men they loved. When the burden of carrying each family's pain on my shoulders became too much, Jacob arrived to relieve me. I watched as he listened with care to the few remaining women and children that I hadn't had the strength to get to. His kind words of encouragement and attentiveness were a balm to their frenzy. I couldn't help but feel my heart swell with pride as I observed him.

The morning passed slowly, excruciatingly, and all work, all progress, stood at a halt while we watched the horizon. Finally, as the sun beat mercilessly on our heads, I saw Isaac's outline appear, followed by a mass of men. Unable to wait, I ran ahead, my veil slipping off and streaming behind me, the sand hot beneath my feet. As I ran, I watched his worn face and couldn't help but remember the day I first saw him, when I had first walked so slowly toward him, toward our future. Before I could reminisce any further, I came to a halt in front of him. "I was worried sick," I said as I fought to catch my breath. "What happened?"

Isaac stared down at me, studying my face before shifting his gaze to the staff he held in his right hand. He twisted it in his fingers, watching as it burrowed deeper into the sand. "The herdsmen of Gerar saw our company from a distance, and followed us. They watched as we dug our well, waited until we left, and attacked our two guards. They claim that the water is theirs, as we are in their country." Anger flashed through Isaac's eyes before he continued. "It took everything in me not to kill them then and there. But I know others will come looking for them, and I must do what is right for our people."

I nodded in understanding. While Isaac could easily kill them for what they did to our own, our group was no match for all of Gerar. Any act of violence would be an act of war; one that we couldn't afford to fight.

"Instead, I've ordered that every man set out to find more water. We found one spring and I am confident that the Lord will provide another. We've come for supplies and respite before heading back out." He placed a kiss on my forehead before trudging slowly past me, his tired shoulders refusing to slouch, his head held high.

After a small lunch of what remained of our dried meat and stale bread, the men departed in search of more water with tools in hand. Unable to sit and wait any longer, the women and I set about putting up the last parts of our camp, savoring the feeling of being home again. If we were to die of dehydration, at least we would die in the comfort of the homes we loved.

Night wrapped its cool, murky arms around us as worries grew over their prolonged absence. Finally, as the women began to put their children to bed, the men arrived. Triumph stretched across their faces, and enthusiasm radiated from every part of their beings. I stood up slowly, watching as Isaac led his camel back to our camp, the fire from his torch illuminating his face. He had left us a tired and worried man, and had returned a reinvigorated warrior. He gracefully swung his leg off of his camel, and in just a few steps, had me in his arms, lifting me so that my feet dangled in the air. His mouth smiled into my neck as he held me tight, and I laughed. For that moment, we were young again. Free from the sorrows and tribulations that life had brought us, simply two young people who loved each other deeply, and had a lifetime ahead.

"I assume you have good news for us," I said playfully as I pushed away to look at him closely.

"We've found another well, and have stationed ten guards there. Should the Lord will that it be so, the herdsmen will be satiated with the well they stole, and leave us to have the one we've found."

Trepidation filled me, making my smile falter. We had already experienced the heartbreak of losing two men today— what would we do if we lost ten more? I pushed the thought out of my mind before taking Isaac's hand and guiding him to the fire, where I'd kept what remained of our supper warm. I sat next to him as he ate, distractedly observing as our camp began its ritual of good nights and dimmed fires.

It wasn't until his voice broke my thoughts to ask if I was ready for bed that I realized that we were blanketed by darkness. I rose slowly, tiptoeing to our tent under the guidance of the moonlight, stopping only to look back and study the dark horizon once more.

✳ ✳ ✳

The bed shifted as Isaac rose quietly in the dark. My eyes flew open and I turned over to find him dressing for the day hurriedly, as if moved by some unknown force.

"Where are you going?" I whispered.

"I had a nightmare. I'm sure it is nothing," he said with an edge to his voice. "Go back to sleep, my love. I am going to take Jacob and Esau with me to the well to check on our men."

Something wasn't right. Isaac would rarely wake others for the sake of a nightmare, especially with the knowledge that ten of our strongest men stood guard at our well. Worry worked its way from my stomach to my chest as I watched him walk away.

After a morning spent foraging, cooking, and weaving, they returned to our camp, requesting the assistance of several nurses. While our guards had not been killed, they were wounded. More herdsmen had shown up in the night, demanding our well, refusing to leave until their wish was granted. Our guards had fought them to the best of their abilities, but were unable to withstand the weaponry that the herdsmen came equipped with. Wounded, they'd found refuge a mile east and had awaited Isaac's arrival.

Losing two wells and seeing our ten strongest men wounded was not just demoralizing, it was terrifying. How could we remain strong enough to fight off the people of Gerar without water to sustain our livestock, which supplied us with food? Outwardly, I managed to maintain a calm and even temper, but inwardly, my panic swirled higher and higher until it threatened to burst through my scalp. As Isaac's wife and the secondary head of our household, I had a duty to lead our women and children. But after several days of worry and turmoil, I had no answers. No plan.

The wounded men were carried home on the backs of our healthiest mules to be nursed in the comfort of their tents. Thankfully, none had sustained life-threatening injuries, though many would need weeks to heal. In the middle of a bleak supper of uncooked grain and wild asparagus, Isaac stood up and raised his arms, calling everyone to attention. He cleared his throat before surveying the eyes of those seated as they awaited what he would say next. "The Lord brought us out of Canaan and into Gerar. From a famine, he brought us years of feast. When our time came to a close in Gerar, He led us to this valley. Many years ago, he promised to bless us, according to the promise He gave my father." He lowered his hands, placing both of them on his staff before continuing. "I realize that I ask a lot of you, of your faith and perseverance, when I say that we must continue to fight. We cannot allow the people of Gerar to keep us from claiming God's promise. We must find water, and we must do so now. And so I ask you," he said as he turned his head slowly, peering into the worn and terrified faces of those who listened. "Who will come?"

I watched his back rise and fall slowly. After what felt like an eternity, Jacob stood, nodding his head as he said, "I will."

Esau, who sat by his own fire with the fury of defeat in his shoulders, finally stood and placed his fist over his heart. And then, as suddenly as a wave of water, I watched as every man stood, his shoulders drawn back with pride, his head held higher than it had been earlier that day.

Isaac looked around with emotion sparkling in his eyes before nodding. "Thank you. Now, let us finish our meals and pack, we will set off within the hour."

Our tents broke out into a flurry of activity, with women pausing their hasty packing to press a kiss to their husbands' foreheads and cheeks, and men rushing to sharpen the knives and arrows that would accompany their shovels. Breathless, I searched for Isaac, finding him just outside the entrance to our tent. I grabbed his hand and pulled him into the darkness, before closing the door behind us.

He grunted with surprise, and I saw the glint of his smile in a patch of moonlight from the small crack in our ceiling. "Why I'm still surprised by your strength, I'll never know," he said teasingly.

"Promise me that you will be careful. Promise me that this time, it'll work," I said, fully realizing just how impossible my request was, but needing to hear him say it anyway. I lifted my hands to cup his cheeks, piercing the shadows with my eyes in an effort to find his.

He didn't answer for a few moments, and we stood there in the silence, breathing in tandem as we listened to the crackle of the fire outside and the sounds of busied preparations. "I promise. I believe that this time, we will find the well that the Lord wants us to keep." Gently, he removed my hands from his face, placing them on his chest instead. His thumbs traced my knuckles softly, and his lips brushed my forehead. "I do love you more than any man should be able to, you know."

"I know," I said with a smile. We laughed quietly, savoring our few moments of peace, before he stepped back. Already, the space between us felt too great, too charged with anticipation and fear of the unknown. When he was near me, I felt safe, as if by clutching him, I could protect the both of us, keep us from harm's way. When he wasn't near me, it felt as if half of my limbs and heart were missing—and without them, how could I shield either of us from the storm that threatened our sky?

Before I could say anything else, he stepped out of our tent and was quickly swallowed up by the questions of the others who depended on him, just as I did. Women stepped out of their tents to bid their husbands a tearful goodbye, and we watched as their receding forms disappeared into the night. With a heavy sigh, I turned to face my bed, accepting another night of fitful sleep with the knowledge that there was nothing to do but wait.

* * *

True to his word, Isaac returned the following day with news of a well, one even bigger than the two before. That evening, we waited with bated breath to see if more men from Gerar would arrive to overtake us. By a miracle, our guards were left unbothered, and after several nights of keeping watch, we began to finally breathe a sigh of relief. It appeared that the herdsmen of Gerar had more than their fair share of water from our two previous wells, and we began to allow ourselves to hope that with this third well, we'd finally be able to begin planting again.

On our eighth evening after digging the well, Isaac named it Rehoboth in honor of the Lord making room for us in our new land. Over the course of our couple of weeks in the valley, it had become clear that we would need more space as well as a second piece of land to farm. After naming Rehoboth, we set off with Jacob, Deborah, and one hundred servants to a new territory which promised to be fruitful, and was only a half day's journey away. While we had only just begun to make Rehoboth home, I couldn't help but feel a twinge of excitement at the idea of expanding into more lush and fertile land.

As the eldest son, Esau had been appointed by Isaac to stay behind and oversee the farming of our land in Rehoboth, while leading our servants there. Privately, I'd believed that the role was rightfully Jacob's, given the fact that he had managed our land and servants for over a decade, and would one day inherit the birthright that Esau gave him. Rather than vocalizing my thoughts, I chose to keep them to myself. History had proven that Isaac and I did not see eye to eye where Esau was concerned, and though he was aware of what the Lord had told me so many years ago, he was still cautious to go against our customs.

Esau and I hadn't spoken since the night we'd found our first well. Our goodbye was stilted, and somewhat forced. Even so, I placed my hands on his broad shoulders and stood on the tips of my toes to press a kiss to his forehead. "Don't go and start a family without inviting us back to celebrate," I said as I peered up at him.

He smiled, excitement flashing through his eyes at the thought of having land and a household to run. "I can't help it if the right woman forces my hand, now can I?"

I sighed, reaching out to pat his cheek gently before turning to follow the others who had already begun their walk. Many had ridden ahead, anxious to get to our new home and to begin to set up camp. Isaac and I chose to walk the distance alone, enjoying the peace of the cool night air and the stars that winked overhead.

"Do you think leaving Esau here was the right decision?" I asked quietly, breaking our silence.

Isaac studied the sky before answering. "I do. Remember, Jacob leaves him with nothing upon my death. I know that Esau's decision to trade his birthright for a bowl of soup was his and his alone, but I think a bit of leadership and responsibility will do him good."

I walked next to him quietly, considering his words. While I was not confident in Esau's wisdom as a leader, I did know that he would do almost anything to gain Isaac's approval. He wouldn't let the land and our household fail. At least, not intentionally.

The sand turned to spongy grass as we finally slowed. I breathed in deeply, savoring the smell of the meadow that surrounded us, remembering our home in Canaan. Deborah had built a fire to boil water for supper, and Selah led the rest of our servants around the site as they discussed where to place our tents.

"Deborah," Isaac said from behind me. "I see that Selah is having my wife's tent built as we speak. Can you see to it that it is placed in that clearing to the east?"

Deborah nodded, before rising to instruct Selah, leaving us alone by the fire.

"What made you do that?" I asked out of curiosity. We'd grown accustomed to having our tent near the rest of our company, ever since leaving Canaan.

"I want you to love our new home as much as you loved our first one. That clearing has a collection of trees surrounding it, similar to the ones that bordered our tent back home. While it is missing our little brook, I thought you might enjoy it."

Tears filled my eyes as I looked up at him. For more than half a century, he had adored, accepted, cherished, and heard me. The fact that he remembered just how much I loved and missed our little oasis shouldn't have come as a surprise, but it did. A welcome one at that.

I looked around us, taking in the swaying trees and greenery that enfolded our campsite with a deep sigh of relief. "We're home, Isaac." I reached out and gave his hand a squeeze, before taking my first step into our next, newest life.

CHAPTER
TWENTY-THREE

It was approaching midnight when we climbed into bed that evening, exhausted from packing and unpacking our tent. We laid in the darkness, listening to the wind as it rustled through the leaves overhead. I began to doze off, only to be woken by Isaac slowly removing the blanket and shifting to stand up.

"What's wrong?" I croaked before struggling to sit up as well.

"I'm just restless. Please go to sleep, my love." As he shrugged on his tunic and walked outside soundlessly, I began to drift off to sleep.

The next morning, I woke to find Isaac's side of the bed cold. It looked exactly the same as when he'd left it the night before. I threw the covers off and ran to look outside, fearing that something had happened to him. As I surveyed our campsite and the brilliance of our lush surroundings, I looked toward the hills to see a man crouched over a pile of what appeared to be large pieces of rock. When he stood up and turned to walk back down the hill in search for more, I realized with a jolt that it was Isaac. While I was accustomed to seeing him do manual labor, it had been years since I'd seen him work in such a frenzy. I watched in confusion and awe—he moved with the same fluidity and strength that he had when we first met. Seeing him work felt as if I had stepped back in time, the only difference being the tiny specks of gray that had begun to streak his hair.

I dressed quickly before venturing out to meet him. His focus was so intent on his task, he didn't seem to hear me approach. "Is this what you've been doing all night?" I wrapped my veil around my shoulders to ward off the morning chill.

He looked up in surprise and smiled. "I spent the night speaking with the Lord. Then, just before sunrise, I decided to build an altar to commemorate it." He studied a large stone he held in his hands before placing it carefully on top of the others.

"What did He say to you?" Normally, I didn't ask Isaac about the details of his conversations with God. But his behavior today was so different, I couldn't restrain my curiosity.

"He assured me that He was with me, with us, and would bless our new life here for my father's sake. He gave me the reassurance I needed to settle here." Isaac wiped the sweat from his brow, finally nodding in satisfaction at the altar he'd built before turning to face me. "So, what do you say to our new home?"

I smiled, reaching out my hands for his. "I'd take any home, as long as it included you—but this just so happens to be very, very agreeable." Amusement shone in his eyes, and I pulled him toward me. "Come, let's get you cleaned up and fed. We have plenty to do."

❋ ❋ ❋

Settling into our new home came naturally. After so many years of living at the mercy of a foreign land with equally foreign people, I had almost forgotten what it felt like to be comfortable in my own skin again. To live without fear for the first time in over twenty years was an inexpressible relief; a gift.

Our first several days passed quickly, with the women working to put the finishing touches on our tents, and the men beginning to plant and hunt. Jacob continued to oversee all that had to do with our livestock and the management of our land and home, and Isaac saw to the hunting and planting. We were in a race against the approaching autumn, fighting against the quickly shortening days to plant just one more seed, to hunt just one more animal. Since everything we sowed wouldn't be reaped until the following summer, we needed to hunt and forage enough to carry us through winter. Our work was made more complex by the fact that we had yet to find a substantial source of water. Because of that, our servants had been taking turns making the journey back to Rehoboth to gather water every few days, and we had a group of men searching and digging throughout the land from sun up to sun down.

In the middle of one particularly backaching day of foraging, I stood up from where I crouched, groaning as I pressed my hands into my lower back. The air around us had changed ever so gently. Its balminess was gone, leaving behind a pleasant crispness as a reminder of the winter to come. While the sun was still strong, I welcomed the beginning of the seasonal change, the feeling of the warm sun on my back as the breeze tickled my hair. I smiled to myself, remembering the times I had played with Laban in weather just like this so many summers ago, when I looked up and saw them.

Three men approached us in the distance, riding atop three huge horses. Each man carried a large spear and leather shield, and the man who led the trio wore a bronze helmet. I stared at the sun that glinted off of it. There was only one person I had ever seen wear something so ornate, the same person who had a direct hand in our new life, and in the trials we'd experienced in Rehoboth.

I dropped my basket, turning to grab Deborah's arm before running home. I found Isaac and Jacob standing by the fire as they warmed their midday meal. Both looked up at me in alarm, and I realized for the first time that I was shouting. "He's here," I panted as I came to a stop. "The king is here."

Isaac studied me, and I watched as understanding crossed his features. The king arriving now, after all that we had endured from his herdsmen, was not a good sign. I fought to keep my breath steady as I considered all we had left in the valley. It was possible that he traveled to us after destroying them.

"Should I get the men and our weapons, Father?" Jacob asked. I could see his anger in his clenched jaw. I had never before seen him so agitated, so ready to fight. He and his brother had long struggled with resentment toward the king, believing that his treatment of us should not go unpunished. At first, their outspoken beliefs had worried me, but Isaac had reassured me that they were only a testament to their youth and lack of foresight.

Without saying a word, Isaac removed the stone pot from the fire and placed it gently on the dirt. He reached for his staff and rolled his shoulders back with a deep breath. He began to walk toward them, with Jacob following suit, pausing briefly to place his palm on my cheek. I stared up at him, pleading him silently for some unknown thing, some impossible control over my greatest fears. The air between us was charged with urgency, greater so than when we had been found out in Gerar, greater than when we'd been banished. As if waking from a deep sleep on a warm summer's day, he remembered himself and began to walk away.

"We need to protect ourselves, to protect our women, Father. We need to arm ourselves before we face them." Jacob stopped in front of Isaac, his legs spread defiantly, his fists clutched at his side.

"No, Jacob. If that were what the Lord wanted us to do, he would have told me so. He promised to protect and increase us. We must meet them with faith." Without another word, he stepped around Jacob and continued his steady walk.

Jacob watched him quietly, dumbfounded, before finally following him.

"If we die, we die together," I called to them hoarsely before running after them. "I won't let you meet them alone. I can't stand here, powerless, and await our fate as I watch my husband and my son die." Without allowing him to answer, I reached out for Isaac's hand, squeezing it firmly.

The king had arrived at the edge of our camp, accompanied by two men in military uniform. Terror filled the faces of the servants who stood on the outskirts of our site, frozen in place as they watched us walk calmly past them. Puzzled by the king's decision to wait outside the boundary of our tents, I stared at him defiantly, watching as he and his companions looked at our new home with obvious admiration.

"King Abimelech, it is an honor to have you here." Isaac bowed his head slightly, showing no signs of distress or confusion over his sudden appearance.

I tipped my head, and Jacob remained silent, staring at our visitors warily.

With a grunt, the king swung his thick leg down from his horse, landing on the ground with a thud. Dazedly, I realized that I had never seen him stand before. He was shorter than I had expected, barely an inch taller than myself, yet he carried himself with the natural pomp and prestige of a king born from a lineage of powerful rulers.

"Isaac, how good it is to see you," he said with a grand sweep of his hand. "Please, allow me to introduce Phichol, the chief captain of my army, and Ahuzzath, a dear friend of mine."

Both men looked at Isaac solemnly before nodding their heads.

"Why are you here, Your Highness? It was my understanding that we were no longer welcome in Gerar after you sent us away from you. So, we made a new home for ourselves in the valley, and here. Is that acceptable to you?"

The king raised his massive hands, showing us his palms in a sign of acquiescence. "You see, my friend, I couldn't help but acknowledge how prosperous you've been. You found water where none of us ever could, after many years of the most successful harvests I've ever seen." He walked slowly toward us, his palms still outstretched. "It would seem that the Lord has been with you all of this time."

Isaac watched him quietly, as if awaiting the first official blow.

When the king saw that he didn't intend to speak, he continued with a shrug. "Phichol, Ahuzzath, and I began to discuss things, and I realized that it would be unwise for me to completely cut Gerar off from you and your people, seeing as how the Lord has blessed you. So, I have come to propose an oath between us. A covenant." He lowered his hands slowly and his jowls wobbled as he nodded. "Seeing as we have sent you away from Gerar in peace, we request that you do us no harm, as we have not touched you, and have been nothing but good to you."

I looked up at Isaac in bewilderment, who continued to stare down at the king as if observing him for the first time.

The king sighed petulantly, frustrated with his lack of response. "Just remember how I welcomed you to Gerar, and how I took pity on you when you were caught in your lies," he looked at me with an arched brow. "Remember how the land I gave you was fertile and fruitful, and how you proceeded to be far more prosperous than any of Gerar's native farmers ever

141

were." He tilted his head to the side as if avoiding an annoying gnat, wiggling the folds of his neck once again as he shook his head. "Now, I cannot take ownership of what some rogue herdsmen might have done"—he waved his hand through the air nonchalantly—"but I can say that I have protected you and your people these twenty years. Today, I call for a covenant."

Isaac breathed in deeply through his nostrils as he stared down at the staff he held in his right hand. When he finally looked back up at the king, I saw amusement dancing through his eyes. "My friend, you will have your covenant, as well as a feast."

I turned to look at Jacob, whose face held a guarded expression, the same one he wore when masking his confusion and frustration.

The king's mouth dropped in surprise, and he turned triumphantly to look at his two friends before clapping his hands. "Now that is more like it. We are famished. Let us eat!"

Stupefied by what had just occurred, I remained rooted in place as all three men slowly guided their horses past me, followed by Isaac, and finally by Jacob. The terror of death and destruction had vanished in mere moments, leaving shock and giddiness in their place. I ran ahead of the men to instruct Deborah and Selah on the feast preparations, and to send a runner to share the good news with our people in the valley.

After some frenzied cleaning and cooking while the men stood under the shade of nearby trees, we enjoyed a feast framed by a pastel sky. Tender cuts of lamb were followed by crisp, cool watermelon dipped in fresh honey. While we didn't have the luxury of a multitude of dishes like we once had in Gerar, I hadn't tasted anything better.

Isaac, King Abimelech, and his men sat on their own, talking and laughing late into the night. The following morning, I watched through bleary eyes as all four stood before the king reached up to pat Isaac on the back. They shook hands, speaking in hushed tones, before finally riding away.

Isaac watched as they departed, standing resolutely, peacefully, as the morning dew soaked the bottom of his garments. After a few minutes, he turned slowly, his lips quirked into a small smile when he finally saw me standing in the doorway. "The Lord is good," he said as he walked toward me.

"I thought you were mad. I thought we were surely walking to our imminent death." I crossed my arms and looked up at him challengingly.

"Part of me believed I had gone mad," he whispered before chuckling. "But how glad am I to know that the contention between ourselves and the people of Gerar can now come to an end." He wrapped his arms around me, drawing me to his chest. I breathed in those same familiar smells of musk and pine, savoring them more than I usually did, and wishing that I could be right there, with him, for eternity.

Later that day, the men we had charged with digging wells came shouting with the news that they had finally struck water. After weeks of digging, searching, and coming up short—and weeks of traveling to draw water in Rehoboth for our new crops and livestock—the news that we had finally struck water made our camp really, truly become our home. It was the missing piece, the final link that would allow us to let the land encircle us in its arms, to soothe us into a lifetime of joy and hardship. The timing of it all wasn't lost on me, either. The king had left with a covenant, and we had gained the water we needed to build and sustain our life.

"Does this mean we will finally be able to put a name to our land?" I asked Isaac as we laid in bed that evening. I listened to his quiet laugh. He knew how much it had bothered me to live in unnamed territory over the last few weeks.

"I've decided to name the well Shebah, and our new land Beersheba."

"Beersheba," I said quietly, enjoying the sound of it as it rolled off my tongue. "That's a nice name, though I think I would've accepted anything you chose after waiting so long."

He rolled over and placed a gentle kiss on my neck while running his fingers through my hair. "Hush, before I leave it nameless for the rest of our days."

I faked a gasp and gently pushed him away. Within a few minutes, I heard his deep, steady breathing as he slipped into sleep. "Beersheba feels right," I whispered into the darkness.

CHAPTER TWENTY-FOUR

Eight more years blinked by. Years full of balmy summers, brisk winters, healthy crops, and more livestock than we'd ever raised. Before we knew it, we settled into a routine and rhythm. Beersheba felt just as much our home as Canaan once had.

I listened to the dull thud of my camel's hooves as they pressed into the sand while I swayed in my saddle. The word *home* crossed my mind as I remembered my parents, and the pain I had felt when I left them all that time ago. I felt a pang at the memory of the last words I exchanged with them both, the sadness on my mother's face, and the pride on my father's as I followed Eliezer to Canaan. That was the last time I ever saw them. When we were living in Gerar, Laban had sent news that my father had passed away in his sleep, followed by my mother just a few days later. Even now, I felt their loss. A flood of tears threatened to spill out of my eyes, and I sniffed in a resolute attempt to maintain my composure.

The fact was that Isaac and I would one day grow old and pass on, just as my parents had, and just as their parents had before them. We were in good health and as active as we had always been, but rooting ourselves into Beersheba had made me crave that next natural progression in our life. I wanted to see our sons married. I wanted to laugh as we bounced their children on our knees, telling them stories their parents never wanted them to hear. I wanted so badly to fill the void my parents had left with the smiles and gurgles of sweet children.

Spring had finally arrived, and I savored the sound of the birds that chirped overhead as we made our way past a grove of trees. Isaac and I were on our way to Rehoboth, a trip that we made every few months. We cherished the opportunity to greet our people, watch their families grow, and catch up with

Esau. When we had first left Rehoboth, I had expected Esau to take a wife almost immediately. Given that he had always had his pick of women both near and far, and the fact that he was well within a marriageable age, it had surprised us when he refrained from taking a wife. We had tried to suggest suitable matches for him; young women we remembered from Canaan who had grown up in well-respected households, even women we'd approved of from Gerar. But time and again, he had refused our suggestions, stating that he would be the one to make the choice when he was ready.

I felt a surge of dread as I thought about the oddness of our visit today. Typically, Isaac and I would send word of our planned arrival to Rehoboth ahead of time. This time, however, Esau had requested our presence. While I prayed that it wasn't to surprise us with the news of his marriage, I knew Esau's tendencies and his record of hasty decisions. None of it sat well with me.

I looked to my right to find Isaac riding next to me, admiring the cerulean sky with a faint smile. I had shared my concerns and hesitations the evening before, which he had assured me were nothing more than a mother's worries. Knowing that he would always be blinded by love and adoration for his eldest son, I held off on speaking further about the subject. We'd find out soon, regardless of what we thought.

We crested a small hill and looked down to find Rehoboth glimmering up at us from the valley below. In the years since its naming, the land had taken on the appearance of a small but thriving city, with guards at the front gate, and colorful textiles adorning every tent. Everywhere I looked, there was a flutter of activity: a group of children playing just outside the walls, a line of women laughing as they carried their wash basins. I could hardly recognize the patch of sand that had once greeted us.

"Mother, Father," came Esau's booming voice as he strode through the gates. Somehow, he appeared to be even bigger and ruddier than the last time I saw him. He gave me a cheerful kiss on the cheek, before clapping Isaac on the back. "I am glad to see you. Thank you for coming at my request." He stood back and held his hand out as if to usher us inside.

Having ridden in behind us, Deborah tossed me a puzzled

look, which I returned. It was rare for Esau to greet us this cheerfully—he usually reserved such behavior for when he needed something from either one of us, or when he had less than desirable news to share.

We followed him past the servants' quarters, stopping briefly to exchange greetings and news. Many of our servants had married and expanded their families; it felt as if every time we arrived in Rehoboth, there was some new birth or marriage to celebrate. Even so, Isaac and I never grew tired of it.

I hugged Resa, Eliezer's daughter whom I had known since she was just a child. As I pulled away, I heard Esau clear his throat and looked up to see him shifting impatiently. "I apologize, am I thwarting our plans for the day?" I said while failing to hide my irritation.

He looked from me to Isaac, and for the first time, I saw what appeared to be worry in his eyes. "I have news to share with you, if you'll please just follow me."

I took a deep breath and nodded, noticing for the first time that lanterns were strung overhead, intermittently broken up by the flutter of colorful pieces of tapestry that flipped in the wind. Deep down, I knew that what he would say next would be unpleasant. When Jacob came bringing news, it was news that Isaac and I wanted or needed to hear. Esau tended to only have news that created strife. I watched as Isaac stopped to peer at the decorations before continuing to follow Esau. We walked the outskirts of the collection of tents, stopping just outside of Esau's quarters.

"Have you gotten a new bed you'd like to show us?" Isaac said teasingly.

I looked around us in confusion, trying to understand why we'd been brought to his door.

"No, much better. I have taken two wives whom I want you to meet." He smiled broadly, puffing his chest out with pride. Suddenly, two women slipped out of his tent and stood on either side of him.

"You took two wives? Two? After years of us begging you for just one?" I blurted out, unable to control my thoughts.

He faltered, looking at Isaac and I anxiously before puffing his chest out once again. "As I told you before, I wanted to wait for the right woman, the right *women*, to marry. Here they are." He nudged them forward, as if they were two small children hiding behind their mother's skirts. "This is Bashemath, the daughter of Elon the Hittite."

She was tall, with deep olive skin and dark eyes and hair. She towered over me, reminding me in a strange way of a warrior. I offered up a polite smile, not wanting to be cruel, while she studied me intently. After a few awkward moments, she grinned slowly, and I watched as her smile stretched across her face. "It's a pleasure, Mother and Father," she said as she bowed dramatically over both of our hands, pausing to kiss Isaac's only.

Esau's eyes raked over her appreciatively as he watched her performance. He snapped back to attention when Isaac cleared his throat. "And this is sweet Judith, daughter of Beeri the Hittite."

Judith was petite, with ivory skin and ebony eyes and hair. She peeked up at the both of us bashfully, before bobbing her head in respect. I couldn't help but look between the women with confusion. It was as if he had chosen two of the most opposite women he could possibly find, and decided to marry them.

My heart thudded furiously as I glared at him silently. Not only had he married two women without informing us, he had married women from families we had never met and had no connection to. It was an act of rebellion, one that we wouldn't be able to remedy. His decision had been made, and his actions were irreversible.

Isaac spoke first, his voice heavy with guarded emotion. "Son, why would you tell us this after the fact? We have always wanted to provide you with a marriage celebration. You've robbed your mother and I of that opportunity."

Anger flashed across Esau's face. "I brought you here today to celebrate the news. It was my decision, and mine to make. As my parents, I expected you to be happy for me, for the felicity I have in my marriage, and for the children my wives will bear me."

"You cannot expect us to welcome the thought of your secret marriage. You must give us time to process and understand." Isaac stepped forward to put his hand on Esau's shoulder, before acknowledging both women with a nod. "We've had a long morning. Why don't we enjoy a good meal?"

"Or have you already had your fill?" I asked through gritted teeth.

Isaac shot me a look of warning.

Esau appeared to not have heard what I said. He smiled broadly, wrapping his arms around the two women once again. "We've prepared a feast for all of us to enjoy, along with a bit of music and dancing." He turned to walk around his tent to the large clearing that was typically used to store equipment and livestock. It had been rearranged to feature a large bonfire, with beams of wood placed in a semicircle around it. It was hardly a setup for a marriage celebration, and already I could feel beads of sweat running down my back from the heat of the fire.

"Come, come," Bashemath sang briskly as she clutched my upper arm in her firm grip and propelled me forward. With a forceful push, she directed me to sit on one of the available beams.

I winced up at her, silenced in my shock at her behavior.

"We have every kind of food and drink you could ever wish for!" she proclaimed loudly, her voice thick with an accent I couldn't place. Looking around as if irritated that the servants had not appeared at her call, she snapped her fingers obnoxiously while watching me from under her lashes. When servants failed to arrive, she stomped her foot before turning to shout. "What must I do to ask for a bit of food on the day of my marriage celebration? Bring it to me now!" The bangles on her wrist clunked heavily as she gesticulated wildly. I realized with astonishment that they traveled up the entirety of both of her arms.

"There is no rush," said Isaac as he lowered himself to sit next to me. "Please, allow them to take their time."

"Really, Father, you are too gentle with your servants. Ever since my arrival, I have been appalled by their lackadaisical behavior. I will allow no more of it in my household." The smile she gave him reminded me of the time I saw a one-eyed cat snap up an unsuspecting mouse after carefully watching it for several minutes. Even that had been more pleasant than this.

The knowledge that she planned to be so rough on our servants, our family, infuriated me. We had striven to treat them with the utmost care and respect. Now that they were in Esau's charge, they were in Bashemath's and Judith's. We no longer had the ability to protect them.

Just then, I realized that Judith hadn't followed us. "Where is Judith?" I asked as I looked around.

"Hm?" Bashemath glanced up from studying one of her bangles, as if just remembering that I was still there. "Oh, Judith is probably being her normal sulky self. She doesn't like sitting in the sun. Says it's too hard on her precious complexion." She rolled her eyes before sauntering with swaying hips toward the table where the servants had begun laying out food and drink. Esau stood at one end, watching hungrily as she approached him.

Thoroughly sickened by the news we'd received as well as her behavior, I knew that I wouldn't be able to stomach anything. When Deborah arrived to ask if I'd like a plate, I shook my head silently, choosing to stare at the fire that blazed in front of us while sweltering in the sunshine. Isaac did his best to work through a plate of food, but left much of his meal untouched. He remained quiet for most of the affair, offering only the occasional nod when prompted.

Just when I had begun to think that we would be allowed to leave, Bashemath planted herself on the beam beside me, landing hard enough to make me jump. She hiccupped, and I reeled back at the stench of her breath. "Tell me about my beloved husband. Tell me stories of his bravery from before we met," she said with an obnoxious giggle. She looked around her as if to make sure that others were paying attention, before finally resting her eyes on me.

"Anything you need to know, I'm sure he has already told you. He's quite the storyteller," I said politely. At that point, all I wanted was for her to leave. And where was Judith?

"That is so, so true." She hiccupped again. "In fact, that's how he first seduced me, you know. I overheard him recounting a story of his bravery as he fought a bear in the wilderness, before carrying home three deer carcasses on his own shoulders. I've never respected a weak man. I knew then and there that I would make him my husband." She looked him over appreciatively, surveying his body as if he were a tower of tropical fruit.

At a loss for words, I remained quiet with Isaac beside me. He appeared to be listening to every word, and I turned to see a hint of amusement cross his face. Clearly the fact that this woman felt comfortable enough to be so forward with her new husband's parents entertained him. I stretched my shoulders to shake off the irritation, wishing that I could find something to laugh at as well.

Bashemath turned to look behind me with a leer. "*There* you are, you little waif." She laughed again, even louder than the first time. "Your new parents have been wondering why you've refused to grace them with your presence. Here, take my place. I have more celebrating to do." She stood up and swayed before stumbling away.

Judith smiled at me shyly before sitting on the very edge of the beam. After a few minutes of waiting and wondering whether she would ever say something, I decided to break the silence. "How have you been liking your new home?"

"It's very nice." She pushed her sandal through the dirt as if tracing a path away from us.

I waited again, expecting her to expand on her thought. When she said nothing else, I asked about her family and upbringing, to which she offered equally succinct, if not mysterious, answers. From what I could glean, she came from a family in Canaan that Abraham had been distantly connected with, though I had never met them myself. Her and Bashemath's polar personalities stood out the more I prodded her for information. While she was by no means the woman I would have chosen for Esau, she was leaps and bounds more pleasant to be around than Bashemath. At the very least, Judith wouldn't make my head ring.

As our conversation lulled, I heard the familiar sounds of the flute and drum begin. Unprompted, Bashemath jumped up and began to dance around the fire, wiggling her hips as she winked at the onlookers who stood frozen in discomfort.

"I think that is our cue to leave," Isaac said suddenly. I breathed a sigh of relief. He reached down to help me up, placing his hand on my lower back reassuringly. "I think it would be best for the both of us to go home to Beersheba. There will be plenty of time to grow accustomed to Esau and his new wives in the future." He turned toward Esau, and raised his voice over the noise of the music as Bashemath wiggled in the background. "We are leaving. As for you, Judith, and you, Bashemath, I look forward to learning more about you as the years go on." To my surprise, he took my hand without a word and guided me back to our camels. The servants who had traveled with us sprang up from their seats in relief, bidding farewell to their friends before following us to the gate.

While I had never expected Esau to want a traditional marriage and ceremony, I had expected him to do so for the sake of his father. Seeing how he treated Isaac, how he treated me, hurt deeply. As we began our journey home, I mourned the thought of what our relationship as mother and son could have been, and where it was now. I thought back to all of those summers in his childhood, when he was once innocent enough to enjoy playing with his brother, too young to fully resent him, too young to think of me as anything but his darling mother. It was as if one evening he had gone to bed as a boy, and woken the next day determined to be a man. An angry and reckless one at that.

I swiped at the tear that rolled down my cheek, forcing down the hurt that sat in my chest until it was nothing more than a dull ache in my stomach. As we trudged back home with the afternoon sun behind us, the ache worked its way across my shoulders and neck. This wasn't the first of the strife Esau had caused, and it wouldn't be the last.

CHAPTER
TWENTY-FIVE

Deborah's snort was loud enough to echo across the clearing. As soon as we had arrived home, Isaac had asked her to draw me a luxurious bath, demanding that I not be allowed to move a muscle for the rest of the night. Deborah had whisked me away with zeal, ordering me to brush my hair as she prepared the water.

And now she was laughing. Or, struggling to hide the fact that she was laughing.

"What on earth are you doing over there?" I asked warily, feigning frustration as I struggled against joining her.

She cleared her throat and hastily brushed her thumbs under her eyes with her back turned to me.

"I saw that, Deborah. I know you were laughing hard enough to be brought to tears. Oh, just tell me." I flung the brush down in annoyance, spinning in my seat to face her. One glance at my face was enough to send her into a fit of laughter again.

"I'm trying not to laugh, I really am. I know that today was terrible, and I am as sorrowful and angry as you are. But I can't stop thinking about that woman, and how she danced by the bonfire. You should have seen your face." She fanned herself with the towel she held in an attempt to gain control.

I felt a grin break across my face and my shoulders began to shake. Although I was still saddened by Esau's decision and perplexed by his choice of wives, in retrospect, the entire situation had been ridiculous.

"I am sitting here in emotional torment, and you are laughing as if you've been told the funniest story you've ever heard. Really, Deborah," I said as I wiped my eyes and fought to catch my breath through the giggles that consumed my body. "For the rest of my life, I will wonder what he was thinking. And for the rest of his life, I fear that he will do the same."

"Judith seemed to be much more agreeable, though." Deborah raised her eyebrow hopefully at me.

"She was certainly easier to get along with, though I would never have expected him to choose her. He's always preferred more outgoing women." Outgoing was putting it kindly.

Deborah nodded thoughtfully as she uncapped a bottle of oil and poured it into the bath. "Perhaps he tried to choose a woman he believed would make you and Isaac happy, so as to soften the blow of his decision to marry Bashemath, the woman he preferred."

I inhaled sharply. The thought had not occurred to me, though it would be a more logical explanation for his decision to marry two such starkly different women. Based on his behavior today, it was clear that he only had eyes for Bashemath. I felt a twinge of pity for Judith—one of my greatest fears when I became Isaac's wife was that he would not want me. I hated the thought of her feeling that way.

"Well, one day we might find out what all of it means. Until then, however, we must learn to accept the decision he's made. It'll only be a matter of time before Rehoboth is teeming with his children." I stepped into the tub, sliding down into the warm water with a sigh. "I am just grateful to know that Jacob would never make that same mistake."

❋ ❋ ❋

My resentment toward Isaac grew over time. First, its roots stretched beneath my surface as deeply and slowly as those of a tree. Over the months that followed, I felt my frustration about his failure to lead Esau, to discipline him, to direct him away from the path that he had taken, continue to build until one day, the resentment no longer sat safely within the confines of my heart. It had sprung to fruition as recklessly as a weed.

Logically, I knew that Esau was his own man. He made his own decisions, and had chosen his own path. But no matter how many times I tried to convince myself to believe that fact, a small voice continued to whisper in the back of my mind. That he had behaved this way as a child, and that Isaac had turned a blind eye. That I had told Isaac what the Lord had told me, and Isaac had never fully accepted it. I had never understood Isaac's preference for Esau, nor his blindness toward some of his greatest flaws. And in a way, I knew that Isaac felt the same about my love for Jacob. The only difference was that Jacob had been chosen by the Lord to be our family's leader, even before he and his brother were born. Esau was never supposed to inherit anything. He was never supposed to have the power and access that he now had.

Look what he's done with it, I thought with a shiver. After meeting Bashemath and Judith, Isaac and I refrained from discussing what had taken place. I would have preferred to speak about it, to vocalize my concerns and frustrations about Esau, to hear Isaac reassure me. But I watched as he continued to grow more distant from me, his face seeming to turn inward whenever I was near. It was as if, overnight, we had lost the openness and warmth we'd always enjoyed in our marriage. The vulnerability we once had with each other was no longer safe nor sacred. So we didn't speak about it, we didn't refer to it. We danced around the topic of Esau, only referring to the things that were the most glaringly difficult to ignore, like Bashemath's ridiculous behavior every time we saw her, or our surprise over Judith's pregnancy.

The years passed in that same way as we dug deeper into our roles, finding solace and comfort in the rigidity of our schedules. Jacob managed our land and servants; I led the women as we reaped, dried, and stored; Isaac oversaw each season of sowing. I pushed past the growing loneliness I felt by rarely having a moment to spare. Much of my time was spent with Jacob, or Deborah, or any number of the women and children that now filled Beersheba. Each evening, Isaac and I still ate a private supper in our room, but it lacked the intimacy and comfort it once offered. He didn't watch me brush my hair in the mirror like he used to, and my heart broke a little more every time he didn't.

I knew that these things were common in marriages, though for some reason, I had always assumed that Isaac and I would never experience it for ourselves. Our love had seemed impenetrable. From the day we married, we adored each other, favoring the other's company over anyone else's. But every time I wanted to ask him if we could drop the guards around our hearts, I couldn't seem to speak. He'd stare at me, as if waiting for the permission to finally be my Isaac again, until all I could do was shake my head. Then he'd walk away with a new slope to his shoulders.

Each day, I'd watch him leave while feeling like a new piece of my heart had been ripped from my chest, a piece that he carried with him, whether he wanted to or not. One evening, I woke in a cold sweat with a racing heart. I struggled to remember my dream, only recalling bits and pieces of it. Isaac had been bedridden, and I had watched him slip farther and farther away from me, until I could no longer see him through the thick fog that surrounded me. I laid back down and listened to his deep, steady breathing, taking comfort in the fact that he was still here with me.

But was he really?

The next morning, I woke up resolved to work past the rift that had grown between us. As he readied for the day, I kindled the fire. I had woken earlier than usual, so I'd taken the opportunity to fetch us some tea.

"I thought we could share our tea in here this morning, rather than with the others," I said as I studied his broad back as he bent over the wash bowl.

He paused, his hands suspended midair, the only movement being the drops of water that tumbled down his forearms and from his elbows. He turned to look at me warily, as if he were looking into the eyes of a wild beast instead of his wife. "If that's what you would like."

My heart stuttered. While I had hoped he would show a bit more interest, I wasn't surprised that he was so hesitant. I nodded before gesturing to the seat across from me, and poured hot water into his cup. I stared at the tea leaves as they unfurled, wondering abstractedly if my heart would ever again do the same.

He dried himself off with a towel and donned his tunic before sitting across from me. After glancing at me briefly, he turned to stare into the fire. Even now, the tones of his eyes mesmerized me; I watched as the flames danced across their surface. I took a deep breath and steeled myself for what I would say next.

"Isaac, it is time that we discuss the pain that is between us. I have been angry with you for some time now, and I admit that I have blamed you for much of Esau's downfall. I asked you to be more stern with him, to make sure that he wouldn't follow his wayward mind and foolhardy ways. But as difficult as it is for me to admit, he's a grown man now, and there is nothing we can do to turn back time."

He continued to stare at the fire, his eyes dropping for just a moment before finding their place again.

"Isaac," I said as my voice tremored, "I miss you. I miss my husband, and I miss the love we shared for so many years."

Slowly, he turned to look at me, and I could see the pain written in his features. His brows were drawn and brooding, the edges of his mouth sloped downward. His eyes carried the look of a wounded animal. It felt as if a knife had cut through my core. I had expected him to be angry and defensive, but seeing him hurt, and knowing I had a hand in it, pained me more than I could bear. We studied each other for a moment, and I forgot to breathe.

"Ever since that day in Rehoboth, I have despised myself for Esau's actions. Seeing the way he behaved with his two wives, and how he spoke to the both of us, it felt as if the son I thought I had never even existed. I knew you were angry with me, and I am ashamed to say that I didn't want to address it. I was already angry enough with Esau, with myself."

Unable to watch the pain that twisted through his features any longer, I spoke up. "He was only a child for a handful of years, Isaac. Yes, we both could have been more strict with him, but we thought—hoped—that he would grow out of it. Much of his behavior now has been at his own fault."

"But I had the ability to shape and mold him when he was young. I focused so much on his hunting, on raising him to be a strong leader, that I forgot to watch out for his heart." Isaac's voice broke. "And for that, I am sorry. Please forgive me, my dear, beautiful wife."

Unable to hold back my tears any longer, I let them stream down my face as my shoulders shook. In one swift movement, he reached across the table and lifted me, placing me on his lap as he cupped my head with his hand. I cried all of the tears that I had been shoring up; the tears I had held in every evening we went to bed, the tears from every thought and apology I wanted to say but couldn't. Finally, I sniffled before looking up at him and saying, "I am so sorry for being so angry. Please forgive me."

He pressed a kiss to my forehead and I closed my eyes, savoring its relief. We stayed that way until the sun was high in the sky, only then stirring at the sound of the servants outside as they worried over Isaac's absence.

"I must go," he said with a sigh before gently helping me to my feet. "I will see you tonight for supper." He caressed my cheek with his thumb, his eyes searching mine, before turning to leave. He held the tent flap over his head as he looked back at me one more time with a small smile on his face.

As if my heart were breaking out of its cocoon, I felt it flutter back to life. Small, tiny beats and flips that reminded me of a long-ago evening, of the shiver of my limbs as I walked toward him in that field that I would always miss, never forget, with my past lying at my feet, and our future on his shoulders.

I was his Rebekah again.

CHAPTER
TWENTY-SIX

"**Y**ou'd think we were two hundred years old by how we're behaving." I fanned myself in exasperation and watched Deborah's fan flap in the corner of my eye. We were leaning against a large tree, taking refuge in its shade on yet another scorching summer's day.

"Is being two hundred years old a prerequisite to being overheated? Besides, we're nearly there anyway," Deborah said as she panted beside me.

I closed my fan and attempted to hit her with it playfully, only to realize that I was far too hot, and far too tired to see it through. We had spent the past month picking and cleaning grapes, and were now nearing the beginning of the bartering season. Soon after that, we'd begin our olive harvest. The moment we breathed a sigh of relief over the fact that our days spent in the blistering sun were drawing to a close, we would turn to find a mountain of work ahead of us. Whatever we kept would need to be stored and preserved. Whatever we sold would need to be cleaned and packed for transport.

"Remember when you once told me that I didn't need to do this, and should leave it to the servants? I'm beginning to think you were right."

Deborah chuckled quietly while staring at the bare field that lay in front of us. We sat in comfortable silence for a few more minutes until the sound of Jacob's shouting broke through my daydream. I turned in the direction of his voice, gasping when I saw him sprinting toward me, his tunic flying behind him, his eyes wide with terror. I stood hastily, dropping my fan in the process, my heart in my throat.

"There's something wrong with Father," he said with his hands on his hips as he walked in circles in an attempt to catch his breath. "Today, when he was overseeing the livestock and choosing ones for the market, he grew confused and he—he stumbled. It was as if he couldn't see."

I clutched Deborah's arm for support, frozen in fear of the thought of Isaac being injured, or worse. He had always been so strong, so capable, but in recent years, he had begun to slow down. At first, in ways that only I ever noticed, but eventually, in ways that Jacob began to pick up on, too. I had tried to ignore it, to tell myself that he was as healthy as he had always been, while turning a blind eye to the gray that now covered his head and beard, and the exhaustion that was deeply and permanently etched in his face. "Take me to him."

Wordlessly, Jacob put his arm around me and walked us slowly home. A few of the men who were nearby had brought Isaac back to my tent to lay down. I ducked inside, instantly relieved by the coolness of the air. He laid on his back with a damp cloth over his forehead as he stared up at the ceiling.

"My love, what happened?" I asked shakily. I sat beside him and placed my hand over his.

"I was evaluating the livestock and checking them as I always do. I had spent the morning doing so, until suddenly I—I couldn't see."

I reeled back, unsure of what to say next. For as long as I could remember, Isaac had never struggled with his eyesight. "Did you faint from the heat?" Even as I said it, I knew that the question was ridiculous. After a lifetime spent outdoors in all conditions, it would be almost impossible for the heat to overwhelm him while he stood in the shade of the stable.

"No, Rebekah. I was coherent and awake. I just couldn't see."

I sat next to him quietly, studying the bridge of his nose and the way it led to his high, sharp cheekbones. His eyes had always been my favorite feature of his—how could they fail?

"Well, we will have the nurses look after you to find out more. It will be all right, Isaac." I squeezed his hand as if to confirm that he was really there, that everything would turn out in the end. The reality was that our age had finally begun to creep up on us, and it had brought all of its effects, both good and bad. I didn't truly know whether all would end well, nor if his loss of vision was momentary, or a sign of times to come.

Isaac looked so tired. Over the course of our marriage, he

had always appeared to have drunk from the fountain of youth. Day after day, he had risen from bed and tackled everything that our land had demanded, never wavering, never showing any signs of strain. I had often jokingly asked whether he was sure he really was twenty years my senior. He never seemed to grow older, save for the occasional wrinkle or gray hair. I wasn't sure when his shoulders had begun to sag in the way they did now. He was still the strong, tall, handsome man I had married, but I saw now that he was weary.

After several prolonged moments of silence, he lifted his weathered hand and patted mine in reassurance. "I'm sure you're right, my love. I'm sure you're right."

❈ ❈ ❈

"How is he?" Jacob stood just outside the door of our tent, his hands still on his hips as he stared at the ground in worry.

"He's resting," I whispered, hesitating before saying anything else. I looked around us before walking toward the trees that bordered where we stood. Once we were a good distance away, I turned to face him. "The truth is that I am concerned about him, Jacob. It seems as if his age has finally caught up with him. I've never seen him look so dejected, so"—I choked back a sob—"tired. I've never known anyone who lost their eyesight, but he seems very sure that he didn't faint. He says that he was completely awake, but just couldn't see a thing."

Jacob dropped his eyes to the ground, staring at his shoe as he kicked his foot through the blades of grass. "What will we do?"

It was only then that I realized that however much we disliked or feared it, everything today had changed. Isaac had set out on his daily work as he always had, and returned a different man. The man we all leaned on, the man who unfailingly shouldered everyone else's burdens without complaint needed our help and our care now. The breeze played with the stray tendrils of hair that framed my face as I considered his question.

"We will need to help him feel purposeful, while ensuring he doesn't strain himself. All I know is that whatever might be happening with his health, it can't make things worse for him to rest a bit. Though, God help the man or woman who tries to take all of his duties from him." Stripping Isaac of his duties, the things he loved only second to myself and his sons, would be a death sentence. He was just as much a part of the land he tilled as he was a welcome sight to our livestock and servants. He needed his job, and we needed him—for as long as we could have him.

"I can step in and slowly pick up some of his duties as time goes on. Hopefully, he will fail to notice," his mouth quirked into a sad smile.

We walked quietly back to the servant's quarters, all of whom had halted what they were doing and were waiting anxiously for news. Jacob shared a brief and filtered announcement, stating that Isaac was merely resting and had overdone things today. While many of the listeners stole glances at each other in concern, the majority were visibly relieved to hear that nothing serious had befallen him.

After Jacob dismissed the group, I fell back from the crowd, allowing the exhaustion that had been threatening my consciousness over the course of the day to overwhelm me. I walked past the servants' tents and out to the crag that overlooked our fields, pausing to take things in for the first time in years. From here, our crops looked like a tapestry that had been woven together in pieces—to the right, the chartreuse shimmer of buds of wheat swaying in the breeze; to the left, the vibrant greens and snippets of yellow from this season's corn that had yet to be picked. Everywhere I looked, life seemed to move, to dance, beneath my feet. Life that at one time hadn't been here; life that had been started by Isaac.

I bent over and clutched my stomach as I began to sob. My shoulders shook and I fought to breathe, until finally, I gave in to the pain and anguish that followed. I kneeled on the sturdy rock beneath me, rocking back and forth as I mourned the beginning of Isaac's loss, the beginning of this new phase of life that neither of us were prepared for. Would we ever have been prepared? Would we ever have been willing to accept our mortality? We had devoted our lives to creating more life. We had welcomed the birth of babies and foals, calfs and chicks; we had mourned the loss of family and friends, and the animals who had worked their way into our hearts.

Yet, none of this felt right. I wasn't ready.

I felt two hands on my shoulders, and looked up to see Deborah's tearful eyes staring back at me. She, like myself, had spent a majority of her life in Isaac's care. If anyone knew even a portion of the sadness I felt, it was her.

"Do you remember how scared I was when we arrived in Canaan? When, after Isaac had left me in Sarah's tent to prepare for the marriage, you helped me wash and dress, and I was terrified. I was so fearful of this new life that had been thrust into my lap. That feeling was nothing compared to this." My knees began to throb dully as I used my veil to wipe my face.

Deborah laughed quietly, her eyes sweeping dreamily over the colorful landscape that lay beneath us. "Of course I do. Even then, after watching you two meet, I knew that you two had something special. I also knew that you'd have to uncover that for yourself with time, so I let you be miserable," she nudged me playfully in an attempt to cheer us both up.

"Well, it worked. Perhaps you'll let me be miserable just now, just for a bit longer?"

"Better yet, I'll join you." She sighed before sitting next to me and wrapping her arms around my shoulders. We remained that way until the sun disappeared behind the mountains, crying quietly as we mourned the loss of our youth and the change of the season.

Finally, as dusk set in, I turned to her with a loud sniff. "And do you remember when you couldn't even bear to let me hug you? Look at us now." Her eyes were swollen and her skin was spotted with blotches of red and pink. How good it was to have a friend, a sister, who could mourn when I mourned, and rejoice when I rejoiced.

"Come, I want to get back to check on Isaac," I said as I stood and pulled her up next to me. "Besides, if we stay out on this crag for any longer, our bones will turn to dust."

We groaned as we stretched our limbs before walking slowly back into the inviting glow of our home.

CHAPTER TWENTY-SEVEN

True to form, Isaac woke the next day and set out on his normal duties. True to his word, Jacob followed him from afar, taking note of how he spent his day and saw to the work that he had yet to share with him. As the weeks passed, Jacob began to slowly incorporate more of Isaac's work into his own, offering his help when and where he could, and many times, convincing him to let him take over so that Isaac could rest.

Though he refused to admit it, I could tell by his behavior that his eyesight was increasingly failing. Sometimes he would gaze at me over the supper table, and I'd see his eyes glaze over as they searched from left to right, as if hoping that I would reappear. Other times, he'd pause in the middle of his work or sentence, staring at what was in front of him until he could see it again. Then his vision would return, and watching it happen was like watching a small child unwrap their first gift.

It was as if his loss of vision made him even more appreciative of the times when he could see. He showered me in compliments, and watched even more intently as I brushed and plaited my hair at night. Once, I snuck up on him in the stables to find him surrounded by baby lambs, his nose pressed to their necks as he murmured into their ears. Watching him take on this new phase of his life, this new challenge, reinvigorated me. The smallest things became blessings, even more so when they were shared with him. Though we witnessed the decline of his sight and stamina, the joy we shared over what remained was insurmountable.

Jacob took to his increased duties with zeal. My heart swelled with pride when I watched him listen to the concerns of our servants as if he had all of the time in the world, before turning to give instructions to those who worked in our fields.

Most importantly, our people remained happy and cared for, and Jacob led them in the way that his father always had.

It wasn't until our customary visit to Rehoboth approached that I realized that word had not been sent to Esau about Isaac's health. It hadn't crossed my mind to send a messenger, but I also knew that Isaac and I couldn't make the journey. Isaac would protest and say that he was fit for the day of travel, but I feared worsening his condition with the strain of a full day on the back of a camel before he endured Esau and his wives' behavior. I knew that Isaac would want to see him, however.

"We should send someone to fetch Esau and to also tell him the news of Isaac's health," I said as I sat in front of the mirror and worked salve into my exhausted hands.

Deborah was tidying the room behind me, fluffing cushions and beating out rugs as she went. She paused and spun to look at me in horror. "You mean to tell me that no one has told Esau yet?"

"No," I said slowly. "It slipped my mind, and we've been so focused on everything here in Beersheba. I haven't been able to think further ahead than a few days at a time."

She nodded in understanding before exhaling slowly. "I'll go and ask a couple of men to travel out to Esau first thing tomorrow."

Inwardly, I hoped that he would come alone. Judith and Bashemath had a brood to look after, and I wanted to make sure that they didn't overwhelm Isaac with their antics. Esau's big, boisterous personality would be more than enough.

The following evening, Esau came on foot, running as if he had a storm to outpace. I squinted to look for our messengers and his camel behind him, but it seemed that no one, including his own wives, had been able to keep up. He slowed down only to take a long drink of water, before storming toward me. "Where is he?" His enormous palms covered each of my shoulders, and he shook me gently as if to encourage me to speak faster.

I led him to our tent, managing to steady my steps though his entire body radiated frenetic energy as he tried to slow himself next to me. In an effort to distract him—and hopefully, to calm him before he met with his father—I inquired after

Judith and Bashemath, as well as our two messengers. He answered my questions gruffly, giving me enough information to know that neither of his wives had been up to leaving as quickly as he had. As for our messengers, they'd left when he had, but given the fact that they traveled with their camels, they wouldn't arrive for some time.

We stopped just outside the door to our tent, where Isaac had laid down for a nap before supper. I gripped Esau's arm as he reached to open the door. "Please, be gentle with him," I whispered imploringly. "We don't know much, and I fear that discussing the subject of his eyesight for too long will only serve to upset him more. We need him to have peace, so that he can rest."

Esau stared at me before finally nodding his head. I breathed a sigh of relief, and watched as he slipped inside.

Normally, I would have left the two of them in privacy. But something about this visit, about Esau's panicked arrival, left me curious to find out what he might say to his father. He and Isaac hadn't spoken in depth since before the announcement of his marriage. The only times they had been around each other had been during our visits to Rehoboth—and even then, myself, Judith, and Bashemath had been present.

I slipped to the side of the doorway, pressing my ear against the skins that lined our tent. I couldn't help but think about how ridiculous I looked listening to through the walls of my own room. I whispered a quick prayer that Deborah wouldn't find me, though she had a knack for seeking me out when I was my most miserable or embarrassed. I heard Isaac's muffled greeting, and the sound of both men clapping each other on the back. The bed creaked, and silence extended for several seconds. Finally, Esau spoke.

"I would have come sooner, had I known you needed me," Esau said.

"Thank you, my son. But we are more than capable of managing things in Beersheba. Your mother and Jacob have been a great help to me, and you have your family, and all of Rehoboth to look after."

"Yes, but—" I heard the struggle in Esau's voice to maintain his composure, and the dull thud of his fist landing against his thigh. "It's my job, Father. It is my duty to take care of you, to step in when you need help. I'm the eldest. You should have told me."

As his voice began to raise, I felt my throat tighten. I prayed quickly, hoping that Isaac would overlook his anger and change the subject.

"My son, while you are the eldest, you handed away your birthright to your brother. Technically, it is Jacob's duty now."

I inhaled sharply. Since the day I had told Isaac about the exchange I had witnessed between Jacob and Esau, he hadn't spoken about it. I had assumed he had wanted to forget that it had happened, or even to overlook it entirely. He had given Esau the job of overseeing Rehoboth, which seemed to indicate that he had every intention of honoring him as his eldest, even after Esau had given Jacob his birthright.

Esau shouted something unintelligible before the sound of shattered pottery broke through my thoughts.

Unable to bear any more, I whipped open the door of the tent. "Stop it! What are you doing coming here and disturbing your father and destroying our home?" I looked behind him and saw that he had thrown a stack of decorative bowls across the room. What remained of the fruit they had held still wobbled on the floor. "Get out," I seethed.

Hurt flashed through Esau's eyes before it turned back into anger. The muscles in his jaw strained against the effort of his silence. Finally, he stormed out of the tent. I turned to look at Isaac for the first time, relieved to see that he was still lounging calmly on our bed, seeming otherwise unperplexed by his son's behavior.

"Are you all right? I can't believe he would come here and treat you in this way." I bent over to pick up the broken shards of pottery, taking care not to cut myself.

"I understand his anger. He grieves his foolishness, and he resents his new life almost as much as he resents his brother. He has no one to blame but himself, I know"—he raised his hands as if to stop my thoughts in their tracks—"but even so, I mourn with him. I, too, wanted to give him everything. He is the eldest, and that is how it is done." He stopped, deep in thought as I continued to clean up the mess Esau had made. "In fact, it is my belief that he has the right to some privileges as the eldest son, even though he gave away his birthright."

"What do you mean? Are you referring to Rehoboth? He has reaped the rewards of your generosity there, and tenfold."

"No, I am not referring to that." He tilted his head as his eyes took on their faraway expression, indicating that his vision had faded once again. "What we all forget is that I still have my father's blessing to offer, and I intend to give it to Esau. It is rightfully his, after all. By bestowing my blessing upon him, I will die with the comfort of knowing that I didn't leave him empty-handed. In fact, I'll be leaving him with almost everything, save our land, crops, and livestock."

In my shock, I nearly dropped the cloth-wrapped shards I held in my hands. I remembered the day I had told Isaac about what the Lord had told me, and his initial dismay over my dishonesty, and his subsequent frustration over the fact that I let him believe that Esau should be favored as the natural heir to his blessing and estate. Back then, he had been reluctant about the idea of breaking a centuries-old tradition, but he had committed himself to prayer over the fact. It had never occurred to me that he would go against something that the Lord had so explicitly stated. *The elder shall serve the younger.* In my eyes, that went far beyond a simple—if stolen—birthright. That included everything.

"But the Lord said—"I began tentatively before Isaac interjected.

"I know what you told me. Trust me, Rebekah, I wouldn't be able to forget that day, and the shock of it, no matter how I might try. But the truth is that I do not have more clarity or peace now than I did that day. So, I am inclined to follow the custom we know, the custom my own father expected when he blessed me, and pass on his blessing to my eldest son."

My hands shook with the betrayal and rage that I fought to keep at bay. Not once had Isaac shared these thoughts with me, or indicated that he had plans to bless Esau, even after the message I had shared with him that had come directly from God, even after Esau had squandered his own birthright. Every fiber of my being wanted to fight back, to speak against Isaac and his logic, but a part of me knew that no good would come of it. All it would do would further cement him in his ways, further solidify his decision to pass on the Abrahamic blessing to Esau. My only hope was to try to convince him over time.

I began to sweep up the crushed and bruised fruit while breathing deeply to steady my thundering heart. After several minutes of thick silence, I finally spoke, forcing my voice above a whisper. "I'm sure that you know what is best."

* * *

As if determined to assume his rightful role as the eldest son and heir, Esau refused to go back to Rehoboth. Instead, he sent for his wives, children, and many of their own servants and nursemaids. Our home was overwhelmed with the sudden influx of people. Everywhere I looked, one of our grandchildren ran screaming through a herd of sheep, or under women's skirts as they bent over their wash for the day. It was as if Esau had been multiplied into tinier, even more energetic and savage versions of himself. While I loved them as a grandmother, his children were completely chaotic and unmanageable. For the first few weeks of their stay, Isaac, Deborah, and I tried to gently discipline them whenever we saw fit. But after a while, it became clear that not only had they been raised to behave however they preferred, their mothers had no intention of stepping in.

So, our lives continued on in that way. Screaming children, overwhelmed servants, frustrated grandparents, and Esau attempting to force his way into the role of the leader for all of Beersheba. At first, he and Jacob remained cordial. Jacob kept to himself, quietly continuing his work from dawn to dusk while avoiding prolonged visits home except for the necessary meal or meeting with our staff. His inability to be deterred from his duties seemed to only frustrate Esau more, leading him to question each of our servants, and then myself, over Jacob's comings and goings. Little by little, he was able to glean enough information about Jacob's duties to begin to meet his brother in each place he arrived, without asking or being asked.

Late in the afternoon, I looked up from the stew I was

preparing to find Jacob walking in with his day pack. Normally, he wouldn't return home until long after nightfall. I wiped my hands off on the cloth that hung from my waist before meeting him just outside the perimeter of our tents. "You're back so soon. Is everything well?"

He avoided eye contact with me as he shrugged his pack off and tried to walk past me. I placed my hand on his chest to bring him to a halt. "What is wrong?"

"I wouldn't have chosen to come back so soon, you are right. Esau has been following me for several days now. He finally demanded that I hand over my responsibilities to him."

I stared up at him, searching his clouded eyes and troubled countenance as my concern grew. While Jacob was strong, he was no match for Esau. If Esau decided to force his way into Jacob's role, Jacob would have no choice but to acquiesce.

Not wanting to embarrass Jacob any further, I stepped aside to let him pass. I stood rooted in that same place, staring at the grass beneath my feet with my hands clenched into fists at my side. What was happening was unacceptable. Esau was completely out of control, full of rage and lust for power. I couldn't let it continue, I couldn't allow Jacob to be treated this way after so many years of loving and working our land, caring for our livestock, and leading our household. And I wouldn't allow my husband to be led blindly to his death by his own son, like a sheep to the slaughter.

Something would have to be done—even if it came at the expense of almost everything and everyone I loved.

CHAPTER TWENTY-EIGHT

I saac continued to lose his eyesight as I continued to lose my patience. The strain of living with Esau's wives and children had grown to an extreme, and watching Jacob live adrift and aimless threatened to be my undoing. Jacob, to his credit, had done his best to keep busy around Beersheba while avoiding his brother. He returned to the things he loved most —cooking, and learning. While I enjoyed having him close by again, it angered me to know that every day he woke up, he was reminded of the fact that he no longer had the blessing of overseeing his father's work.

As for myself, I was busier than I had ever been. Each day was filled with whatever tasks were necessary for that season— picking, pruning, cleaning, drying, storing, and weaving. Many of our servants began to call me a whirlwind, saying that I stopped only to check on Isaac, or to eat a quick meal. Though my body wanted me to slow down, I still preferred to keep busy. To avoid the pain that had worked its way through my family and home. To avoid the realization that somehow, the beautiful life Isaac and I built had shattered, replaced only by strife.

"There you are," Deborah called from across the field of wheat that lay between us.

I had taken my time picking and looking over the crops that day, ignoring the sweat that trickled down my back as the heat baked through the veil atop my head. Ever since Esau had assumed Jacob's role, I hadn't trusted that our crops would be cared for in the way that they needed to be. So, I had used my daily visits as an excuse to stay away from home until evening.

"Here I am. I'm surprised you found me, I'm quite a distance away from home." I watched as she hurried toward me, her chest heaving with the exertion. I smiled to myself as I remembered how young we once were. Our minds were as agile as ever, but our bodies hadn't followed suit.

"Yes, you are. I'm sure that was completely unintentional as well. You would never want to make yourself nearly impossible to find when others actually needed to find you, now would you?"

"No, of course not." I kicked at a nonexistent rock at my feet while avoiding her gaze.

"Well, the good news is that I merely came to check on you. You're worrying me, you know. You're never home, you rarely rest. Isaac was asking for you earlier."

I felt a prick of guilt at the thought of him lying in our dark tent with little more to do than to stare at the ceiling—if it was even visible to him. But to me, that trade off was preferable to what might happen if I finally took the time to sit next to him, undistracted and free to speak my mind. I feared what I might say, and I feared how it might hurt him and what remained of the love and trust we had built. For months, I had fumed over his decision to bless Esau. Every waking thought had been consumed by my determination to find a way to dissuade him. But no matter what idea I came up with, nothing ended well for all of us. Regardless of the method I implemented, someone would hurt, whether that was Isaac, Esau, Jacob, or even myself.

"Was he?" I asked in a show of concern. "Did he need something?"

"Just his wife," Deborah said as she met my eyes meaningfully. "Rebekah. . . I know you're hurting, and you have every right to be. But his condition is only getting worse. Do you want your anger to take the place of whatever time he has left?"

I felt my shoulders rise in defensiveness even as I realized that she was right. I shook my head, unable to speak for fear of dissolving into my emotions.

"Good. Come home with me, then. You've done enough today. Spend time with the man who loves you deeply." She held out her hand to me, waiting until I joined her side before she wrapped her arm around my shoulders.

We walked home together, stopping intermittently to catch our breath and enjoy the scenery. Deborah filled our conversation with stories about the servants, and snippets of gossip that I typically wouldn't be privy to. As we walked up the hill to our tents, I found Jacob speaking to one of our overseers. Every bit of his demeanor and manner of speaking seemed urgent, and without thinking, I handed Deborah my basket before running to him.

He looked up from his conversation, relief flooding his face before it settled back into the same mask of sadness and exhaustion. "There you are, I've been searching for you. You need to come quick—something's wrong with Father. He asked for you, and then he requested Esau's presence."

I swallowed as my mind began to race. What if he had asked for me earlier for more serious reasons than he had let on? His request for myself, and then Esau, sounded like more than loneliness. It sounded as if he had something he needed to say, to the both of us. Before it was too late.

On wobbly legs, I began to walk slowly toward our tent, the home we had loved and cherished since the beginning of our marriage, the very one that Sarah had so artfully adorned. I wanted to run, to scream, to fight whatever and whomever I could in order to stave off what I feared and believed was about to take place. Instead I walked slowly, terribly, to the door of our tent, stopping just outside when I heard Esau's deep voice.

"I'm here, Father." Esau's voice was muffled, but the emotion in it was unmistakable.

"My son, I am old. I am tired. My eyes are giving up on me, and I don't know how long I have left." Isaac paused to take a deep breath, which I could barely hear over the thrum of my own pulse. "Please, take your bow and get me some fresh venison to make the meat that I love. Bring it back to me, and I will eat it and bless you. Before I die."

I clapped my hand to my mouth and stepped back in horror. My sweet, dependable, strong Isaac. How could I have ignored the signs that his health was declining so poorly? I thought back to the evenings we spent together, trying to remember if he had shown any symptoms of illness other than his worsening eyesight, and understandable exhaustion. I realized then that Isaac had likely hid the worst of it, not wanting to worry me or to taint our time together.

I clenched my fist to my stomach, sick with grief, before I realized what his instructions entailed. He planned to pass on the Abrahamic blessing as soon as Esau returned with fresh venison. My determination to find a way to change his mind hadn't worked. I had failed, and thus I had failed Jacob. I had to do something, and quickly. Before it was too late. Before he went against the plans that God had intended for Jacob.

I heard Esau walk toward the door, and I spun around to the other side of the tent. As I faced the stables to the east, I was struck with an idea. For just a moment, my mind faltered and I questioned whether what I intended to do was wise. But then my panic consumed me, and I forced myself forward in search of Jacob.

I ran back in the direction of where I had met him, finding him on the path that led to his tent. "Jacob! Come here." I gesticulated wildly, beckoning him to pick up his pace.

He started to jog, his concern only growing as he took in my agitated behavior. "What is wrong? Has something happened?"

I shook my head and pressed my finger to my lips. "I need you to listen, and then I need you to trust me and do whatever I say. Can you do that?"

He stared at me warily, and I watched as his mind worked furiously through all of the questions that he wanted to ask. Instead, he nodded quietly, his hands on his hips as he awaited what would come next.

"I overheard your father speaking with Esau. He told him to bring a fresh meal of venison, so that he could bless him before he died." Jacob's eyes widened and I forced myself to look away, knowing that if I gave in to the emotion that swirled through my chest, I'd never see this through. "And this is the part where I need you to trust me, and to do everything I say. Go to our flock, and fetch two of our best kid goats. I will make your father's favorite stew. You will then bring it to him, and he will bless you instead."

Jacob stared at me as if I were a woman possessed. "I look and sound nothing like Esau, Mother. He is hairy and loud. I might be able to muffle my voice, but if Father touches even my hand or forearm, he will know it isn't me. He will curse me when he finds out." Jacob ran his hands through his hair, making it stand on end in his distress.

"Look at me, Jacob." I pulled his hands away from his head,

forcing his attention to return to me. "If your Father curses anyone, let it be me. Just listen to what I'm telling you to do, and go fetch those two kids. I'll do the rest."

The corners of his mouth turned down in concern. After a few long, torturous moments, he finally shook my hands off of his and walked purposefully toward the stables.

I watched as he walked away, paralyzed with disbelief over what I had just done and what I still planned to do; praying that it would not all come to naught. I shivered at the thought of Esau's fury if—no, when—he found out. But Esau's anger would be nothing compared to the torment that Jacob and I would experience if he didn't receive Isaac's blessing. I had to see this through. I had a duty to my son, and the Lord, to ensure that Jacob was the chosen one.

Didn't I?

CHAPTER TWENTY-NINE

My hands shook as I passed the steaming bowl of soup to Jacob. In my frenzy to outpace Esau, I hadn't stopped skinning, cleaning, prepping, and cooking for the last several hours. Esau was a quick and skilled hunter, so it was only a matter of time before he returned home and prepared his meal. I had to send Jacob to Isaac with enough time to allow Isaac to enjoy his meal and give his blessing before Esau returned.

The servants' tent I worked in looked as if a crime had been committed. Blood and stray fur littered the ground around the fire. It hadn't been an easy process, nor a pretty one, but in the end I made the stew and came up with a way to ensure that when Isaac reached out for Jacob's hand, he would feel Esau's hairiness.

"Lift up your arms."

Jacob did as I asked, his cheeks burning with a mixture of shame and excitement.

I wrapped the skins of the kid goats around his forearms and wrists, securing them with small straps of leather. I ran my hand through them—they were downy to the touch, and the leather straps could easily pass for what Esau typically wore when on a hunt. I gave them a final pat before I looked up at Jacob.

In my rush to prepare the meal, I realized that I had taken care of making Jacob feel like Esau, but I had overlooked one important thing: his smell. Esau had a unique musk, and had never cared to wash his clothing frequently, nor even bathe more than once a week. Jacob, on the other hand, always smelled of soap and fresh linens. The moment that Isaac hugged Jacob, he would know he was trying to fool him. So, while the stew had simmered over the fire, I'd snuck into Esau's room to find his favorite tunic. One sniff had been enough to tell me that its scent would easily convince Isaac that it was Esau standing in front of him, rather than Jacob.

Dwarfed by the tunic, Jacob stood in front of me with his arms awkwardly floating at his sides as if to keep the skins away from his clothing. I fought to control my nervous laughter—he looked like a young boy playing a ridiculous game of dress up. Though he was as tall and broad as Isaac, he was no match for his brother's clothing.

"This'll do," I said with a nod.

He turned his head to sniff his shoulder, wrinkling his nose in disgust. "I smell terrible."

"You smell like your brother, which is exactly what we want. Do you think you'll be able to sound like him?"

He nodded before furrowing his brow in concentration and mimicking Esau's deep, gravelly voice.

"That'll have to do as well," I sighed. "Remember to try to speak as little as possible. Place the bowl in his hands, and let him smell it. Then, when he reaches out to bless you, make sure he feels your lower arms only."

Jacob held eye contact with me before shifting his gaze over my head.

"I know that this is uncomfortable for you, and that you doubt whether it'll even work. As I said, should anything happen, I will be sure that your father knows it was my doing, and not yours. But we must go through with this, Jacob. It's our only hope of securing the blessing that is rightfully yours." I realized I was clutching his arms at this point and released him with a deep breath. "Let's go before his food gets cold." I placed my finger over my lips, before nodding for him to follow me. Though the sun was beginning to set, it was still bright enough for everyone to see us and question what on earth Jacob was doing wearing his brother's clothing and goat skin around his arms. We had to get to Isaac without being seen.

I made my way to the back of the tent, lifting it to usher Jacob through before following behind him. We were next to small copse with dense underbrush. The moment I dropped the wall of the tent, I felt the scratch of the bushes against my ankles. "Hug the underbrush and stay as crouched as you can," I whispered before turning forward at an awkward, hunched run. I did my best to ignore the sting of the twigs that slapped my legs as we raced ahead, stopping to check and make sure no one could see us before scurrying between each walkway.

Finally, we arrived at the back of my tent. I paused to take a breath and steady my heart while peeking around both sides to make sure no one was near. "It's time. Sneak around the front, and check to make sure no one can see you before you enter. Remember, try to speak as little as possible. Go!"

Jacob was wild eyed, and I watched his throat bob as he swallowed. After just a moment's hesitation, he stepped swiftly around the corner of the tent, walking at a leisurely pace to the front while surreptitiously glancing around him to ensure no one could see. In a split second, he was gone.

I looked down, surprised to find that my hands were trembling. I counted until ten before rounding the corner, trying to appear as relaxed as Jacob had been. A couple of women walked by, chatting cheerfully with a basket of freshly picked corn held between them. Thankfully, they didn't seem to notice me. Seeing me come around the back of my own tent would have appeared suspicious.

I glanced around for something to hold or do to steady my nerves, grateful to find the unfinished palm basket I had been working on the evening before sitting to the side of the entrance. I dragged a stool to the doorway, close enough for me to hear their conversation, but not so close that I would look strange to passersby. Hopefully, those who saw me would figure that I was sitting outside for anything Isaac might need. I picked up the basket and began to absentmindedly weave when I heard the sound of stone on wood, and Isaac clearing his throat.

"Who are you, Son?"

I nearly dropped my basket at the sound of Isaac's voice. He sounded wary, if not completely suspicious. I silently chastised Jacob—had he walked in and spoken before his father could smell and feel him?

Jacob cleared his throat, before beginning an imitation of Esau's deep, resonant voice. "It is me, Esau, your firstborn. I've done as you asked, and have brought you venison to enjoy.

Please, sit and eat so that your soul can be refreshed, and then you can bless me."

I nearly rolled my eyes. While he almost sounded like Esau, he spoke far too eloquently.

"How did you find venison so quickly? I expected it to take at least a day of hunting."

"Well," Jacob hesitated as if searching the dark room for an answer. "The Lord brought it to me."

"Come closer to me and let me feel you." The bed creaked as Jacob leaned forward, and Isaac shifted against the pillows that lined the back of our bed. "You sound like Jacob, but these are Esau's hands. Are you Esau, my son?"

Jacob answered without skipping a beat. "I am."

The silence grew as Isaac seemed to consider what Jacob had said. Finally, Isaac spoke. "Bring it to me. I will eat it before I bless you."

Jacob walked to retrieve the bowl from our tea table. After he helped his father sit up in a more comfortable position, I heard the sound of Isaac's stone spoon against the clay bowl. I took a deep breath, only then realizing that I had been holding it. I listened to Isaac's quiet slurps and murmurs of contentment as he ate, waiting impatiently for him to proceed. It took him much longer to finish a meal than it had when he was young.

"I have some wine for you as well, Father," Jacob said as he broke the silence.

I furrowed my brow in confusion. While I didn't remember sending him with anything for Isaac to drink, we did have a small decanter of fresh wine sitting on our table from the evening before. Isaac thanked him quietly before taking a sip. The scrape of the bowl against our wooden table met my ears, and I steeled myself for what was to come.

"The meal was delicious, my son, though it didn't taste like your venison," Isaac said.

I could have sworn that I heard a small smile in his voice, though my heart lodged in my throat at his words. Of course, I hadn't considered the fact that Isaac had asked for Esau's venison, his favorite meal, specifically. While he couldn't see, he could certainly feel, smell, and taste. I had taken those first two senses into account, while completely overlooking the last.

I heard Jacob shift forward slightly as the silence stretched on. I breathed in and out three times, trying to do so quietly for fear of being overheard by Isaac even from outside the tent.

Finally, he spoke. "Come closer and kiss me, my son."

I listened as Jacob leaned forward once more and placed a kiss on Isaac's forehead.

"Though I might not be able to see, I would know your smell anywhere—the scent of the field, which the Lord has blessed, and a hard day's work."

I held my breath once more and leaned backward, straining to hear as Isaac blessed Jacob quietly. In a few minutes, it was done. I heard Jacob rise before helping Isaac lay back down to rest and clearing away his dishes. He walked calmly out of the tent, his eyes aglow with victory. Relief caught up with me as I realized that we had done it, that Jacob had earned the blessing in the end.

I reached up to pat his cheek lovingly. "You did it," I whispered. "And what a blessing it is for me to say that. Come, we must hide you away and clean you up before your brother returns."

As I watched him walk along the perimeter of the tents once more, I felt the hair on the back of my neck stand up. I turned and found Esau walking toward me, a broad smile on his face as he carried a tray of food. I had known that I would have to face the consequences of his anger, but in my panic and hurry to make sure that Jacob received the blessing before Esau came home, I hadn't stopped to fully consider how I would handle him. Until now, it hadn't occurred to me just what Esau might do to Jacob when he found out. He had been furious, beside himself with rage over his decision to give Jacob his birthright so many years ago—and that had been at his own doing. What would he do now, when he realized that his final right as a firstborn son had been given to Jacob?

I had to stall him. I had to give Jacob enough time to clean up and hide the evidence of what we had done.

I rushed to Esau, feigning excitement over his arrival while attempting to block his path with my body. "My son, how good it is to see you! How was your hunt?"

Esau looked down at me questioningly before raising the

tray he held to my face. "It went well. I've brought the venison that Father requested, and am taking it to him now." He sidestepped me, and I stumbled in my attempt to catch up.

"He's resting now, why don't we keep that warm over the fire?"

"He told me to bring it back to him as soon as it was cooked," Esau said brusquely. "Which is exactly what I intend to do."

I reached out to grab his arm, and he turned to look at me impatiently before gently nudging my hand away. We stood just outside Isaac's tent. I knew that the moment Esau stepped inside, he would realize what Jacob had done. I also knew that when Esau's mind was made up, it was impossible to hold him back. I had made my bed, and it was time to lie in it.

I patted his arm before letting go, offering him a small smile of apology as I watched him disappear through the door. The guilt I had silenced for so many years rose to the surface, threatening to overcome me completely. While Jacob and I had always been close, I loved Esau too. For his wildness, for his simplicity, for the fact that though he looked nothing like Isaac or I, he was undeniably our son. Our firstborn. I remembered what it had been like to hold him, his plump, swaddled form wiggling in my arms as I petted his soft red hair. In my hurry to protect one son, I had hurt the other. While I felt in my heart that what I had done was right, was justified, it hurt me to know that I had hurt Esau so badly in exchange. The fact that he had done so well in Rehoboth offered me a bit of consolation. He had a family he loved, and land he had done well in. Surely, over time, he would forgive his father—if not me and his brother— and live a long and healthy life. He was a fighter; giving up was not in him.

The sound of Esau's yell of anguish broke through my thoughts. Though I stood away from our tent, I could clearly hear what he was saying.

"Bless me, Father," he pleaded.

"Your brother came and took your blessing." Isaac's voice was thick with emotion. Tears sprang to my eyes as I heard the last whisper-thin part of our trust break.

Esau roared in anger before throwing his tray against the farthest wall. I listened as it hit the ground with a thud. "He took my birthright, and now he has taken my blessing. How well his name suits him," he said as his voice shook. He breathed in deeply, before speaking again with a slight quiver in his voice. "Have you really not reserved a blessing for me?"

"I have made Jacob lord over everything: the land, the servants, our crops and livestock. I have passed on the blessing of my father, whose blessing came directly from God. What do I have left to give you now?"

Never had I heard Isaac sound so broken. Even after losing his father, he hadn't shown such despair. The knowledge that I had brought on this level of grief was enough to make me want to turn and run through the fields we called our home, into the desert, and far past that. To some unknown, far-off land where regret and disappointment couldn't live; where the knowledge that I had broken my husband's heart and wounded one son in exchange for the happiness of the other wouldn't sit in my bones for the rest of my life. Instead, I stood rooted in place as my nails dug into my palms.

I heard a rustle and realized that Esau had fallen to his knees in front of Isaac and begun to weep. "Don't you have one blessing for me, Father? Please," he begged. "Bless me too."

Isaac continued to console him as best as he could, hushing him intermittently while listening as his eldest son cried over a future he had lost. A few minutes passed, and Esau's weeping finally subsided.

"My son," Isaac said slowly. "I will bless you as best I can." I heard him shift forward slowly to place a hand on Esau's head before murmuring a quiet blessing, almost like a prayer.

Though he could not offer him the Abrahamic blessing, Isaac did his best to bless Esau, his home, his land, and his success with what power and will that remained. It seemed to calm Esau, who listened quietly before thanking him. I heard him stand and begin to pick up the tray of food he had thrown, realizing with a start that he would find me outside and know immediately that it had been me who had put Jacob up to everything. I turned to leave, but my feet remained frozen in place as I came to the realization that if he didn't find me, he would certainly find his brother. While I feared Esau's wrath, I feared his violence toward Jacob more.

I lifted my chin and faced the entrance to our tent, waiting for Esau to walk out. Finally, he ducked his head under the frame and came outside. I caught a glint of sadness in his eyes, which transformed into anger the moment he saw me. He studied me quietly, as if unsurprised by my presence, before nodding in understanding. "It was you, wasn't it?" he said, his voice hoarse with emotion.

I nodded, unable to say a word.

"How could you do this to me? He already had my birthright, wasn't that enough for you? Do you hate me enough to take everything from me?"

Slowly I unstuck my tongue from the roof of my mouth, shaking my head as I spoke. "I have never hated you, Esau. Far from it. I love you, I have always loved you. But this was the Lord's will. He told me it would be so even before you were born. I didn't want to have to do it this way, but I had no other choice —"

"You had plenty of choice," he said in a chilling voice. His eyes glazed over as he refused to look at me, staring at the purple horizon instead. When I said nothing more, he walked past me, stopping only to hand Judith the tray he held. He grabbed his spear from where it lay against his tent and began to walk in the direction of his favorite hunting grounds. It appeared that he planned to expend his frustration while hunting, rather than on his brother. While it would work to keep his anger at bay for a short while, I knew from experience that his resentment would only grow with each passing day. I had to work out a way to protect Jacob.

I looked at the basket I clutched in my hands, its unruly palm fronds sticking out in every direction. Somehow, it looked worse now than it had when I began working on it earlier in the day. I tucked it to the side of our tent before walking in. While I wanted to prolong having to face Isaac, I couldn't avoid him forever. It was time.

I peered into our cave-like tent, its only light source being the dim fire in our hearth. I bent over to stir it, and the smell of fresh venison met my nostrils. I turned to see that it littered our floor and the cushions nearby. Isaac laid in bed, staring with glassy eyes at the air above him.

"Isaac—" I said, unable to continue. I watched him, my lip quivering as I took a moment to let the weight of what had happened today fall on my shoulders.

He sighed before shifting to sit up. Though he faced me, he couldn't see me. Oh, how I missed seeing the light that flooded his eyes every time his gaze rested on me. When had been the last time?

"I don't know what to say, Rebekah, other than the fact that I am awestruck by what happened today. The moment that Esau arrived, I had a feeling you were involved. But"—he held up a hand to silence me—"I heard everything I needed to between the both of you. You have broken my heart."

I began to cry, my chest rising and falling rapidly as I fell to my knees beside where he lay in bed. "You have to know that I only did what I felt was best, according to what God told me. You didn't listen, Isaac, when I told you all of those years ago. It seemed like you did, but then we never spoke of it again until only a few weeks ago when you mentioned that you would still bless Esau." I lifted my head from where it lay on the bed, staring at him resolutely while steadying my voice. "I did what I had to in order to protect you from going against God's will."

Isaac looked weary now, too tired to be angry, which hurt my heart even more. I would give anything to be able to argue with him, and to know that he was healthy and whole again. This, seeing him so exhausted, so weak, was more of a punishment than I could bear. He didn't say anything for a moment, and I listened to his shallow breathing until he spoke again.

"Whether I went against the Lord's will or not, that was my decision to make. Not yours. What you have done now is irreparable. You have broken mine and Esau's hearts, while uplifting Jacob. I have always loved you so, Rebekah"—a tear fell down his cheek as his voice tremored—"but I don't know if I'll ever be able to look past this."

His words were the final break in my dam. I fell into my tears, allowing them to drown out any sense of time or reality, settling fully into the pain caused by my own hand, and the bittersweet relief of knowing my duty was done. It was as if the decades leading up to this moment had been practice, training, and they had amounted to this one, final moment.

Those moments of boundless joy and pure heartache had been nothing compared to the magnitude of what I felt now. While his words broke me, I understood them. I understood him. What would I have felt if he had done to me what I did to him?

"I understand. I can only beg for your forgiveness over time. Please know that it hurts me to know how badly I have hurt you —you have been so good to me, so loving, so caring, so patient. Though I do not regret the fact that Jacob now has what was intended to be his, I accept that I will spend the rest of my life making up for my actions. I love you, Isaac," I said as I fought to keep my voice steady. I reached out for his hand, but he let it lay motionless under my palm.

"I love you, Rebekah," he said quietly as I walked into the comfort of the evening air.

CHAPTER THIRTY

Deborah found me huddled just outside the perimeter of servants' tents that lined our site. I had come here in an attempt to get away from Bashemath, who followed me while vehemently cursing as Judith watched with wide eyes. I had known nowhere else to go other than away. As I had stumbled through the crowd of concerned faces, I'd felt a tightening sensation in my chest followed by the dull, uncomfortable feeling of my heart stopping then starting again. It was as if it had done a cartwheel inside my ribs, pausing only when it reached the confines of its cage. The feeling was so foreign to me that I'd dropped to the ground, right where I stood.

As I crouched, I felt reassuring hands on my shoulders, and turned to find Deborah. She was an oasis in a desert of emotion, and without another thought, I threw my arms around her neck, sobbing into her shoulder as she shooed the onlookers away.

"What has happened, Rebekah? You're scaring me. Tell me what's wrong." We had walked a distance away and were sitting on a large rock with our backs turned to the rest of the tents. At our feet lay the rows and rows of golden wheat, which gleamed and shifted in the evening breeze.

"I've finally done it. I've finally hurt Isaac enough to ensure that he will never forgive me." I sniffed, unable to continue speaking.

"Surely you are wrong. He loves you more than anything in this world. Can you tell me what happened?"

I took a deep breath, steeling myself to disappoint yet another person I loved. I told her everything, leaving nothing out. In a way, it was cleansing to tell her everything I had done. I watched as her face transformed from compassion, to amusement, to horror. When I finished, she looked ahead, thinking deeply before speaking.

"So, what now?"

"What do you mean?" I asked in confusion.

"What will you do now? Esau might hunt for the next couple of days, but he will return. What will you do about Jacob? What will you do about Isaac?"

I thought about it for a moment, letting her words sink in. As I watched the heads of wheat shift beneath us, I heard the soft tinkling of bells behind me. I turned to find them, fighting a rising sense of familiarity. "Did you hear that?" I said.

"Hear what?"

"Those bells. There they are again—can you hear them?"

Deborah stared at me as if I had gone completely mad before her face softened in pity. "You're tired and have gone through enough today, Rebekah. You need food and rest," she stood up and held her hand out to me, but I shook my head.

"I'm not ready to go back yet. Go home, please. I hate to make you stay out here when you must be exhausted from the day. I'll be fine."

She looked at me in concern, before tucking a strand of graying hair behind her ear. "I'll go back and fetch us something to eat and drink. Wait here," she said. "Promise me you won't move."

I promised and watched her walk away before turning back to study the landscape. As I observed the way the breeze moved through the grass and listened to an owl overhead, I heard those same bells, growing louder until I felt the urge to cover my ears. Then, just as suddenly as they started, they stopped. A chill came over me as I remembered, finally, when I had last heard them. Not knowing what else to do, I fell to my knees, pressing my face into the grass, and waited. This time, there was no voice to hear, other than the small one in the back of my mind.

Esau will withhold his rage, but only until Isaac passes away, Rebekah. You must save Jacob before it is too late.

I laid with my face in the ground, the grass tickling my cheeks as I worked through what I had just heard. While the Lord hadn't spoken as loudly as he had the first time, I couldn't deny how clear the voice had been in my head. The urgency with which the message had been relayed sent a shiver through me, followed only by anguish. Not only did it mean that Isaac's death was imminent, but my fears of Esau seeking revenge were confirmed. My thoughts began to spin as I laid motionless, abstractedly noticing that the dew had dampened my dress and veil, and that my knees ached.

"What on earth are you doing?" I hadn't heard Deborah walk up behind me.

I lifted myself slowly and stretched my neck before rising to sit beside her. "When you left, I heard those bells again. I couldn't place them, but they were familiar. Then I remembered that I heard those same bells when I was pregnant and the Lord spoke to me. As soon as I realized that, the Lord told me that Esau is planning to kill Jacob as soon as Isaac dies. He—He told me to save Jacob before it is too late."

Deborah's eyes widened in disbelief. "You can't mean—does this mean that Isaac will die soon?"

I swallowed in an attempt to quell my tears. I couldn't think about the fact that Isaac would die so soon after I broke his trust, and subsequently, his heart. I couldn't save Isaac, I couldn't stop death's pull. But I could save Jacob.

"Esau has connections from here to Gerar, and far past that. How can we hide Jacob?" Deborah asked as she rubbed her temples, the food she brought growing cold as it sat forgotten on her lap.

"He'll need to go somewhere that Esau has never gone, far enough away that hopefully, over time, he will forget his anger and allow him to come back." While I hoped that it would be a matter of months, I knew in my heart that Esau's resentment wouldn't diminish so quickly. "He will need to go where he will be protected. He needs to go to Laban."

* * *

It took three weeks to receive word from our messenger. Each day, I watched the horizon with bated breath, pleading silently for his approach. We had managed to keep Jacob and Esau away from each other, with Jacob camping out in different places each evening in the valley of Beersheba, while Esau continued to manage our land and crops. Every day, I watched as he pushed through his duties, his brow set as if he refused to accept the fact that the work he did now was no longer rightfully his to do. I kept out of his way as much as possible, working the fields in between checking on Isaac's health.

Isaac and I had hardly spoken, other than for him to request a certain meal when he was finally hungry, or for me to provide him with updates on how Beersheba was faring. No longer did I receive the affectionate squeeze of the hand, or the gentle tickle of his fingers through my hair each night. While he didn't ask me to, I made a bed at the foot of his, not wanting to disturb or further distress him by sleeping beside him. Loving him from afar was foreign to me—we'd been so close, so inseparable, all of our marriage. The space between us now felt insurmountable. Even so, I was determined to show him the love and care that he deserved, though I knew that nothing could ever rectify what I had done.

So, each day passed like the one before. I rose before dawn and tended to Isaac, before walking out with food and drink to meet Jacob in the location we chose the day prior. He'd wait for me, looking more and more like a wild man, hoping each day that I had some good news to share. I hadn't told him that I'd sent a messenger to Laban to request his blessing over Jacob's journey to him. All I'd said was that I was awaiting news, and until then, he needed to stay hidden from Esau. After our meeting, I'd trudge out to our fields to oversee whatever needed to be done that day, before coming back to tend to things around our home. Every evening, I laid my head down at Isaac's feet, listening as the silence between us deafened me.

Today, as I stood by the fire at the center of our tents and stretched my back, my eye caught movement on the horizon. The sun was just beginning to rise behind me, and I squinted as I made out the outline of a man on a camel. Thank God, I thought. I ran toward him, stopping only when others began to poke their heads out of their tents in confusion. "What news do you have?" I panted. I wiped the back of my hand across my forehead while staring up at our messenger's exhausted, sunburned face.

"Your brother has asked me to tell you that he has a room ready and waiting for Jacob."

I nearly cried out with relief, but stopped myself so as not to alarm him. "Thank you. I am sure I do not have to ask this of you, but still I will. Please keep this message between the two of us."

He nodded, the only thing on his mind being going home to his wife and children. I stepped aside and watched as he dismounted and walked his camel to the stables.

While I had prayed, and waited, and hoped for the good news he shared, I now had to accept what would happen next. The thought of losing Jacob, of missing him, was enough to make me lose my breath. But in order to save his life, to ensure that God's will came to pass, it had to be done. There was no other way around the sorrow; I had to walk through it.

I turned to walk back, exchanging pleasantries and smiles of greeting with those who had already begun their day. A few of the women cast concerned looks at me, registering that something was wrong from the fact that I didn't stop to speak with them as I normally would. When I arrived at the door of our tent, I stopped to look around me, inhaling deeply before stepping inside. Isaac was awake and sitting up today, which was an improvement. I began to gather the food, water, and clothing I had set aside for Jacob.

"Where are you going?" Isaac asked. I turned in surprise to see him watching me with clouded eyes. While he could no longer see, he was able to follow the sounds of those around him. Knowing he watched me without seeing was still something that I struggled to accept and understand.

"I'm gathering a bit of food and clothing for Jacob." While it had hurt to tell Isaac that Jacob was in hiding, I refused to be anything but truthful to him any longer. Isaac had seemed unaffected, if not slightly relieved by the knowledge that Jacob and Esau weren't to cross paths. I knew that I needed to tell him the news I received from Laban, but I wanted to get to Jacob before he grew too worried. "Is there anything you need from me before I leave for the day?"

He folded his hands in his lap, staring blankly ahead. "No. At least, nothing that you have the power to give me."

I hesitated before stepping forward and pressing a kiss to his cheek—the first time I had done so since the day he blessed Jacob. I turned away, nearly gasping when I felt him catch my hand. Slowly, I turned to face him, fearing that my acknowledgement of his affection would make it all go away.

He held my hand in his palm as gently as he would a dove, stroking it with his thumb. "I do not need eyes to see this hand I know so well. I have held it through years of plenty, and years of pain. It has been at my side through everything, unfailingly." He lifted my palm to his lips and pressed a kiss in it, sending a shock wave through my arm. "Please stop sleeping at the foot of the bed, Rebekah."

A stray tear rolled down my cheek and I nodded silently before realizing what I was doing. "Do you really mean that you would like me to sleep beside you?"

"That is where you belong, is it not?" I saw the whisper of a smile make its way across his mouth, before he set it back into its neutral line. "At least, that is where I think you belong."

"It is, my love. It is," I said with a sob. Forgetting to worry first, I sat beside him and wrapped my arms around his neck. Though he was bedridden and tired, he was still strong and sinewy beneath my arms. If I closed my eyes, I could imagine us fifty years younger, free of the way life had weathered us. After a few minutes of holding him, I felt his arms encircle my back. We stayed that way for a while, until I finally sat up with a resounding sniff.

"I really must go, he will be worried sick," I said.

"Yes, go. You'll know where to find me."

I laughed quietly as I placed my palm to his cheek before saying goodbye. Leaving him now, after our first moment of reconciliation, felt nearly impossible. But the knowledge of what lay ahead of me, and the fact that Jacob was relying on me, pushed me forward.

Jacob sat against a large outcrop with one leg outstretched, his elbow propped against the other. He looked deep in thought, something that he had done little else of in these last weeks. As I approached, he turned toward me, relief showing in his face. "There you are. I was worried when you weren't here at the time you said. You're usually earlier than I am," he said. His smile fell. "What is wrong, Mother?"

"Nothing, nothing. In fact, I have good news to share. My brother, Laban, has invited you to stay with him in Haran. After you've had your breakfast, we can make our way back to prepare for your departure."

He stepped back as if stung by my words. "What do you mean? I can't leave what's rightfully mine, not now, not when Father's health is increasingly failing and he's given me his blessing."

"You and I both know that the blessing he gave you was not originally intended for you. Though it worked out for good in the end, we must be cautious of how your presence here might affect others."

"By that, you refer to Esau," the muscle in his jaw popped, and he placed his hands on his hips before turning away. "At what point will he be forced to accept what has happened?"

"We can ask ourselves that until we are blue in the face, Jacob. But that doesn't change the fact that he is furious, and that he intends to seek revenge the moment your father is not here to see him do so." I hadn't planned on telling him what I knew, but it had been necessary in ensuring that Jacob understood just how dire his departure really was.

I watched his shoulders drop in acceptance before he turned to face me. "There truly is no other way?"

I shook my head slowly. "Jacob, I have deliberated, planned, and calculated what to do to keep you safe every minute of every day. This is the only way." I reached out to place my hand on his shoulder. "Stay with him for a little while, just a few days, really, until your brother's fury passes. It'll give me peace to know you're safely away from here. When Esau has calmed down, I will send for you immediately. Trust me—" my voice broke, and my lip quivered as I continued "—I lost your brother long ago. I can't lose you, too."

He looked at me with sadness in his eyes, and I knew that he would go, if even just for me. Wordlessly, he reached out and accepted his breakfast and change of clothes. I sat beside him as he ate, enjoying the sunshine overhead and the breeze that ruffled through my hair.

"It's strange, but sending you to Laban is bringing back so many memories of when I came to meet your father," I said.

"You must have been terrified."

"I was, but maybe not for the reasons you would expect. You

see, I was young. So, so young. I'd had my share of turning away suitors, I enjoyed my independence and the freedom I had while living with my mother and father. I had no real responsibilities. And then one day, it all changed. My daily chore took on an entirely different meaning; I went to the well for water, and came back betrothed." I smiled, remembering Eliezer and my wonder over the jewelry he had given me. "In many ways, today feels similar to that day."

"The only difference being that you weren't running for your life, and you had a spouse to meet," Jacob attempted to joke, but I watched as his smile fell.

"That was my lot in life, and this is yours. However much it hurts, this is what we are supposed to do. This way, you can fully step into the blessing your father has given you, and become a father and leader to many."

We sat side by side for an interminable time, staring at everything and nothing, allowing ourselves one final moment to enjoy each other's company while pretending that nothing and no one else needed us. When the sun grew higher overhead, we finally turned to each other with a nod before standing up. Jacob held out his hand to me, and I clasped it, grateful for the assistance.

We walked home slowly, thoughtfully, parting when we came to his tent so that he could pack. I instructed him to only bring what could fit on his one camel, and to leave room for a gift for Laban as well. I planned to send him with jewelry for Laban's wives, and a tapestry I knew he would love. He gave me a quick hug before stepping into his tent, and I fought the weariness that threatened to overwhelm me.

You can be tired tomorrow, after he's gone, I thought. Just not today.

❊ ❊ ❊

Deborah and I spent the afternoon preparing Jacob's camel, and gathering my gifts for Laban. We worked silently together, and I knew that she was giving me time to process my feelings about his departure. In many ways, I knew that she was doing the same. She had raised Jacob alongside me, and having never had a child of her own, felt the loss of his presence nearly as deeply as I did.

While we packed, I forced myself to consider how I would tell Isaac. Though he had accepted—though not approved of—Jacob's life in the wilderness these last three weeks, I feared that he wouldn't take well to the thought of him leaving completely. Given the fact that Jacob had Esau's birthright and blessing, his place was here, leading our people, and starting a family. Isaac had always seen Esau differently than the rest of the world. "He can be given to violence when angry, yes, but he has control over it," he'd said to me on a few occasions. Convincing him of Esau's plan to kill Jacob, especially since I only knew of it through the Lord, would be nearly impossible.

As I wrapped Laban's tapestry tightly in protective cloth, a thought occurred to me. There was one way to convince Isaac to accept Jacob's departure.

❊ ❊ ❊

"Are you awake, my love?" I whispered into the dark room.

"Yes, come in. Do you need something?"

"I do, actually. I was hoping to speak with you. You see, I'm a bit worried about Jacob."

"What for? If this is about Esau, you have to know that while they might need to fight it out, he would never do more than that to his brother, Rebekah. He loves the both of us too much for that," he said firmly, as if hoping that by doing so, I would finally believe it too.

I looked down at my twisted hands, not wanting to hurt him by arguing back. "No, it's not that. The thing is that I haven't spoken with you about Judith and Bashemath. They have been a strain, to put it lightly. Jacob, now that he has your blessing, will be looking for a wife. I fear that he will choose a woman like Esau has chosen, and I don't think I will be able to stand it. I am so tired, and just want peace. Adding another contentious daughter to the family will be my undoing." While my main motivation was to keep Jacob safe, sending him to Laban would allow him to choose a good wife from an honorable family. I hated the thought of him leaving, but I hated the possibility of what would happen if he stayed here even more.

"I knew that Bashemath was trouble, but to hear that Judith is placing a strain on you as well is a surprise to me," he said.

"You are right, Judith is as quiet as she's always been," I admitted. "However, Bashemath has been troublesome enough for the both of them. And that is why I want our son to find a wife in Haran, where I grew up. Laban will ensure that he chooses the right woman for him, for our family, and we won't have to worry any longer."

Isaac studied the ceiling quietly, as if he were drawing out the plan in his mind. "His duty is here, to the land he inherited, to the people he leads. When I am gone, he is all they will have left."

I felt my heart squeeze in that same, uncomfortable way as I sat down beside him. I placed my hand over his, forcing myself to shake off the feeling of dread, and whatever else was beginning to grow like a weed, just behind my heart. "It is my hope that he will have more than enough time to find a proper wife and return to us before we ever need to consider that. You are getting better by the day, my love. Though you don't have your vision, you have more energy than you have had in months. Please, allow me to send him to Laban so he can find a good wife."

He flipped his hand over and cradled my palm in his while running his forefinger over my pulse. "Very well, but I will only give him my blessing so long as he chooses one of Laban's daughters to become his wife. Only then will I feel that his departure will be worthwhile."

I felt my face break into a smile, unable to contain itself over the relief I felt. I pressed a swift kiss to his cheek. "I will go and fetch Jacob now, so he can speak with you before he leaves." Jacob and Isaac had not been near each other since the day of his blessing. A part of me feared that their speaking would place more strain on Isaac, but a larger part was overjoyed to know that Isaac would not die before he and Jacob could make amends.

I found Jacob outside his tent, crouched over his pack as

he filled it with dried meat, vegetables, and fruit. After a bit of coercion, he followed me reluctantly, reminding me of when he was young and had to face Isaac after being caught tricking Esau out of his dessert.

"Remember," I said as I turned to him to block his path into our tent. "This could be the last time you two speak. Please, make amends with your father so you can go in peace." He nodded, his face looking pale and drawn.

This time I walked away. I wanted to give them privacy, something that I had stolen from the both of them previously. I also was in desperate need of some water and rest—the burden of the last few weeks had taken its toll on me. I found Deborah sitting under the shade of our favorite tree, smiling to herself as she listened to the birds singing overhead.

"I'll miss him, you know," she said as she broke our silence. I stared down at my water jug, choosing to focus on what was in my hand, rather than the pain that awaited me.

"I know. And I think you know that I can't put how I feel into words, other than to say that I feel as if my heart is being torn out of my chest, chunk by chunk, and that when he leaves, nothing will be left."

"I understand." She turned to me suddenly, urgency filling her features. "Rebekah, I've known you the longest of anyone here, second only to Laban. I've been with you through every trial, every journey, over every mountain, and through every valley. Are you sure this is right? What if—what if he never comes back?"

"You don't think that I haven't sat here, wondering the same thing, every single day since I sent that messenger?" My voice was shaking from misdirected anger and grief. "The truth is that if he stays, and if Isaac dies, Esau will kill him. And then what will my life have been for? What will I have done, except break my husband's heart, and cause my son to turn on his brother? I can't live with that thought, Deborah. It'll kill me."

"You're right, I'm sorry," she said. "I let my feelings get the best of me. You know best, and are stronger than I'll ever be."

"Thank you for staying by my side, even when I do foolish things." I nudged her shoulder with mine, and we fell into a comfortable silence. Memories of us as young girls, laughing and talking into the wee hours of the night, floated through my mind. What I would give to go back and live just one more day of that, to give my mother and father one last hug, to enjoy one last meal under the guise of childlike innocence.

Because no matter what I told myself or how I looked at the present I had created, I knew that tonight, when I watched Jacob leave, a part of me would be broken beyond repair.

CHAPTER THIRTY-ONE

I spent the rest of the day wishing that time would stand still. Even as I pet the camel that had been prepared for Jacob, remembering the friend I had made in Chazo fondly, I found myself bargaining with time. Asking it to stop, begging it to go elsewhere—to just give me a bit longer, a little more.

But the sun was determined to set, and the stars still appeared, twinkling as if resolute in reminding me that time was up.

Jacob had found me sitting with Deborah, overjoyed with Isaac's blessing over his journey. This time, Jacob had the relief of knowing that his father had blessed him, and him alone. His happiness was enough to overshadow my growing sense of dread.

The three of us walked slowly home, and Deborah began cooking Jacob his favorite supper. We watched as she cleaned and prepared the meat, spices, and vegetables, enjoying the sound of her comforting ministrations. I told Jacob stories about our youth while she worked, and she intermittently jumped in to refute or correct my memory. Even then, I knew that I would carry the moments we were sharing with me for the rest of my life.

Every time the conversation lulled and sadness began to sneak up on us, one of us would say, "after supper, not now." Deborah had said it first, in an effort to help us remain focused on the present, and on enjoying each other's company before Jacob left. So, we chatted, laughed, cried a little, and said, "after supper, not now."

We had our supper with Isaac, and invited Deborah to sit with us. Initially, she had been reluctant to accept our offer, but had finally done so at Isaac's insistence. "You are family, Deborah. After all, I've known you just as long as I've known my wife," he had said with a smile.

So, she had made herself comfortable on some of the luxurious cushions she had always admired, right beside Jacob. I listened to the three of them talk companionably as I helped Isaac eat, fighting down the rising tide of emotion that seemed to start from my feet, and work its way into my soul.

"Are you all right, my love?" Hearing him call me that brought a smile to my face.

"Hmm? Oh, yes. I was in another world just then." I raised another spoonful of food to his lips, but he pushed it away.

"No, I can sense your worry. As you said, he will be back before we know it. Unless something's changed, he's a good-looking man. He's never had difficulty attracting the attention of many women," he said as he chuckled quietly at his joke. I couldn't help but join in.

"Yes, you are right. It's just a mother's job to meddle and worry." What I didn't say was that his return was dependent on the abatement of Esau's wrath, or the delay of Isaac's death. Either way, it felt as if I were being ripped in two.

"After dessert, not now," Deborah called from where she sat. I smiled at her in appreciation, endlessly grateful for her ability to tune into my emotions and look ahead for me when I couldn't.

After supper, we enjoyed a dessert of sweet cakes topped with the sugary syrup I made from the last of our figs. I laughed as Isaac took his first bite, his eyes growing wide with enjoyment.

"That was easily the best dessert I've ever had, Mother," Jacob said after he cleaned off his plate.

"I'll make sure to give the recipe to your new wife," I teased, before my stomach dropped. We had pushed off the inevitable for long enough. I sighed before breaking the silence. "Dessert has ended, and now's the time." I rose slowly, stacking Isaac's plate over mine before setting them to the side. Deborah and I exchanged knowing glances before stepping out of the tent. It was important for Jacob to have one final moment with Isaac. Our tears could wait that long.

We stood like sentries outside the tent, guarding it from some unknown evil. Finally, Jacob came to find us, tears glistening in his eyes. He gave us a resolute nod, and the three of us began to walk to where Jacob's camel waited patiently.

"Wait," Deborah said. "I want to say goodbye here. You two deserve your own farewell."

I swallowed, attempting to force the tears that flooded my eyes back into my body, and walked a distance away to allow the two of them a moment. Deborah spoke quietly, looking up at Jacob as he listened intently. I heard the low murmur of his voice, and watched as she reached up to fling her arms around his neck in the same way that he once had with her. He hugged her swiftly, as if embarrassed by the emotion that was written across his face, before walking to me.

We fell into step with each other, and I listened as our feet scuffed through the spongy grass, acutely aware of the dew that wet the hem of my dress. I looked up, pleased to see that the moon was full—it would afford him plenty of light tonight. I forced myself not to think about the loneliness that awaited him, or how long it might take for me to find out if he made it safely to Haran. Instead, I looked at the stars overhead, awestruck as they shimmered and blinked as if they were suspended in water. "I've always loved the stars, you know. When I was little, they reminded me of sparkling gems. It wasn't until I was older that I realized that it was the other way around: Stars don't resemble gemstones; gemstones resemble stars. Every night of my journey to Canaan, I studied the stars, and drew comfort from the way that they lit my path. They felt like friends to me, guardians watching over me from heaven. When you look at those stars, I want you to think of me, to know that I'm there with you, praying over you, lighting your way." Unable to speak further, I wiped the tears that spilled down my cheeks.

"I will, Mother. I will make you and Father proud by serving my uncle well, and bringing home a wife. You have done so much for me," his voice quivered. "I'll never be able to repay any of it. But I promise you, I'll be back to take care of you."

Pride swelled inside me as I looked up at him, seeing him for the first time as a capable man, not just my son. I reached out to him, forcing him to stoop as I clutched his head to my shoulder, right over my heart.

As we stood there, blanketed by moonlight and cocooned by the land we cherished, I remembered what it had felt like when I first held him, when I first met him, when Isaac had smiled down at the two of us with love written on his features; the entire world spilling out of our shared heart. I remembered the nights I rocked him, so gently, so carefully, until he slipped into a warm slumber. I remembered the years that I watched him run and play as the sun glinted off of his soft curls. I remembered the times he had smiled at me, the triumph of his newfound skill or fact winning over his otherwise introspective demeanor.

Those years were gone. I had been given my fill, and now it was time to do the thing that hurt most: Watch as he left with a piece of my heart that would never grow back. I thought about my parents, remembering the pain they had fought to conceal when they watched me leave, never to return. I had thought I'd known sadness then.

It was time. I loosened my grip, carefully rearranging the curls that had escaped from his head covering as I studied his face one final time. My beautiful, courageous, clever boy. I pressed a kiss to his forehead, choking back a sob. "Go. Go now," I said as I nudged him forward.

He stared back at me with those soulful eyes, his mouth shaking slightly before settling into a firm, determined line. For a moment, the world receded. It was just us, refusing to speak of the pain that carved a pathway between where we stood. And then, with a deep heave of his chest, time resumed. Then he was walking, away from me, away from his home and everyone he'd ever loved.

I watched the horizon until I could no longer see his outline, and until he became a speck in the sand, and long past that. I watched until the sky decided I couldn't watch anymore, its darkness extinguishing any connection I had to him.

"Rebekah, let's get you inside." Deborah placed a trembling hand on my shoulder, squeezing it gently, acknowledging my anguish without saying a word.

With a final, shaky sigh, I tore my eyes from the horizon and turned to face her before we began our slow walk home. "May God guide him better than I ever could."

Afterword

It is unlikely that Rebekah ever saw Jacob again.

The Bible has a funny way about it. It makes sure to mention some things, while also making sure to not mention others. While many will choose to pay attention to the things that are mentioned, I've found that homing in on those unmentioned things can be just as important. In this case, Rebekah's unmentioned death was as much a sign to me—as a non-sign can be—that her ending wasn't quite as rosy as one would hope.

Do I pray that I'm wrong? Of course I do. I loved Rebekah before writing this book, and I love her even more now. What a complex, beautiful, and layered woman. A brave and bullheaded one, at that. Thinking that she might have spent the rest of her days tending to her ailing husband while missing one son and dealing with the wrath of the other is almost more than I can bear. But that doesn't mean that the facts, both mentioned and unmentioned, don't deserve to be shared.

Much prayer and research went into my interpretation and portrayal of Rebekah's story. However, this final part feels too important for my own mere interpretation; so I leave it to you. Below, I've jotted down just a few important moments that are mentioned in the Bible after Jacob's departure. I encourage you to piece them together in your heart, stew on them, pray on them, and understand her story in your own way.

Jacob's Twenty-Year Absence

"Thus have I been twenty years in thy house; I served thee fourteen years for thy two daughters, and six years for thy cattle: and thou hast changed my wages ten times." Genesis 31:41

Jacob And Esau's Reconciliation

"And Jacob lifted up his eyes, and looked, and, behold, Esau came, and with him four hundred men. And he divided the children unto Leah, and unto Rachel, and unto the two handmaids.

"And he put the handmaids and their children foremost, and Leah and her children after, and Rachel and Joseph hindermost.

"And he passed over before them, and bowed himself to the ground seven times, until he came near to his brother.

"And Esau ran to meet him, and embraced him, and fell on his neck, and kissed him: and they wept." Genesis 33:1–4

Jacob's Return Home; Deborah's Death

"So Jacob came to Luz, which is in the land of Canaan, that is, Beth-el, he and all the people that were with him.

"And he built there an altar, and called the place El-beth-el: because there God appeared unto him, when he fled from the face of his brother.

"But Deborah Rebekah's nurse died, and she was buried beneath Beth-el under an oak: and the name of it was called Allon-bachuth." Genesis 35:6-8

Isaac's Death

"And Isaac gave up the ghost and died, and was gathered unto his people, being old and full of days: and his sons Esau and Jacob buried him." Genesis 35:29

❋ ❋ ❋

It's interesting, isn't it, that Deborah and Isaac's deaths were recorded, but Rebekah's wasn't. In fact, the mention of Deborah's death—the only reference to her name in the Bible, specifically—was so intriguing to me, that it inspired Deborah's character in *Rebekah's Way*. What a good and loyal friend she must have been, after having spent a lifetime with Rebekah, for the Lord to bring attention to her death in the Bible.

While the Bible doesn't explicitly say that Jacob returned home after Rebekah's death, it doesn't say that he returned home to find her alive, either. Again, it is my belief that what is left unsaid can be just as important, if not more so, than what is said.

So, how did Rebekah's story end? Did she and Isaac find a way to stitch together the frayed strings of their trust and live another twenty years in harmony? Did she spend each day watching the horizon, waiting for word from her son? Deep down, did she know that she wouldn't see him again—at least, not in this life?

I have my hunch about what transpired, though I'm cautious about ever being too sure. However, one thing I feel confident in is that Rebekah had peace, if not pain, about her lot. She lived a full, adventurous, pulse-quickening life. She was imperfect; she was flawed; she was like us.

She was Rebekah, and she had her way.

Are you saved?

The Bible is just a book of fairy tales—albeit lovely ones—if you don't believe it. While the death and resurrection of Jesus Christ might sound like that of a fairy tale, it was real. It happened. Even historians and scientists have backed the Bible up.

But do you believe it?

The downfall of modern humanity is our inability to believe that miracles really, truly happen. The world has conditioned us to think that anything miraculous must have happened at the hand of technological advancement. That thought process is stealing souls, one by one. I refuse to leave you here without making sure that it doesn't steal yours, too.

Modern humanity has also muddied up the waters with different religious ideologies, and I need you to know that it's quite simple, really. Jesus died for your sins and went to hell —and then pulled a disappearing act—for you so that you wouldn't have to. Because we were all given the same lot in life— sin, and the punishment for sin, hell.

But here's the beautiful, wonderful, tear-inducing fairy tale of it all: You and I don't have to go there, because Jesus took care of it all. All we have to do is accept His free gift. Really.

So, all you need to do to let Jesus save your soul is, well, to let him. He's waiting to hear from you—offer up a quick prayer asking for His forgiveness, thanking Him for dying for you, telling Him that you believe He really did die and come back to life. Finally, ask to receive His free gift of eternal life. Cry if it feels good. Laugh if it feels better.

Then open your eyes and realize that you've been saved. And remember—salvation is not only free, it's eternal. You'll never lose it. He'll never forsake you.

"And I give unto them eternal life; and they shall never perish, neither shall any man pluck them out of my hand.

"My Father, which gave them me, is greater than all; and no man is able to pluck them out of my Father's hand." John 10:28-29

ABOUT THE AUTHOR

Kirsten Lawler

Kirsten is a mom to three rescue dogs, a wife to one loving man, a fiction editor, and now, a self-proclaimed author. After spending years serving the creative small business community as a copywriter and marketer, she decided to chase her passion for literature by writing historical fiction that helps others fall back in love with their Bibles. When she isn't (re)reading any and all of Jane Austen's works, she's studying her Bible and using her Peloton. . . before promptly laying on the floor to invite her pups to smother her.

@authorkirstenlawler | www.alwayservices.com

Made in the USA
Las Vegas, NV
13 October 2024

96822968R00125